Through Other Eyes

By

Jan Hawkins

This is a Companion Book
Rating MA

A companion book is a given set of circumstance in which there are two accounts from very different outlooks.

This story is told through the eyes of Tom.
You can also find the tale as told through the eyes of young Jeremy
In Book 1

Lands Edge

The Dreaming Series

Book 1 - **Shadow Dreaming**
       Taipan & Aine

Book 2 - **Sky Song**
       Sean & Jenna

Book 3 - **Spirits of the Rock**
       Andrew & Ngaire

Book 4 - **Caverns of The Dreamtime**
       Tom

The Spirit Children

Book 2
Those Born of the
The Dreaming Series

© 2014 Jan Hawkins
All Rights Reserved
ISBN 978-0-9874654-3-6

ABOUT THE AUTHOR
Jan Hawkins

Australian Author, Jan Hawkins, was raised in the Australian bush on the outskirts of Sydney on the Georges River. Now residing in Queensland, she spent 20 years in education at secondary level in the IT field. Her love of computers pales in comparison to her love of the Australian bush and Jan now has quite a portfolio of photographs, which form the basis of her covers.

She is passionate about the history of her country and a strong desire to discover and experience new places fuels her desire to travel extensively throughout the land. Along the way she relishes being able to listen to people and to share and enjoy the adventure she calls life.

Sydney Town

Tom:

I was always meant to be what I am; I could have been none other. I know now to be otherwise would have destroyed me in the same way that it had destroyed my father. He tried to be other than he was, he turned his back on his world and the world he was born too and it destroyed him. There's always a price to pay for being of the Kadaitcha Lore but it is a price that I am now comfortable with.

We buried my old man the other week and the memory holds me quiet at different times such as now, it was so recent. It had been a quiet ceremony. My Grandfather and I said our farewells in the way of our mob along with some of the family and friends. It had been a small gathering as he had no place, no home anymore. So we chose to say our goodbyes and send off his shade into the bush where he had found peace in the end.

That was a fitting place for our ceremony to clear the breath of his Shadow from the rivers edge. This was after we had the other service, the one that was expected. We had his ashes scattered to the winds.

His world had been his own type of tortured existence for these last months or perhaps even years. Those same months had seemed endless to me, though not as endless as they had been for him.

His Shadow no longer lingers here. He has faced his demons and been claimed by the Spirit Serpent. He is with Wolgaru and the dark dogs of the Shades, the Djaranin. He will be cleaned in the sacred fires of the caverns and walk amongst us again one day as a Spirit Child, reborn and renewed. I look forward to that day when he returns to us even though I may never know if I will meet him again.

He too will have no memory of me, of what he was and what he did, but I will remember the man, the Shadow who no longer lives. That man is truly dead. Even his spirit has faced the shame of his death in the fires, which will cleanse him, making him whole once more.

I no longer can feel the burn of anger within me. I have learnt to tame that anger, that which scored through my childhood. I have pulled it apart, examined it and while I will not forget, while I have learnt lessons that have made me who I am, I can at least now feel the freedoms of acceptance.

What I do feel instead is the fire of hate for what he had become, the arrogance and self-importance that man can wear like a mantle. This hate I will need to tame to be everything that I can be and I know this for myself. I have no need to have this told to me.

It is my challenge in life and this hatred will not tame easily so I will fight to temper it some. It is a small step each time. This is what my Grandfather and others have advised and I'll listen to what they tell me.

Some say you should forgive fully, but that is not possible for me as the scars of my childhood live within me always. They made me who I am; they are a part of me. I know this and it has nothing to do with the anger I had, but more to do with accepting the type of man he was and coming to accept that without pain.

I don't need to forgive him as he made his own choices and he could not ask this of me, nor could anyone really. The Caverns of the Dreamtime will always hold my secrets.

In life you choose what you are and forgiveness has no part in that choice. He accepted what he was and so do I now. It's more about acceptance. I, more than anyone, knew what he was and had become. Even if he didn't realize in the addle of what drugs had made of his mind.

I can give myself what was stolen from me as a child. I can make a better job of being a father to the child within me. I can be a better father than my own father was. Every now and then I can set my own man-child free and each time I gain something that lives and breathes in an adult world, my world. This brings my world into the sunlight.

It feels like this now as I sit and wait, watching the people of the city go about their day. I feel the freedoms of the child within me wanting to venture out and explore the world I'm watching.

Here in the Botanical Gardens in the heart of the city it is a fitting place to set the kid in me free, allowing him time to heal. It's green and lush, not quite the beautiful olive tones of the bush that I loved but certainly this place makes me smile.

Sydney is a beautiful city. Even in the concrete jungle that it is in places, you can still feel the heartbeat of the old world if you close your eyes. Particularly here amongst the gardens, even despite the ordered paths and curious tourists.

It is a world many often don't see, a world where men and women have walked since the Dreamtime, not only in the last paltry two hundred years. Yet even this world has changed so many times.

Now it's a city, a bursting hub of business and commerce but the harbour waters still move along at their own timeless pace, free and unfettered. There is a quiet beauty here, you can still feel the echo of a time long past. So I can relax and let this knowledge wrap around me.

I knew the Cadi mob had lived here, this was their land, their Country. My eldest brother Taipan had told me a lot of their history. It was much more than the last two hundred years.

However I hadn't heard before the songs or stories of the Eora people whose Country this had been. This apart from a few stories others had spoken about while I was in ceremony with my Grandfather Apari and my teacher Badjimala or Big Jim as we knew him by his familiar name.

The history of the Cadigal, who were a family of the Eora people was in many ways a tragedy, although their descendants still lived here in the city. Their mob had been some of the first to be truly decimated by diseases bought from other worlds.

Disease had spread throughout this land killing whole mobs and complete families. They had spread with the step of the whitefellas and with others who had come to this land even earlier. I had the blood of the whitefellas mixed with that of the blackfella in me, so it was my history too. It was now the history of this land. It was now the history of my Country, a Country that now belonged to many.

The Cadigal had been a water people, living by the ocean and mixing with the forest mobs, or the people of the trees, in the ways that the people had back then. It would've been a good life I think. We might have warred over women and sometimes over Lore but it was a ritual fighting in which there were rules and structure as well as honour and justice for the men. It was the way of men then, and women.

There was little honour in the city today I decided, not as it was in past times. Everything was bought to rights back then and there was a natural balance to these things. This same balance could no longer be easily found in the laws the whitefellas had bought to our country.

So it was that the Kadaitcha, the men of Lore were now bringing this balance back to our land. It was a secret thing, a silent and sacred thing as it had always been. A value taught and judged by the Spirit Creatures of the Dreamtime who had always governed the people of this land.

It was the whitefellas law that was corrupt and useless in the balance of life and country. The whitefellas had imposed their Law but it was so often unjust and unbalanced. We were now at last growing strong enough once more, to impose our Lore back upon this land.

It was a Lore that had lived here since the Dreamtime and one that had always been the Lore of the people. I could see how our Lore was more just, in many ways. It too had changed as people have changed but there are some things that will always remain the same. Some Lore's that should never be broken.

I knew near where I sat now, in the city gardens was an ancient Bora Ring that was buried by these formal gardens and I had been curious about that. You could still feel the power of the Earth here, the power of the Spirit world where the Elders and the Kadaitcha of the different mobs had once made judgements over thousands of years and I wondered about that too.

Couldn't others who sat around on the grass, those who walked over the ground feel it too? Perhaps they didn't understand what it was that they felt mingling, with the sense of peace in these gardens. Perhaps they just didn't know what to make of these things anymore.

It felt good; like the welcome of a mother to a place as ancient to our mob as any had ever been. It was a place where the Spirits reached up through the earth and touched you, leaving the power of the earth flowing through you.

As the warmth of the sun washed over me, warming me, I eased back onto the grass and considered my knowledge. That which I had gained over the past few years.

I could sleep here quite easily I thought as my mob had done for eons. If Kelly didn't hurry up she would find me asleep for sure and that thought made me grin, I wonder what she would do about that?

I liked Sundays, it was a good day because you had Saturday to ease you into doing bugger all on Sunday. Mondays weren't so hot, it was hump day I figured. The day that was hardest to get over, when you began the slog through the week. Yep Sunday was good.

Thinking about Kelly I wondered what my mate Jeremy would make of this meeting of ours. Kelly hadn't wanted him to know about it and I could see why, they were friends. Just friends from college she had said but he was a special friend to her. She didn't want to lose his friendship. She also didn't want their friendship to be other than a friendship. He was young, as young as she and at that thought I pursed my lips.

She might be a shade off eighteen but she was a nice kid and I liked her. She had seemed troubled I had thought and I wasn't so keen on the bloke she was seeing, what was his name? Paul... Peter... something along those lines.

When she had invited me to meet her this weekend I hadn't been so keen, she was a good few years younger than me after all. When I had pointed out the distance in our ages she had laughed though. Her boyfriend what's-his-name was even older than me and that surprised me a bit. I figured then that she liked her guys older, maybe that was why she wanted to be just friends with Jeremy.

For a moment I considered what her boyfriend what's-his-name would make of this business. Did he even know of our meeting or was Kelly on her own and going behind his back. I would ask her outright I decided. It was one thing to keep this from Jeremy but another to keep it from a guy she had been seeing for months. That just didn't sit right, he seemed a bit odd actually when I thought about it.

I sat, my thoughts quiet for a moment as I watched a couple in the park stroll by with their kid in a pram. I couldn't help thinking about my little girl Ellie then, and that memory flicked a wistful thought through my mind.

The last time I had seen her she had been at the point of crawling about, even at so young an age. Cute as a button I had been enchanted by her smile and her sweet little giggle. It had made me wish my life could have been different in some ways but then... no. Ellie would have everything she would need. Andrew was a great dad and Yindi his young daughter now accepted Ellie as her sister. They were like a pigeon pair those two and Alex her mum was happier than I had ever seen her.

The prospect of another baby with Andrew hadn't phased her at all, she was born to be a mum I thought to myself and then just for a moment I considered what I had given up.

There were regrets there for sure, but no regrets for the happiness Alex had found, nor for the life Andrew now had, even if it could have been mine. I hadn't chosen that life I reminded myself. I could not be what I was, what I wanted most in the world to be and hold that life together. It was an impossible dream to even consider.

"Hey you. There you are, I had just about given up looking for you."

"Hey, Kelly." Grinning up at her I patted the ground beside me and then chuckled at her grimace. "Come-on girl. Sit... the grass won't kill you." I added sitting up myself, leaving my thoughts behind.

Kelly shrugged after barely a minute and then sat down beside me easily, folding her long legs in front of her.

"I was wondering if you were gunna turn up." I challenged with a grin filled with cheek.

"Me! I said I'd meet you here."

"Yeah, an hour ago."

Giggling hesitantly she dropped her eyes. "Yeah well I only got up an hour ago. It was a late night."

"What's-his-name keeping you up then?" It was a good introduction into the subject I wanted to know more about and I waited hopeful that she would feed me more information.

"Pete. His name's Pete."

"Yeah well Pete then."

Kelly looked up, a strange thought reflected in her eyes. One touched by a frown and then suddenly she avoided the curiosity in my own eyes, turning away to watch the crowd as though it was of more interest.

"What is it? The Dodger giving you trouble?" I asked insistently, teasing her. This bought her glance swinging back to me as I chuckled uneasy at her reaction.

"The what! Dodger...?"

"Yeah. Seems he is a bit of a dodger?"

She laughed at that, her grin broad and sweet. "He does? I never thought of it."

I shrugged. "So what's the problem with him an' you?" This is what I had figured; it had to be something to do with her bloke for her to ask me to meet up.

For a minute, just a glancing second there was a fear in her eyes and then it was gone. "I don't know... I just...?"

"Just what?" I coaxed insistent as I lounged back on my elbow and watched her, curious about her reactions.

"I don't know. He's just... different sometimes. I'm never sure of him."

"Yeah well... aren't we all?"

Kelly grinned at that and seemed to relax a bit. "Yeah I guess. If I tell you something, you wont tell anyone will you? Especially Jeremy. I don't think he would understand." She spoke a tone full of confidence that I would unstintingly do what she asked of me. It was flattering really I decided.

"Yeah sure. I don't tell Jeremy everything you know. I mean he and I are mates but it isn't like that. We are like brothers, but we respect each other's privacy. He's a lot younger," I shrugged. "He doesn't always think like me, about the things I do and why I do them. I wouldn't expect him to."

Nodding she caught my eyes. "I know, that's why I wanted to talk to you, sort of... ask you stuff."

"Ask away." I invited after a moment still curious and growing more so as I listened to her.

"Pete... well he is older too. He thinks different I think. I mean it's different when I am with him. He expects different things and I don't know. I mean it's good, I like him but he wants... he asks me about doing things."

"What things?"

Again she shrugged, not meeting my eyes. "I mean it's not so bad. A lot of the girls do it. They go with different guys and have parties and stuff. It's good, I mean I enjoy the parties and Pete says it's OK if I like a guy and if I want to I can earn money. Not just a little bit but lots... lots of money. Sorta like a job really."

I eased myself up quite suddenly as I considered what she had said. This was no simple matter I suspected and my thoughts had me frowning. "He wants you to hostess at these parties?"

"Yes. That's what he said. A lot of the girls do it and it... well it's fun too sometimes and the money is great."

"He's pimping you out?" I added, a little incredulous now.

"No! No it's not like that! He says I don't have to do it if I don't want. But if I do I can make a lot of money. I mean I have to want to... if I don't like the guy then..." Again she shrugged.

"He's pimping you out Kelly."

Kelly breathed out a long sigh and then looked away her thoughts obviously warring with my words. It was as though she didn't want to believe what was plain to see. But it was a tolerant expression that settled about her features.

"He's not," she said finally. "It's not like that. That sounds horrible."

"Well then what is it, if it isn't that? You're invited to private parties and sex is on the menu. You get paid... that's pimping you out. He gets a cut and you get a cut... that is what it is. It's prostitution."

"No!" Shaking her head with determination she glared at me. "It isn't like that. I don't have to do anything. You don't understand..."

"Kelly I'm not judging you but I am not gunna' pretend it is different than it is. The guy's a pimp and you... you're an attractive girl, young, fresh... what this bloke is looking for. You're right up his alley... just what a pimp needs."

"No! He asked me, and... and he said it was OK. Lots of the girls do it. I'm not the only one."

I shrugged. "So? It's probably the circle of his friend's. They could all be doing this. What...? Do you think prostitution is all about dark rooms and stuff? How do you think these guys get... a hostess. They don't walk up and advertise. It's a mutual thing. It takes a bit of grooming I guess. It's a business and they have to look after their harem or whatever it is, or they are out of business."

"Harem!" Her laughter was a curious mix of shock and amusement. "It's not a harem," she protested after a time but you could still see the doubt, the confusion in her manner.

I settled back again on my elbows and tried to workout just what it was that Kelly was trying to ask me, telling me even. "OK tell me what it is. Explain it to me."

"You won't tell anyone, not Jeremy?"

"Not gunna happen. This is between you and me. I promise."

"OK. Well there is a place, it's not far really but we go there sometimes, well most weekends and..." she shrugged again. "Well there are lots of friends, girls and different guys, mostly the girls have their boyfriends. I know them... maybe a half dozen and there are always people there. Pete has a room or maybe two there and he buys me stuff and lets me keep it there 'cause my ... my Aunt wouldn't understand. It's really nice, not sleazy or anything. It's like my apartment really, mine and his too. We both stay over sometimes. But lately we have been going to these parties and it's not like what you think. They are real parties with normal people and it's a lot of fun sometimes."

"Do they do drugs at these places?"

"Sometimes ... yes. It's like at a lot of parties. But they don't do that all the time and it's fun. Nothing hard I don't think just joints and... stuff and sometimes we have pills, uppers really. Pete always looks after me and makes sure I don't take anything bad or anything like that."

"Protecting his interests I think." I challenged.

"No! You're being horrible. He isn't like that."

"You're the one telling the story Kelly, I'm just interpreting it."

"Well it isn't like that at all. Not like what you think."

Easing myself back again I looked up at the sky, partly shading my eyes as I considered what Kelly had said. I wasn't sure what to advise her, and she obviously wanted advice of some type.

"What is it you want me to tell you?" I asked suddenly, catching her eyes.

Again, there was that careless shift of her shoulders. A small shrug and I realized she didn't even know what she wanted, or what she was dealing with.

"I just wanted to ask someone if it was... seemed OK? You don't hate me do you... it's not like that or like I'm doing anything wrong. No one is getting hurt or anything"

"I'm not your father, I can't give you permission."

"I don't want permission!" Her voice was resentful but still she sat there.

"You want my opinion, well you've heard that. I'm not judging you Kelly, you do your own thing."

"Well... what do you think?"

I considered it. "You don't like what I think. This guy is pimping you out. It's probably been going on at this house for ages. I guess they make a lucrative living at it, the guys an' the girls."

"It isn't like that." She answered rebuking me, she was defensive but you could see that it was just like this. It was the interpretation that you put on it. She just didn't like my interpretation much. She probably thought along similar lines, or had at least seen the comparisons or she wouldn't be sitting here with me asking me about it I figured.

I wondered then how it was that she couldn't see it clearly for what it was and then I guessed that maybe she didn't want to see it. My next thought was how long would it be before she would see it and then how long before it would make no difference to her.

"OK. I need a drink, there has to be somewhere around here?"

Climbing to my feet I stood for a second looking down at her and then offered her a hand-up. She seemed so young and that irritated me for some reason. "Come on, let's find a place. There has to be a bar around here or a club or something."

"Yeah there is. I'm hungry too."

"OK... food it is."

We found a small bar and bistro further up the main drag towards Kings Cross, though I didn't want to get too far into the Cross precinct where the prices tended to hike. They served a tapas spread at the place so I decided that this would do us, something simple and quick. Though it wasn't until I got back to the table, where Kelly had picked at the back of the bistro and set her beer on the coaster in front of her that I remembered that she was likely under-aged. I could have kicked myself for my lack of thought about that.

I don't know whether it was my look of guilt that I tossed around the room or a natural process but the barman was at the table within minutes asking for ID. This was not looking good.

Kelly however was not at all concerned and pulling out her wallet from her shoulder bag she was able to produce a provisional licence readily. Glancing across at me with what could only be described as a cheeky smile.

Incredulous I watched as he checked her ID and age, then nodding he left us to move on in a manner that clearly told me he thought there was nothing wrong with the whole process.

"What's that?" I asked curious and somewhat nonplussed, indicating the ID she was now stowing in her cavernous shoulder bag.

"My drivers licence."

"You don't drive!"

"Yeah I know, but don't tell him." She giggled, obviously happy to have fooled the guy.

"Give me a look."

"Not now... shhh... in a minute." She answered, giggling again. "He'll be watching I think."

Looking up, I saw that she was right. He was doing just that from the bar and not trying to even look as though he was doing other than that.

"The Dodger got you that?" I asked behind a casually folded hand, knowing the answer even before I asked her.

"Yeah. It says I am nineteen, great isn't it?"

"Yeah … if you don't want to end up in the tank. Jeezus Kelly… who is this guy you are hanging with?"

"He's nice really. Really he is!" She protested, despite my look of doubt. "He does look after me and… and it's nice. That… really!"

"Just like he looks after the rest of his harem I am sure." I added with serious scepticism, hopefully softened with a smile.

"He doesn't have a harem, I tell you it isn't like that."

I remained sceptical. "Does Jeremy know you only want to be friends with him? Seems to me he has other plans. He likes you, you know." Again I smiled, companionably. Not wanting to see my mate hurt in the business although he wouldn't thank me for it I was sure.

Kelly looked up with all the endearment of a child. She had that look about her and it was probably the most attractive asset for the Dodger. She could carry a look of maturity when she wanted. Reverting to an almost childish charm was one of her endearing ways.

"Yes. We're really open about everything but… but Jeremy wouldn't understand this I don't think."

"Yeah… I don't think either. Not yet anyways, maybe in a few years when the city has hardened him a bit."

A restless silence settled between us for a moment, and the questions rolling about in my head got the better of me.

"So you don't mind this business of other guys?" I asked curious.

Kelly just shrugged. "I give it away anyway so what's the difference. Guys expect this kind of stuff and you never see them again, well mostly anyway. Besides, do you even think about it? I bet you give it away too. It's the same thing."

I laughed at that and then shook my head indulgently. "Not lately." I added.

Kelly frowned. "You got a problem or something?"

That really made me laugh. She was game this girl and I'd often thought that was the case, now I knew it. I liked candid talk though, as there was an honesty about it.

"No. I recently had a sort of… well sort of a circumcision." I answered, watching the curiosity in her eyes.

"At your age? That musta' hurt!"

"Yeah, well it was all part of it. Still healing but it's OK. It was my decision, no one else's."

"Why?"

I shrugged. "It had a meaning for me, it's a cultural thing in many ways."

"Oh. What did your girlfriend think about that?"

I grinned. "No girlfriend. Life's complicated enough."

Kelly smiled, and it lit the space between us. She had a lovely smile I thought to myself. "Jeremy said once that you both were in some type of training, like kung-fu stuff. So you mean I have the two of you all to myself then?"

Again I laughed at the challenge in her grin, it was like a game and it was fun in its own way. "Yep. I guess you do, if you want to look at it like that."

It was a good afternoon and I was glad I had met up with Kelly though she worried me a bit. There was no way Jeremy would understand what she was doing, he was way too young and for him it would be tragic, that his friend had got mixed up in this. But it was her choice and I agreed that this was something Jeremy didn't need to know about.

At least while the two of them remained just friends. Not unless she decided to tell him, after all he already accepted that she had the Dodger in her life. Jeremy and her were just friends after all.

Hours later I walked her back to the place she had spoken about. It didn't look like a brothel of any kind I had ever seen, just a house really even if it was sort of scrappy. There were a few people around but they mostly took no notice as I waved her off. People in The Cross usually kept to themselves. Your business was nobodies business.

It took a time to find where I had parked the ute, up in around the residential blocks and it was on the edge of dark when I got to the car, but I could see I had company even as I approached.

Jep had little regard for anything to do with property, particularly if it was city-side. He was perched up on the bonnet of the ute, lounging back in the shadows of the buildings around us.

My Jongorrie was something of a nuisance although he was handy to have around. We had settled into a companionship, which while it wasn't quite a friendship it was definitely more an association of wits. But it worked for us.

The salacious little forest man of the Spirit lands, who had engorged tastes and questionable habits, he kept tabs on me and I had to admit that he was of help at times. More a second set of eyes and hands to help me when I needed help.

I had inherited him from my father when I had begun my initiations. He had tormented him mercilessly in his time and it was my grandfather who had helped me see that this was the Jongorrie's role in life. He had as much choice in it all as I did, but he was a type of helper for the Kadaitcha. I needed to treat him with respect, as much as he accorded me his own brand of consideration.

The Jongorrie were creatures of the shadows, part of his way was to keep me safe, even if it was from myself. He wasn't above carrying tales to Apari, my Grandfather, I had discovered. But I had my own ways of dealing with him.

I took a moment to check if there was anyone about within hearing. I had been caught-out before and people didn't take well to hearing someone talk away to an imaginary friend, particularly if you weren't a child. Finding no one about I greeted him with a nod.

A creature of the spirit world, he lived within the shadows and people saw little of him, if anything at all. He was a shadow of another world, a creature of the forests and caverns from where he ventured in his service to me. He was just a part of this spiritual world that was mine, this gift that was almost like another dimension to my sight. It was a gift I had discovered as a young man and I could discern him easily because of this sight. This had come with my Initiations and my growth into my manhood.

"How is the possum?" I asked easily. It was a task I had set him to keep my little girl Ellie safe. It was his task to ensure at all times that she had no need of me. He knew I liked to hear often about my little daughter and even how Alex was getting on. Though she was more Andrews concern now than mine.

"Ahh Tomtom, the little one is fine. Teething, driving everyone batty she is." He commented as he set to jump down from the bonnet of my ute with the gleeful way he managed to move about. "She sees me ya' know. It reminds me of young Debbie it does and it is a wonderful thing. But we have business you and I. I can feel the pull of trouble in me bones Tomtom." He warned me, impatient with my questions.

"Trouble?" I asked, as I climbed into the old ute and watched Jep clamber in through the open window. It seemed he never did anything conventionally and I had about given up commenting on it.

Jep didn't need the convention of transport, he moved easily across the land in his own time and space. But that he clambered inside the ute told me that he felt he had serious business he wanted to discuss and I was curious about it now.

Car travel generally never agreed with him and I was surprised that he was choosing to travel with me at all.

"Yes. Can't you feel it... in your gut Tomtom? Feel the weight of it surround you. The Moogie Eye should be warning you. Telling you these things."

I felt the spirit weight of the death stone I carried within me, deep in my gut. A weapon of the Lore and I recognized that there was a certain heat about it, which I had overlooked. It could be nothing and then it could be everything.

"Have you spoken to Apari?"

"No… no nono. Your Grandfather is busy but he knows anyways, he would feel the weight of the trouble but it's of no concern for him ya' know. This is your business Ariaka. Your Grandfather wants little of this world of yours and he concerns himself with other things … other things. It is all your business now and he has other concerns."

At his use of my spirit name I frowned. This was the business of the Kadaitcha or he would never have used the name.

As we wound our way through the city streets and out towards the southern suburbs of Sydney, I considered what the business could be all about. I had recently passed through my initiations and was free of many of the constraints placed on me but you never really finished with this business. It was like a birth, a childhood and a growth into maturity and then the onset of a measure of wisdom. My training would go on for many years to come.

I knew I had passed through the first stages some time ago, left behind fear and tamed my anger but within me somewhere was the animal which was hate. One more trial I had to face before my acceptance as a Kadaitcha and I had only recently decided that this trial had little to do with my father's death.

Hate was not a part of what I felt for the man who had sired me and yet, hate was the one thing that was left to test me. Perhaps this coming trouble was the measure of how I could deal with my control when it came to hate.

For the Kadaitcha and particularly for the Shadow Walkers amongst us, controlling the most dangerous of passions was essential to wield the skills and powers we did. Our control was the measure or our place in our world.

As we slipped along the dark tar of the highway, Jep gripped the door in panic and squeezed his eyes tight while I struggled to suppress my grin. He hated car travel and had never become accustomed to it. But in dealing with me, he had to deal with travelling about and many of the other trappings of my world. This irked him tremendously and he rarely gave up the opportunity to remind me of it.

"Slow down Tomtom… Slow this flippin' thing!"

"I'm barely moving as it is." I complained with a smirk. "We're going well below the limit. You just have to deal with it."

With a jarring mumble of cuss words delivered in mixed dialects beyond me, he grabbed at the jacket I kept at the back of the cab. Dragging it down with him he scrambled into the foot-well where he curled up and buried his head beneath the jacket as though it would protect him.

I couldn't help it, I laughed out loud in what was a sympathetic derision and then I slowed down even more. He wouldn't even notice it I knew but at least I felt I was helping him with his irrational fears.

"Look. I'm going slower now! If I get into a blue with another driver because of it, it will be all your fault." I warned.

"We will see… we'll see," he whimpered barely coherent. Peeping out for the smallest moment before he hid his head again just like the old man emu.

We had this discussion any number of times and I knew that he wouldn't be settled at least until we neared the bush. There was little for it, he would just have to stay in the foot-well. I really couldn't go any slower. As it was the cars about me were growing impatient and I tried to smile it off as they cut around me, signalling their frustrations.

We finally approached the ridge near where I lived some time later. Arriving at the place where we usually left the cars parked high above the river on the old Shackles Estate, here Jep popped his head up feeling the weave of the car as it negotiated the track. He was happy to be here, happy his trial in my old ute was coming to an end.

He followed me on foot down along the track and into the house with a certain delight. He liked hanging around here and as much as I often sent him off on some errand to get him out of the way, he would always return to this place with a measure of anticipated ease.

I guessed it was the river, the calming sound of the bush all about him. This married with the comfort of the house although his favourite place was amongst the damp heat and cover of the rainforests.

Jeremy was home, I caught sight of him lounging on the verandah that stretched along the full width of the back of the cottage and overhung the river. He was enjoying the solitude of the evening with what looked to be books or homework from TAFE scattered all around him. Of Big Jim there was no sight, so grabbing a piece of fruit from the kitchen I moved out to join my mate.

"Hey… Howz' it going?"

"Good. You're back late?"

Settling down on the wooden bench seat along with him, lounging back without comment, I propped my feet against the railing. I noted that Jep too squatted quite content. He had moved into the very corner of the railing around the verandah where it was the deepest in shade. His interest was in the flow of the river and he felt himself part of our company. We both knew that Jeremy's sight was not such that he could easily discern the shadow that was the secretive little bushman.

For a moment I wondered how long my Jongorrie would hang about this time and restlessly I began to consider what it was that might have drawn him here to my side. I would have to think of an errand for him, one that would keep him out of mischief but serve whatever ends were of an interest to both him and I.

I had a need to work through this restless heat building in my gut with the death-stone, I was aware of it and there was something afoot for sure.

"Big Jim around?" I asked after a moment.

"Haven't seen him. Should be in soon though."

"I ran into Kelly in town, down around the gardens. She must have a place around there where she goes on the weekend." I offered. Wondering just how much Jeremy knew of his friend from college. Maybe he really did consider her a girlfriend. It would be good to know for sure either way.

"Yeah? Was she with a boyfriend?" He looked up interested and I read the question in his glance. He hadn't met the Dodger either I realized.

"With some guy. Looked to be a friend, a few years older than she is." It was the truth, I might have been the guy but I was conscious of keeping her confidence. "Don't think it was the boyfriend though."

"Oh. OK."

"You've not been to her place, the one where she stays with this guy of hers in town?"

"No. She keeps that pretty much to herself, and she doesn't like anyone going to where she lives. Seems her Aunty is a bit of a skitzo' so we hang out at the park or beach when we catch up. Suits us both."

I nodded. I had thought as much and I found it comforting that their friendship was still pretty platonic. Jeremy might be quiet in nature but he was still my mate and I liked to keep an eye out for him. He was still fairly young and growing up in the forest around Nimbin did little to prepare you for the many cut-throat ways of the big city.

Settling myself back I watched the flow of the Woronora River from our vantage point while my mind messed with the question of what trouble could be brewing. Big Jim would be able to help me with that I knew and I was impatient to see him. For a moment I wondered if I was going to get involved in a hunt or other business. Had the Kadaitcha found someone or something else that had moved into their sights I wondered?

This business could take weeks, or days. It was dependent on what we were dealing with. It would be what the Lore demanded of us to make things right in our world. After all things considered I knew time was nothing to the Kadaitcha, it simply didn't exist. So the evil or wrong that we dealt with could be in any place and in any form.

Whatever it was though, it was obviously brewing and it concerned me if the Moogie Eye was warming to its task. I just had to figure out where it was and what it was about.

This all felt as though it was some type of test, another trial? Could this be the test of what would measure my worth amongst the Kadaitcha I wondered? It was time, and yet time was irrelevant. What was important was the balance of our world.

For a moment my thoughts went back to the evil we had dealt with last year, that which had bought judgement down on my father. We had all been involved in that, my brothers Taipan and Sean. Apari as well and back then I had yet to choose my path fully. It was good that Apari, my Grandfather, had been at hand to show me what would be my life.

Andrew, he too had been so big a part of my choices then. Did he even understand that at the time I wondered absently? I hadn't understood it fully although Apari had known all for sure.

Alex... my mind tripped over the thought of her and then I schooled my thoughts to release her. She was no longer mine. I had no claim at all and I would not stir the images I decided.

Who would have thought that I would have returned to this river so soon after the birth of Ellie, the arrival of my little daughter; certainly not me! With that thought I grinned with the secret pride of a father.

It was a pride that I would claim only with a few who truly knew the history of Alex, my daughter and I. Most people thought of Ellie as being Andrew's child, Andrew and Alex's. It was the best way I figured but she would know the truth of it. I guess in the long run it accounted for little and there was no problem in having a couple of fathers to care for a young girl. It could even be an advantage particularly if they had skills to help her in life and with someone as special as Ellie, it was a good thing.

Time was a funny thing like that, it didn't exist in truth but then it was our reality. A reality of this world, but I knew that it was not so for the other worlds. Each world had its own measure of space and time. It was experience that governed all things, the lessons of life.

Experience and the choices you made in your life. Time was nothing, as was the possession of material things. It had been a hard lesson to learn for me, as much as it was for most.

The Shadows

Tom

It was late when I finally got out of bed the next morning. Jeremy and I had talked late into the night and I had drawn him out about Kelly. He knew nothing of her life in the city, didn't even suspect anything in the crowd she now mixed with. But my suspicion about the truth of it had made my night a restless one.

Jeremy was still snoring quietly in the other room. We had come to an arrangement he and I, and I was glad to have the master bedroom all to myself. Big Jim lived out in the boathouse and he came and went as he chose. He kept a general eye on us both, often spending time at our training but mostly now other things seemed to keep him busy and he was away a lot these days.

His interest was more with Jeremy generally it seemed now, aside from training me in the use of the small stock whip. That was something I was getting quite adept at but I was a long stretch from his skill for sure.

Since our last initiation ceremony it had become a skill I was interested in learning and Apari had encouraged me. A weapon of choice he had said, and I was comfortable with my choice.

I had the opportunity to watch both Jeremy and Big Jim control the Djaranin with their whips at the Bora Rings deep in the Blue Mountains. I had admired how they had both handled the dark dogs of the serpent. These were the dogs of death from the realm of the Dreamtime and having such mastery over these creatures was something I wanted for myself. It was something that could serve me well in the future I thought.

They were shades from the Caverns and controlling them was what I was keen to learn how to do. I knew the dogs travelled with Wolgaru the serpent. My Grandfather had spoken of these things with me, telling me of this Lore and the ways of the Serpent. The Wolgaru serpent was no threat to me as long as I could control the Djaranin or at the very least stay out of their way while my mate worked to control them.

I would meet Wolgaru again. This serpent held men in judgement and moving as close to death as he did made him a serpent to be wary of. He was a spirit creature of the caverns, one the Kadaitcha Men understood well.

Wolgaru often moved around those who walked in the shadows and it was my calling, the reaping of the harvest of evil in man. The men of the

Kadaitcha and the Shadow Walkers hunted evil. It was a harvest amongst men and women who came under the scrutiny of the Kadaitcha because of their ways. It was the balance of things that we fought to set right.

We were called to be a control on the evil that could be found in man and because of this it was often a harvest of death that we dealt with.

I was at the breakfast table, watching the river through the glass doors while the morning light crept through the house behind me, when I turned to notice that my Jongorrie had returned. Settling himself on the floor near the glass where he too could watch the river, he looked across at me silent and curious.

I had no idea where he went during the night hours, no idea what he did with his own time but at least the night had given me an answer to what to do with him in the moment.

"I have a job for you Jep. Can you see to it for me or are there other things you need to do?" I asked, conscious as I was that I didn't even know what his interests were when he took time to relax, if he ever did.

"What? Little Ellie is good... fine... no need... "

"Not Ellie," I grinned tolerantly. "It's something else and the thought of this task settles my belly."

Interested now, Jep jumped up. Knowing that this was something that was of importance. Knowing that the Moogie Eye, often restless within me was responding to the line of my thoughts in cooling its heat. This made all the difference to Jep. This was important business.

"What? What is it Tomtom...?"

"Your gunna like this one."

"Hmm..." Looking at me speculatively he fidgeted impatiently, dancing from foot to foot while I enjoyed his enthusiasm and curiosity.

"There is someone I want you to keep an eye on for me, seek her out and watch that she doesn't get into strife for a time."

"There is? Who! A girl... it's a girl isn't it?"

"Yes, it's a girl I know. The one I met yesterday in the city. Kelly is her name and she is a friend but I don't much like the sound of the crowd she is with. I want to know more."

"The city... the girl. Yes I saw her... nice looking girl too."

"Don't go getting any ideas. She's just a girl but I want to know what she gets up to when she's in the city. Make sure she's safe."

"Ohhh... I can do that. I can tell you, I can."

"Then you know the girl I mean."

"Yes I saw her... I saw her I did. I can find her." He said with a certain glee, warming to the idea quickly I could see.

"Well stay out of trouble. I don't want Kelly knowing you're there, or even suspecting that you're about for that matter. She stays at the house where I dropped her off, are you sure you can find it?"

"I can find it... I can find it Tomtom, it's easy. I can borrow your memory... in your head. I can... I can do that."

Frowning I looked across at him. "My memory?"

"Yes, it is there and I can borrow it. I can do that... it is easy for me to do that."

"I don't think I like that idea, you messing in my head."

"Don't worry Tomtom, there is not much there that I care to see." He reassured me with some delight. "You keep your thoughts to yourself, I'll just get the memory... easy it is."

I looked across at him suspiciously for a moment. "How long have you been messing around in my head?"

"Me!" He squeaked as he edged towards the long glass doors. "Hardly at all... hardly at all Tomtom. I don't do that messing around not with you... not with you."

"With my Dad? You did that?" I questioned suspiciously as more pieces of this puzzle that was my life fell into place

Jep continued to fidget, avoiding my eyes. "I gotta go... go find this Kelly girl for you... but yes. Yes a little bit but not much. It was different, he was different... not smart... he was too easy... too brain bushed..."

"Go! Before I get angry." I warned, somewhat disturbed by this new revelation.

"I's going. I'll look out for her... don't you worry. I'll do good..."

The next moment he was gone, a flick of a shadow and I knew he had gone to wherever it was he went, in the manner that he moved. That was something I was going to ask Apari about I decided. My Grandfather would know about this mind meddling and I didn't much like the sound of it at all.

It was the Tuesday next, before I even gave my Jongorrie another thought. Life had a way of doing that to you, moving on before you felt you had even caught up. I was still working on the building site not far from the Cronulla beach and despite the overcast sky I had decided on a run down to the surf when we finished up early in the afternoon.

I had thought to meet Jeremy down at the beach, he knew where I usually parked and if he wanted a lift home he would more often than not meet me here. However he hadn't been anywhere to be seen when I finally climbed out of the surf with the old surfboard under my arm.

My board wasn't anything flash but that was OK, I wasn't much of a rider anyway. I just enjoyed the surf and the freedoms I felt sitting out beyond the waves with others, watching the roll of the ocean about me and catching the movement and pull of the restless waves.

Floating about in the surf as though I was part of the dance that was the movement and power of the clear blue water. There was something invigorating or renewing in that feeling.

It wasn't far off sunset and that it was still overcast made it something of a grey afternoon. I preferred to be out of the surf well before the sun dropped behind the horizon and the big fish came in to feed, as did most of the surfers. Jeremy's absence was fairly normal, he might well have something else to do today and it didn't worry me.

Making my way across the shifting sand and up to where I had parked the ute, my thoughts were easy and as fresh as I felt.

The evening chill was beginning to bite, the spring evenings still had a winter nip at times. There was the promise of summer to come and that promise was enough to entice most of the young guys into the surf at the end of their day.

It was the camaraderie that you found out beyond the waves that drew many of the surfers and it was an enjoyable release to the pressures of the day. It wasn't until I got up close to the ute, having left the others, that I realized that Kelly was leaning against the bonnet waiting patiently for me.

"Hey you?" I said easily, greeting her with a small sense of pleasure. "Jeremy not around?"

"No, he headed out to check on something straight from TAFE. He's thinking of getting his tattoo done I think."

"Yeah? I had begun to wonder about that, he seems to have been planning it for ages."

It was unusual to have Kelly here down at the beach without Jeremy off side, but it didn't surprise me. It just perhaps added another dimension to our friendship, one that I didn't mind. I liked Kelly, even if she was a little mixed up in some things.

The chill of the late afternoon was beginning to bite and as I partially peeled off my tight wetsuit to better dry myself, I was conscious of Kelly watching me. More than once I challenged her playfully with my eyes but she broke into a light chatter about her day, about TAFE and about anything but what was going on, her eyes playful as she talked. It left me intrigued.

Opening the driver's door I stepped in behind it to better deal with my wetsuit somewhat out of the public eye. As much as the rubber suit kept you warm in the surf it was not practical to drive about in. Like many, I wore little underneath it. Not bothering with swimmers while there were so few people on the beaches.

Peeling the rubber from my chest once I had dried my skin roughly I swung the towel about me before I finally peeled out of the rubber to climb into my board-shorts. Kelly had stepped away from the bonnet and had come over to lean up against the other side door of the door near me. Her move wholly had my attention.

It was a bold move on her part and yet it amused me. I could play this game too I thought and all but ignored her playful attention. But when I was through stripping under the shelter of the towel about my hips and was negotiating my board-shorts having donned my shirt, I stood easily facing her as I dropped the towel in the process, rather than face the street I had turned towards the door and Kelly as I fixed the waist of my shorts uncaring of her attention.

"You done?" I asked raising a brow as I stood in front of her now dressed, challenging her with my eyes along with a cheeky smirk of my own, indicating the cab of the ute with a nod.

Kelly grinned and moved around the front of the vehicle to climb into the cab. My words had been an invitation, a challenge and a subtle question about what we were doing next.

That she so easily accepted my question sent a warm thrill of promise through my body but I wondered if she really understood what I had asked her in those few seconds, those few words.

I flicked the engine to life and then curious, I looked across as she settled herself in the seat belt.

"I'm up for fish and chips. You wanna' join me?" I asked in invitation, my eyes suggesting more than my simple words. It was more than fish and chips I was offering. Did she know it?

"Yeah. Sounds nice."

She was young, though with more experience than most. Perhaps she could read the subtle questions, the innuendo in the words and actions. Was I sure though? Was I willing to take the chance? I never knew what girls were really thinking?

It had been too long since I had really enjoyed the company of a woman, that which went beyond simple conversations and simple friendship. I didn't doubt that Kelly would be willing to take this wherever it went, but did she really know what she was doing?

Swinging the ute about I headed down the road to the fish and chip shop. It wasn't far, but the questions filled my mind completely. It was some time later, with Kelly nursing the parcel of hot fish and chips that I swung into the drive-through at the local bottle shop and picked up a half dozen cold stubbies, then headed off to the other side of the peninsula.

There was a nice sheltered spot near where the Bundeena ferry pulled in, a small car park and a quiet area. It would be a neat little place to enjoy a feed and maybe… just maybe… my thoughts wandered irreverently. The promise in her eyes had captured my thoughts and there was little else I could think about in that moment aside from Kelly and the smell of hot food.

Kelly sat quietly and said nothing about what I was doing or where we were headed. She would know surely what was on my mind I figured. She would understand the implications of what I was suggesting and where this was going. After all she knew the area well and would know what was happening here as we approached the well-known lovers park.

Pulling up in the small parking area with the calmer bay waters on the other side of the peninsula spread out before us, we for a time just sat there in the cab enjoying the scene unfolding like a pantomime playing out.

We had pulled into a quieter corner of the parking lot and nearby there was the small park. The parking lot was emptying fast of the last of the cars, those workers and day-trippers using the Bundeena ferry. Soon there would be no one to disturb us. It was quiet early in the week and night was beginning to fall offering us the privacy that was welcome under the darker cloak of starlight.

I didn't bother turning on the cab light, the light from the street lamp was enough and it was a soft yellow glow that was inviting us outside.

"You wanna eat in here or out in the park maybe?"

"We could eat outside, there are less people about in the park near the old pool," she suggested. Watching the people milling at the terminal boarding and leaving the last ferry.

I loved this area. Gunnamatta Park was green and well wooded, bordering on the bay waters. It was quiet usually, once you got past the public baths at the waters edge. This was where I led us while we chatted away. The night wasn't too cold and the shelter of the trees kept the breeze off the water from nipping at our skin. I looked for a sheltered spot closer to the bay beachside, yet one out of the breeze and the ready view of others who might be using the park.

The hot fish and chips were good, our fingers ending up salty and savoury, the taste washed with beer simply swigged from a stubbie. We sat relaxing and laughing at the simple things as we sat on the grass under the shelter in the soft nightshade and joked about life. Once we were finished I gathered up the paper, crumpled it and set it aside. Then turned my attention to Kelly as she lounged beside me, shifting back at leisure against the old arms of what were the large buttress roots of the tree.

I reached for her, determined to discover her mood and her thoughts, moving in towards her carefully. Slowly gathering her to me as I explored her lips lazily with my own. The question was plain in my look as I eased back to consider her mood.

"You in a hurry?" I asked of her, curious.

Shaking her head, she smiled when I shifted her in towards me once more.

"Good then." I whispered breathing against her neck nuzzling the soft skin, my hand tracing the gentle curve of her waist. I shifted and teased her playfully, which had her giggling. My intention was clear and she seemed to like the idea.

Her lips were salty and soft, her touch restless as it too roved about me discovering the strength of my need for her almost immediately.

Kelly was adventurous I had already discovered, but I was surprised when she pushed me back into the shadowy shelter of the tree and began to deal with the buttons and lacing of my shorts without preamble.

Slipping her much smaller hand down on an adventurous path, I caught my breath chuckling at her invite and at her antics, letting her small hand explore my body. Kelly tugged restlessly at the lacings of my shorts, freeing me from the constraints of fabric and decorum as I eased back to enjoy her play.

What had me amused was what she would make of me. Since my initiation there were changes and as her fingers found these she stopped, pulling back to better see the strangeness in what she felt.

"What... happened...?" she whispered astounded.

I laughed outright at her expression and answered her still chuckling.

"It's OK, it is a head cut, a subincision Kelly... it still works woman."

"Christ. I have never seen that!" In wonderment she looked up at me.

"I chose to do it, with help of course. It's OK, you might even like it?"

Teasing her I shifted about to encourage her before she got to talking too much, but she stopped me by pressing her small hand against my chest. Hauling my shirt high she dropped her lips to my skin adventurously.

I felt the spill of her hair once more as her lips moved down over my chest and midriff and then dipped slowly to my belly. The feel of her hair falling against the skin of my hips and stomach as she tugged at my board-shorts was a delight. Her lips were warm, wet and soft and the promise they offered was everything in that moment.

Surrendering completely to the sweet sensation I eased back with a small growl of appreciation deep in my throat. Her tongue and mouth were exploring my body and my fast swelling erection. My body became a toy that seemed to amuse her. Her touch was hot, wet and entirely intoxicating.

The heat of her mouth was a delight, her tongue adventurous as it swept over me. It was insanely sweet and as much as I enjoyed it, thrilling to the torrid sensations, I knew I couldn't take much more of this after even a short time. I tried to warn her, though I didn't want too... I knew I had to. It had been too long since I had felt the pleasure of a woman.

"Kelly... ease up..." The whisper was more a plea, a delight and as much as I didn't want it to stop, it was a sweet relief when she did. I was then at least able to take control from her hands quickly.

I wanted to punish her for her sweet torment, which had bought me so quickly to an edge. Reward her for the dance of her lips over my body and more than anything satisfy her in a way she could not forget easily.

Roughly pulling the scrap of her small knickers down her legs, tangling them in her feet, I shifted my touch and the lap of my tongue up along her inner thigh. Nestling into the warmth of her legs as they moved about my shoulders and back, accommodating my intent.

When my lips found the svelte places along her body, those hidden well, I sort out what I most wanted. Roughly easing her skirt high out of my way my hands danced along her upper legs and the cheeks, exploring the upper reach of her thighs with my mouth. I guided her movements with determination and obvious intent. I could feel the thrill of her body engorge and then heat in its dance with my touch.

Kelly opened her long legs to me as a butterfly would open its wings and I lifted her hips into the pressure of my lips, ravaging the silken skin with my tongue and lips hungrily. Yet sheltering well my teeth from hurting her. Her groans were sweet and wildly abandoned and it drove me on inspiring the dance of my lips and heavy weight of my tongue.

I wanted to take her to the heights and I knew how. I was learning now what she liked me to do and I wanted to free her mind from her body. I gave her no quarter as she wriggled out of, and then back into my touch. The torture and pressure of my mouth and tongue was driving her relentlessly and I could sense that it was a new dance for her.

Abandoning herself to the sensations sweeping her body she couldn't have stopped me if she had wanted to. Her breath, the sweet moans were a gift. She wrapped her legs about my shoulders and as her muscles strained and shivered I felt the grip of her hands in my hair. She was trying to stop me but not wanting to let me move away. The thrill that her pleasure bought me, warmed me.

The heat racing through my own body quickly burnt a path along my belly and groin making control difficult but I wanted to consume her, enjoy each small sound, each moan and each shudder that gripped her as it raced through her body.

She began to beg in the end, it was a soft sound, a breathless plea on the edge of abandonment. With a completely helpless cry she had my hair in a tight and painful grip. I don't think she realized I couldn't have moved. Instead of fighting her, I slipped my fingers into the warm pool of her body, teasing her.

I threaded the pressure and weight of my touch within her restlessly as she wriggled once more groaning lost to the heat of pleasure felt within her own body, but she did release me at last. Kelly had abandoned herself to the pleasure with breathless small moans that were sweet to my ears, as her body arched seeking the heat and weight of my own.

I moved over her swiftly before she could grip my hair again and plunged the swollen weight of my body into hers. It was swift, a torrid ecstasy, which carried us both to a height quickly. One that was blind to anything else around us.

It was almost savage and I didn't care... she didn't care who heard us either as she became lost to the ecstasy of our passion for each other. Later I was thankful we had sort out this place deep in the shadow of the night.

It was a sweeping passion, which strangely in some way bound us to each other. The like of which was beyond my understanding or even care. I knew it was a strange relationship we shared. One we were now nurturing in an even stranger way between us.

She was a friend, a lover but she was not mine. Love had nothing to do with this and we both knew it. I wanted her, I wanted to consume all the sweet treats of her body and I knew I was not the only one in her life... far from it. What is more I knew she understood that. She understood that I was as free as she.

She didn't look at me with love, or even tenderness but with sated hunger that made me chuckle breathless, when she once more opened her eyes and sort my own in gratitude and pleasure. I lay sunken in the sweet exhaustion that came after such a swift and heated pounding of both our hearts and our bodies. Our skin was wet with a salty sweat as we became welded together for that moment of sweet exhaustion.

After a time we lay still with the weight of me pinning her helplessly beneath me, once I had surrendered to my spent strength. I knew I should move but it took a monumental effort to do so.

Shifting I struggled to ease my body from hers but again she groaned softly when the chill night air swept in between us, my body abandoned hers. In the separation we both felt the fine sweaty film left on our damp skin grab at the night air.

When we were apart and I had settled onto my side facing her, she moved again into my heat. Her hand was moving up about my shoulders and chest. Her fingers testing my damp skin as I tried to cover her reluctantly, using the small scraps of her dishevelled clothes. It was pretty useless though.

Not wanting to let the chill touch of the night air bite at her, I never the less gave up. Perhaps I was still reluctant to hide her from my senses and it seemed a pointless exercise anyway. Easing myself back I rested as she moved deeper into the shelter of my body, nestling replete now she seemed content snuggling into my side.

We were silent for an age, yet time didn't have much of a measure at the moment. It was all relative to our body's exhaustion. I felt her hand skip across the edge of my jaw and in turn I smiled and moved to sweep my own through her hair, bringing it to some order.

"Hmmm?"

Kelly eased herself up slowly. "I've not felt that... like that ever before?"

With a frown I eased my head back to better see her, then grinned wildly at the expression in her eyes as I added, "It was something... Hey?"

Nodding she slipped back into the shelter of my arm, her head resting on my shoulder as her hand slipped over my chest again, travelling, looking for the edge of the crumpled shirt I still wore as she tugged it down to cover my skin.

"We should do it again," she teased.

"What now? I don't..."

"No. I mean again sometime. It was... was good."

"Yeah. Why not? It was good... we were good together." I said in a whisper, prepared to agree to most anything this woman said in this moment.

We lay silent as our blood slowed and settled, contemplating these words and the memory of the passions between us until my mind was exhausted with it. Then I moved.

"Com'on, we better make a move." Stretching suddenly I slapped her hind lightly and playfully, my grin making my excuse. "It's getting cold and I don't want you to get crook because of me. I better get you home."

"Yes... I guess."

I offered her the tiny scrap that was her knickers I had picked up from the grass, dangling them between my fingers. With a cheeky grin she took them. Smiling as she too climbed to her feet attempting to straighten her clothes. Scrunching the slip of fabric tight into her hand she tucked it away amongst her clothing.

I dragged my mind from the thought of her without those knickers on as we walked back slowly towards the ute retracing our steps. I didn't know what to say, my mind was too busy with that scrap of fabric still tucked somewhere and the silken memory of her skin.

When I settled her into the seat I even stretched the car seatbelt about her, ensuring she was safe. I wanted her safe and I wanted to smell the bittersweet twang of her skin again as well. That action of buckling her in allowed me this without me even making an effort.

It was a silent drive back to her place and this time, for the first time she allowed me to drop her off at the front gate. That was unusual and something she had never allowed before. I wondered at that, as she turned back to me and popped her head down to the level of the front passenger window.

"Will I see you again later this week?"

I thought about it then smiled with hope. "I can get down maybe Friday. Will you be about then?"

Kelly bit her lip. "No. Pete... He's picking me up."

"Well then how about I meet up with you in town, will you have free time? Or do you have other plans on the weekend maybe?"

Suddenly she smiled. "Yeah. Sunday, I could meet you. Perhaps in the gardens where we met last... or you could text when you get there."

"OK. I'll do that. Sounds good."

"I'll see you then." Stepping back from the curb she waited and obediently I waved and swung the old ute about to head off. My mind was still flighty with spent passion, my body still warm and at ease in tune with my thoughts.

It felt strange leaving I decided, particularly in this way. Next time... next time it will be different I promised myself. Next time I'll get a place, a room or something where we can take time, relax and enjoy each other more easily. I didn't doubt that there would be a next time and I didn't doubt that this was what Kelly would agree to.

It was just the way it was.

Justice Born

Tom

My Jongorrie was waiting for me when I got back to the cottage on the old Shackles Estate beside the river. It didn't surprise me for some reason. I half suspected that he would know what had happened between Kelly and I and my glance warned him before he even opened his mouth.

I had no intention of speaking to him much when I walked into my bedroom and he was there. Jeremy had greeted me and I him, when I had stepped into the house. He was settled on the lounge with the telly droning away mindlessly while he watched it without much interest and tucking into what looked like dinner. It was an easy companionship we had, one we enjoyed and I wasn't about to do anything that might change that so I had no intention of telling him about Kelly and I. Besides, I knew it would be the way she would want to keep it.

I was beat and although it was still relatively early all I could think about was a hot shower and tumbling into bed. My body and mind was simply exhausted. Jep however had other ideas once I got to the bedroom.

"I've been doing as you said, and it is good. I like this job Tomtom an... an so do you." He comment gleefully in his inceptive tone, words said with his own peculiar delighted expression as I stripped off and headed for the shower.

"Yeah well that part is none of your business." I warned, knowing he knew what I had been up to this evening. In some way I understood that he knew all about it without a doubt and for a moment I wondered if he may even have come in search of me earlier.

Jep just leered and followed me, restless in his step. "I like this job." He chuckled again. "It's a joss house... a cat house it is Tomtom!"

"I thought you might like that."

"You shoulda said... shoulda said and I woulda... woulda'..."

"Woulda' what?" I asked curious.

"Well I woulda' gone earlier. Done what you wanted..."

"Took your time did you?" I chuckled, realizing he had put off attending to the task I had set him and for some obviously less rewarding activity too it would seem.

"Well yes. But I didna' know... you shoulda' said Tomtom."

The belligerent tone in his words had me grinning with irony again.

Under the shower, as the hot water spilt over me, I thought about those words. They were the usual odd interpretation of what he had seen and heard perhaps, knowing as I did the reputation of the Jongorrie.

"So what did you find? Aside from the joss house side of things."

"Well. That was interesting too. I don't like this friend of hers... don't like him one bit. Nasty, mean type of fella'."

"Yeah? Tell me."

"Well... well he is a 'orrible sort of bloke Tomtom... 'orrible sort. T's not just your girl he has... not just 'er and he's not kind to his women. Not at all, he gives them to too many others. Too many wives he has an' he's broken the Lore too... done bad things."

"Oh?" I prompted as I stepped out of the steaming cubicle and reached for a towel absently.

"Yes. Yes... 'e has a few wives. Couldn't count 'em, might not be all his but some is. Has too many wives, he has." Jep reassured me. "He might not miss the one you like much... she is only there part o' the time. Might not miss her I'm thinkin'. He's kind to her... well most o' the time."

Hanging the towel carelessly I wandered back into the bedroom reflecting on his words. I had come up against this before. I knew that the Jongorrie's concept of the world wasn't necessarily the way I would see it and I often had to untangle what he said. I knew he was long lived, timeless it seemed often and he didn't always understand what he was looking at in today's world. He judged things by older standards, older Lore's and ways.

Reaching for the latest book, which I used to settle my mind at night I climbed under the covers of the bed. Mostly ignoring the little man fidgeting about as he too climbed up on the end of the bed watching me, waiting patiently.

He was sitting seemingly awkward in his way, his small legs oddly placed but apparently finding a seat of comfort while my mind ticked over trying to interpret his words. I was not following at all what I was supposedly reading.

Jep would view any woman, or girl for that matter, who showed allegiance to the Dodger as likely being a wife. After all, in his world as with the old ways, women were to be controlled largely by their men and sex was a commodity. It had little to do with love or affection and more to do with desire, entertainment or trade. The only loyalty in relationships was to be found in the Lore. He would consider Kelly as one of the Dodgers young wives no doubt.

He would assume that Kelly had been given to the Dodger as a wife, likely when she was a child. It would be his belief that what Kelly and I had between us was of our own choosing and of little concern to the Dodger.

Women in the old ways had more autonomy in their own choices often.

It wasn't uncommon in the old world for older men to acquire many women over time. Particularly those men who had resources or skills and who could support any number of wives and their extended families with food in the way of survival.

In the old way it was the elders who taught the young women the ways of life, sex and men in general. What was between a man and a woman was not as it is arranged in the world today.

Women traditionally belonged to themselves in their choice of partners. Sex was a natural thing, much the same as breathing or eating. Though their allegiances belonged to their husbands and sex was a trade commodity the husband could often choose to use. It was as a negotiated service in arrangements between others and in return for something of value to them.

In lending their women to others, it wasn't like they lost anything because the woman remained their wife. Often the arrangement had advantage in trade and other things such as those found in healthy children when mates were lacking in diversity. Besides, babies were born of their Country, not their fathers. It was the spirit that mattered, not the physical. They had belonged to Country with loyalty to their totem and in the care of their mothers or the family of their mothers while young.

This point of Lore and relationships had caused a lot of problems with the colonists. They hadn't understood this ancient relationship between men and women. In the bush, where white women were commonly rare, the whitefellas had often disliked returning what they saw as their own black women to their rightful husbands.

"So he has a few women at the house?" I prompted after a moments thought.

"Yes... yes a few... maybe that many. Different houses too... different places." Holding up his hand he presented me with four of his fingers.

"All Kelly's age. Or older?"

"She..., your woman is a lesser wife, but not the youngest. Not at all... there's a younger wife but she is not happy. Not happy by far."

"Younger? How young?"

"Little chested." Jep said salaciously indicating what he meant. "Not yet grown proper... not old enough for initiation."

The inflection and meaning of his words danced along with his mobile expressions. As he prattled on I felt my gut tighten and heat realizing that there were children involved here who should not be in what was essentially a brothel. The death stone warmed suddenly at my own thoughts, reacting to my response to the Jongorrie's words.

It seemed the Dodger's interests extended into young girls and the very thought fired every trigger in my interest in him. Even I was surprised at my reaction, which deepened as the very concept became more real to me.

Under the Lore we had once followed, children would often belong to a husband but they remained with their people until they had fully grown. It was for the husband to support the child and often her family as well. It was an obligation, one with offerings of food and particularly meat during her childhood. The Dodger was a poor husband, one without these loyalties I didn't doubt, but that was something to check on.

As hunters, the men provided much of the big meat and protein items in the mob. A husband would only take a young girl after her initiation, after she had become a woman proper. It was against the Lore to claim a child before her time.

The Lore would judge a man harshly for such a thing as robbing a girl-child of her innocence and childhood, which was rightfully hers alone. A childhood should be something enjoyed and appreciated by all.

"I want you to find out more about this young girl. Where she stays and what she is to him. But you will not go near her... not frighten her." I said tersely. "And I want you back by the end of the week, you have four days Jep and then I want you back to tell me what you have found out."

"You're interested in this one?" The Jongorrie asked surprised at my request.

"Yes, but only because she would not be such a wife yet. This is a child he has stolen from someone. A child he has no right too and I would return her to her mob."

My words held intolerance and this more than anything would convey to the Jongorrie my intent. I could see this already in his face, the added glee; the excitement flashing keenly in his eyes.

To him this would be a matter of Lore, a matter of payback, a judgement I had made as a keeper of the Lore. Not a moral judgement at all but the result would be the same. To him this would be the first time I had made a judgement, the first time I would maybe step out of my own choice in a hunt as a Kadaitcha Man if I judged the Lore breeched.

There would be a certain pride in that for him amongst his kind. It perhaps had been a long time since he had been involved in a full hunt. After all, that was his purpose in life and fascinated I watched his glee steadily build.

"I can do that... I can. I will... I will be back soon with what you want to know. I can... I will..."

Excited he scrambled from the end of the bed and in a shift of the dark light between times, he was gone. Then for the very first time I felt the true weight of my Lore settle about me. I was surprisingly calm, surprisingly set on a path I had so easily chosen and it was only for me to be sure of what I was stumbling into before I acted as I had seen my Grandfather do, in defending the Lore and bringing things to a rightness.

The only other time I had felt such a sense of being steadfast in my thoughts and path was when I had sat at the end of the small wharf outside, in what now seemed to me to be a lifetime ago. It was when I had seen the truth about my own father and I had known I was set on my first real trial as a Shadow Walker, a man of the Kadaitcha. It was when I had been gifted the Moogie Eye, when I first hosted this death stone within me that had so changed my life.

There was something about having my Jongorrie about me now, doing my bidding at this time. It was something that strangely settled me too. It was an odd realization.

When I at first opened my eyes the next morning I realized I had slept well. My rest had been settled and solid. I woke up refreshed and set on my path with my mind having sorted through the complexities of the Lore. If I was right in what the Dodger was up to then I knew beyond doubt that I would be on a hunt and something about that was thrilling.

Perhaps it was the thought of bringing a form of justice to the world where there was often no real justice at times. What the Dodger was doing broke the Lore in my world, and the law in his. Yet there was little true justice being found in any of it at the moment.

Little did he know it but he might well see justice done for stealing a child, one who was too young yet to be a woman and this for his own purposes. The Lore felt good to me in that moment particularly if this crime of his was found to be true.

My mood over the next few days became one of no nonsense and it was a good mood to be working with in my job. I achieved a great deal and even the boss was impressed though I couldn't have been bothered less with him. I simply did what needed to be done while I waited for Jep's return. Mostly people simply stayed out of my way and I guessed that it was something about my manner or maybe my expression that warned them off.

I saw little of Jeremy for some reason, it wasn't that he was away, just that he tended to spend time in his room, something which he had never done before and I wondered if Kelly had said something that may have upset him.

When I probed at it lightly, he brushed such a idea off very easily and I figured I had been wrong. There was something else going on though and after my curiosity he seemed to be about even less than before. In the end I decided that he must be spending time with his mates elsewhere, after all he was of that age when these things became important. Plus I had other things to brood over.

Jep got back to me on Saturday night and I was impatient to hear from him, which made my temper shorter than usual. That the Moogie Eye was growing warmer and heavier by the day, fed by my temper and imagination, wasn't a comfortable thing.

"You're cutting it fine!" I chipped at him, when he turned up in the lounge room in the manner of his kind. Tossing the book aside I had been reading with little interest I studied him silently, waiting.

"My you're in a temper... a temper is not good Tomtom... not good."

I breathed steadily, reaching for breath to tame my impatient mood, acknowledging my temper as I did so. "Yes. Sorry... and?"

"Well he has taken her, stolen her for sure. He doesn't use her himself but sends her to others. She doesn't like it much. Not at all much."

"How do you know this?" I asked softly, still struggling to temper my anger knowing that there was no point in directing it towards the Jongorrie.

"I had to wait... wait I did an that is why... why I'm late. Not that you know that." He added in something of a sulk that eased my mood quickly. "You shoulda' knowed that Tomtom. I was waiting to see... to be sure."

"OK. Sorry... but for chrise-sake tell me what you found without all this other crap Jep. Or... or I will throttle you."

I was kidding, back-peddling my mood but still he wasn't fully sure on that. He fidgeted and then suddenly settled to the floor not far from me as though the weight of his words and thoughts had become too heavy.

"Yep he stole her. She cries at night for her people still and she doesn't like him much, not even the things he gives her most of the time. I don't know where her mob be at though... I don't know. She is white this one, a whitefella's kid."

"She is a kid then?"

"Yes... yes. Too young... too young to do what she does. It is dangerous Tomtom... too young... it would kill her and the men who..."

"Yes. Enough, I can figure the rest."

Impatiently I stood, stepping around the small coffee table and over towards the darkness outside, casting my glance through the balcony windows. Jeremy had gone out earlier and I had the house to myself.

Big Jim was still over in the boat-shed though and I wondered if I should talk to him, talk to Apari even? But then I knew what they would judge me uncertain of myself if I did.

As a man I should do this, be sure in my own mind. I had to be sure of what Jep was telling me, sure that the Lore had been broken before I acted.

"Jep. Tomorrow I want you around, close. I might need you. There are things I want to do in town, in the city and I might need your help. Stay close..." then I swung back to him. "But not too close... hear!"

"Yep I hear... I hear..." he answered clambering to his feet with an unholy glee as he began to all but dance around in his fidgeting manner. "I'll be close... but not too close I promise. Ohh... good. This is good Tomtom. I don't like this fella... he's not nice. Not nice at all to his women I think. A bad man... bad temper he has. Liar too... lies he does to get his way. You can have this woman of his if you want her... have her. You would be better for her."

"It's not the woman Jep." I said quickly scolding him, impatient with his words. "That's not it, but he shouldn't have stolen the child. The women can do as they choose. It isn't only the women that I'm thinking on doing this for. It is the Lore Jep, you should remember that."

"Not the women? Are you sure?" He asked suspiciously.

I just laughed and dismissed him impatiently as my mind sped through weaving together the information I had.

The next day, sitting on the grass down near the ponds in the Botanical Gardens of the city, I was waiting for Kelly. It was like returning once again to where I had been before, only things were subtly different.

I had a plan and while it wasn't one I would be sharing with Kelly, it involved her anyway, though she may never know it. She might never even realise what was on my mind but she would surely bear the consequence of it.

I had seen little of Jep today and I wasn't sure where he was now but I didn't doubt that he was about somewhere. What I did know was that I could just call on the little forest man if I needed him and I knew that just maybe I might. I would need him certainly if things went horribly pear shaped.

When I had finally got up this morning, Jeremy had already gone off on some business of his own and this had made things much easier for me. I also had sent a text to Kelly asking her to meet me here and I didn't expect her to be much longer. She had text me back, so it was just a matter of waiting now.

I liked it here, it somehow felt right. Almost like home and I knew it had a lot to do with the old Bora Ring in the Botanical Gardens. Even though it was in the heart of the city on the shoreline of Sydney Harbour. This was why I liked this spot in particular. Even now I could feel the strengths in the land beneath my feet and hands.

It was a sense of clarity, of the spirit in the earth and land, a sense of Country and of story. It was a history that welcomed me and knew who I was.

Watching Kelly as she approached had me climbing to my feet. She was a pretty girl, her hair mousy and long. I watched as she flipped it around restlessly but she had lost weight in the last few weeks I thought absently. Maybe she was on one of the crazy diets girls get into and the thinner mould of her didn't suit her frame as much.

"Hi," she greeted me pleased with herself.

"Hey there. Wanna coffee or drink? We can get something at the café. I haven't eaten yet I thought I would wait."

"Yeah. That would be nice. Iced coffee if they have it."

Ushering her ahead of me, along the path she had just walked I noticed a free table over by the garden edge and pointed it out. I left her to claim it while I popped inside with our order.

It wasn't long before I was joining her, setting the plate of chips in the centre of the table for both of us. The least I could do was encourage her to eat. I knew better than to tell her that I thought she was getting too thin. Girls took comments like that weirdly.

"So how's tricks?" I quipped, and then laughed. "I didn't mean…"

Kelly just grinned as she cut me off. "It's OK. I know you didn't mean anything like that. I've been having a good time actually. I was at a party last night. It was good… I got something for us too."

Shuffling around in her shoulder pack she pulled out a small wrapped package, her eyes challenging me with a curious smile as she shook out two small tablets. There were four tablets in all, tablets the like of which I was not unfamiliar and I suddenly pursed my lips not so happy about her offer.

"What is it?"

"Just uppers… they're great. I got them last night These were everywhere and they didn't even notice I nicked a few." Popping one into her mouth she offered me the other as she leaned across the table cheekily.

Shaking my head, a small gesture just for her, I frowned. "No. Not for me Kelly, sorry. You never know what's in that stuff and I've heard…"

"Oh come on. They're good, I took some and it is just an upper really. I thought you would enjoy it?" She protested lightly as she played with the small pill in her mouth, teasing me. Still trying to tempt me.

I shrugged. "I don't do that stuff woman. It's madness in a big way."

"Oh it's harmless!" she added laughing at me.

Quite unexpectedly she straightened up. Leaning to me she stretched across the table, wrapping her small hand about my neck, pulling me in for a kiss. My lips met hers at first delighted but then I felt the small pill as her tongue darted into my mouth, playing around my own tongue.

Surprised I jarred my head back in protest but I had swallowed before I even knew it. Realizing unexpectedly that I had taken and swallowed the dam thing anyway.

"Shit!" I swore, glaring across at her as I coughed and wiped my mouth leaving her to laugh as she sank back into her seat amused."

"Oh don't be such a dag." She tormented as she popped the other pill still in her hand into her mouth and swallowed with a swig from her coffee. Her eyes taunted me in my indignation. "They're harmless, I've already had some."

"You don't know what they are cut with." I protested, shaking my head as I swallowed reluctantly again, wiping my mouth in distaste. "I'm supposed to stay away from that stuff Kelly!"

She just shrugged as though it was nothing. "Oh... Well it won't kill you, you might even like it." Putting the package away she looked across smiling, accepting my annoyance as par for the course. "Don't be such a pain... it is just a pill. All it's gunna do is make you relax."

"Yeah but it should be my bloody decision!"

I cut the conversation short while I got over my annoyance. It wasn't the first time I had taken something like this but I had decided a long time ago that I was finished with that stuff. There came a time in life I had found when you just stepped away from the candy store and my time had come and gone years ago.

There was little I could do about it now though, so I resigned myself to just enjoying it. After all I wasn't going to be going anywhere much and it would wear off soon.

"Did you have any plans for this arvo', anything you wanted to do?" I asked after a while, once I had calmed down a bit.

"No. Thought I would leave it up to you."

I grinned suddenly, feeling my mood ease up. "I thought we might have something to eat and then take a walk. I'm curious about this bloke of yours, the Dodger."

"His not a Dodger... that sounds sorta bad," she laughed easily. "He's OK. You just don't like him because of... well of us."

"You could be right there." I added with humour. "Anyway, you can tell me about him later. Have some chips, you look half starved."

Her eyes flashed, but she was in a good mood now and along with me she picked at the chips, eating more than I thought she would in the end.

We headed off for a walk around towards Lady Macquarie's Chair following the pathway that edged the harbour, once we had eaten our fill of chips. Tourists were milling around us but I knew we would move past them soon so they didn't concern me. They rarely got beyond the old landmark at the head of the gardens and once you had found your way through them and down into Woolloomooloo Bay you were pretty much on your own mostly.

I liked the walk around this way even though the tourists commonly got in the way of private conversation. Once we had got past the popular site on the headland we followed the path on around towards the old baths. Here it was much quieter.

The harbour views were pretty special and the strip of natural bushland that grew to the side of the track afforded quiet places to chat as well. You could imagine yourself well away from the beat of the city here, even though the city still surrounded you.

"So tell me about him." I prompted without care. Knowing without doubt that the question was made easier by the small pill popping session earlier. I was hoping she was going to be candid in her answers, as candid as I was going to be persistent.

"What is it you want to know?"

"Well, for one, are you serious or is it a casual thing."

Kelly bit her lip and glanced up from under her eyelashes playfully. "Not serious. He's just a friend really, he sees other girls. But it is good that he lets me use his room in the city, that's really handy. He's even talking about sending me overseas for a holiday."

"He gets a cut of your work?"

"No. No he doesn't," she protested defensively. "You have him wrong. You never did say what you think of it really, you know... now you've had time to think on it. On what I do with ... when I'm with other guys. Does it bother you any? The other girls said that you might be angling for a cut of the money I make maybe. Some of the boyfriends the girls have, do that you know."

"Jeezus. No! That is your business. If it is what you want, why would I want to get in on it. So you told the other girls about us?"

Nodding she glanced away and then stopped, leaning up against the fence quietly reflective. "I told only one other girl, she's a friend. Some of the girls say that it's usually the way it is with guys they go out with. If they know what we do, that is. They think that they are loosing something that is theirs I guess, like we belonged to them."

"No. Not with me Kelly. As I said, I don't much like it, but it's your business girl. If that's the kind of life you've chosen, then who am I to try and stop you? It's not like we're serious or anything is it?"

"So you don't like it? That's too bad. It's not a bad way to earn money. Pete looks out for me and that makes it safer. It would be harder without him you know. We need someone I think, to sorta organize I reckon."

"Hmm. He has others you say? Many?"

"No, just a few girls. Some of them live at the house full time. Others... they come and go." Shrugging she turned back to me with a quip of a smile. "It's a casual arrangement I think, he likes it that way."

"Does he let you have visitors of your own?"

"Yeah... he doesn't mind. He's like you in a way. He sees it as my business and well... He brings lots of the girls to parties. I wondered if he gets money that way? I think that he might, or maybe other things."

"Like what?"

"I don't know. You tell me," she challenged suddenly shrugging. "I don't want to talk about him anyway."

Reaching up she trailed her fingers down my shirt, stopping short at my hip band of my jeans then looked up playfully. "We can find a place. And... play some. I like what you do you know."

I chuckled. "You do hey?"

She bit her lip with a cute coquettish smile. "Yep. It was nice."

My glance swept the bush as my thoughts followed her words. There were quiet places here but... none that wouldn't serve my ends. "We could go back to your place if you want?"

Pursing her lips she considered my suggestion. "I don't know?"

"I thought you said he didn't mind what you did?"

"Mmm. I guess we could, it's just it's a bit of a mess. He went out this morning anyway, said he'd see me tonight sometime."

"I'll ignore the mess." I offered, teasing her.

"OK then. If you like," she agreed suddenly.

I left the ute where I had parked it earlier, not even mentioning it as we headed down through the parks edge, across the ovals and up the main street towards Kings Cross. I knew where Kelly stayed and it seemed simpler to walk even if it was a good stretch.

Kelly was chatty as we walked along talking about the private party she had been to the night before in the Cross. The unit where they had partied had overlooked the harbour and even if I didn't want to hear about it, it was interesting as she talked on about the other girls, most of who were her friends it seemed.

This had all worked out well for me. I had wanted to get into the place she stayed at and in doing so I could have a good look around. Work out what the arrangement was and see what I could find out for myself. Kelly had unwittingly taken me right there, exactly where I wanted to be and I was rather pleased about that.

The semi-detached house when we reached it had the same cramped old feel about it that I expected. It was one in a row of like houses built like so many of the old colonial buildings had been at the turn of the century. It didn't look anything much but it was a narrow two-story place with a high roof and pokey small rooms running off a narrow side hall.

There was a stairway at the door that led up to the second floor, this being below the roof cavity, which would have a small dormer window for venting no doubt. There would be some kind of access into the roof I knew as these high spaces had been used for storage and mean quarters for servants in colonial times.

The architecture of these buildings had always been of an interest to me. Many of these late colonial era buildings utilised the roof space. Some even dug beneath the floor in root cellars that also offered shortfall rooms. These were usually either hot and pretty airless or cold and damp. It was entertaining to guess at what another time had made of these buildings.

It was quiet and there seemed to be few people around, though there were voices coming from one of the ground floor rooms. Kelly led me up the stairs to the second floor and then along right down towards the back of the house, ducking into the room right at the end that seemed to block the hallway.

Moving over to the window curious, I pushed the heavy curtain aside. They kept the room in an evening gloom but they could be used for cooling too, keeping the harsh afternoon sun out. Glancing out across an old tin roof of an annex below I heard her slip the bolt on the door.

That got my attention and dropping the curtain I stepped back towards her, she obviously had something in mind and hadn't just been playful in her words.

The room had overlooked an uninteresting cramped backyard through two pokey windows. Inside it was twilight and airless, but we weren't here for the décor, I could see that plainly in her eyes. I reached for her but she evaded my hands playfully and skipped about. This was a game and she giggled with invite.

The covers of the large bed were awry. Obviously it hadn't been straightened from the night before. There were clothes and other oddities strewn about the floor. These Kelly mostly kicked under the bed or out of the way, making more room seemingly. She picked up only a few of the clothes scattered about, tossing them onto the chair and onto the end of the bed more in play than any serious attempt to tidy.

"Sorry about the mess. I didn't think I was going to get visitors up here." Sitting down with a teasing smile she settled on the bed with ease.

Having caught my eyes she reached over grabbing at my shirt when I approached, pulling me towards her. Slipping her smaller hands up under the fabric of my shirt she swept her fingers against my skin in a teasing fashion until she found the button of my jeans. There she began to fiddle firing my blood easily.

Chuckling I shifted the hair from her shoulder and bent to the temptation of her delicately curved neck. My lips playing along her shoulder as I lent in, bracing myself with my hands on the bed but resisting falling into the already messed up covers. "Not doing anything with you on this bed Kelly." I said softly.

She froze then, sitting back a little surprised. "What! Why not?"

"You heard." Pulling her up off the bed I gathered her back into my arms, reassuring her. "I don't like your bed, it is where you entertain others than me." I teased on a determined and annoying chuckle.

She was disconcerted, but I ignored her slipping my hands restlessly about her as I flicked the buttons and pulled at the zip of her jeans.

Dropping down before her suddenly I hauled these to the floor leaving her to step out of them, while she used my shoulder for balance.

Giggling she reached across to the small table by the bed and took a rubber from the small bowl there, waving it in front of me playfully. "What do you mean you don't like my bed?" She demanded dropping onto it easily again.

"Just what I said." Challenging her I straightened to take the small packet from her fingers. Ripping it open I tossed the wrap to the floor putting the rubber between my lips while I knelt back down to run my hands slowly up the length of her legs as she sat on the edge of the bed.

I reached up over her hips and when I drew her towards me, again forcing her to her feet, she giggled uncertain. Perhaps even a little annoyed with me.

It took a second to finish the job she had started on the button and zip of my own jeans as I kicked them aside. I could feel the light lace of her knickers beneath my touch when I drew her towards me again, away from the bed, my body hardened in its excitement. I sorted the rubber out while she waited for me patiently as we stood there facing each other. I was more than ready and as keen as mustard.

Then turning her about suddenly, keeping her still in the circle of my arms I chuckled at her surprise. Nuzzling her neck I stood behind her, settling her against me so she knew what it was that I intended. Then I slipped the light lace from her hips as she giggled letting her knickers fall while I chuckled softly against her skin at her curious and uncertain manner.

Confused she allowed me to shift her about easily. I think she was curious about what I was up too but she caught on and laughing, she made no objections when I bent her gently, facing her playfully towards the bed.

My hands played about her hips, running over her skin and shifting up about her thighs. My touch sweeping along her inner thigh, travelling up between her legs, was restless and eager.

She caught her breath when my venturing fingers felt the moist invite of her body, slipping down through the moistness along her skin, exploring gently and playing with the silken warmth there as I chuckled in delight against the heat of her back. My hot breath flushing along her back at finding her already excited under my touch.

I was impatient, eager and she was ready. Kelly could do that to me easily I realized and her small chatter about the party earlier had been excruciating in its own way. It was the invite in her glances however, which had egged me on.

Kelly had a firm balance on the side of the bed. Lifting one of her knees up onto the bed at the nudge of my own she spread her thighs to my touch. Easing back I moved my body into hers impatiently with an urgency that was irresistible, meeting the delightful heat of her body with my own.

I hadn't meant it to be this quick, our coming together this salient. The ready moisture of her body had been too great a promise. My hands swept to the tightening tension in her breasts as I moved her more firmly towards me.

Playfully I squeezed and moulded her nipples and breasts with my fingers and palm teasing her gently. Growling again with pleasure and the delight of finding her so ready and compliant, her body firm, moist and inviting.

Her small gasps, almost a squeals of delight, were fired with the edge of pain from the nip of my fingers. It drove the movement of her hips into mine as she arched delicately. Kelly moaned; a deep throaty sound that was music and my hands dropped to guide her, feeling the warmth of her body and the moistness of her welcome me.

The strain of her muscles was evident when I spanned her slender waist with my hands, finding a fine tenseness beneath my fingers. I felt the demand of her hips in a growing and eagre dance against my own.

"Harder... please...! Oh god please..." she begged in a breathless whisper as she dropped her shoulders towards the bed, opening her body fully to mine.

The swell of my body filled hers eagerly and I moved against her in an impetuous beat, a pace that was growing torrid. "Yes... oh yes like that..." It was almost a gasp and I pushed my body deeply into the sweetness of hers. I felt my control slipping and I groaned defenceless in the primitive drive I felt to fill her as I exhausted myself.

It was useless to try and tame the drive of my body against hers as I felt the tightness, the sudden tension in reaching the heights of pleasure. I just didn't care anymore once the tide began to sweep through me.

Too soon I felt the strain and spill of my body. I heard Kelly complain softly in a small moan of protest that it might be over. I should have known, should have tried to ease up but the pleasure was too welcome.

I tried to maintain my body's drive, but it was something of a feeble attempt. Lacking the fire of need, Kelly knew at once when the race of my passion began to subside. She eased away from me eventually, stretching and rolling about on the crumpled dark covers of the bed. Then she swung to catch my glance in annoyance, in a frustration edged with humour.

"Sorry..." I whispered breathing deeply, "That was too hard..." I found myself laughing softly at her annoyance, her impatience as I surrendered to the keen exhaustion of my body. It left me propped leaning against the bed with a small apologetic grin finding its way about my lips.

I tried to straighten slowly but she shifted and I reached for her instinctively as I sank slowly to the floor laughing. I bent my weight to my knees refusing the bed that she attempted to drag me onto. She was put out, certainly disappointed in being robbed of much of her own pleasure I could see, a fine pleasure now knew from the last dance between us.

I reached for her chuckling, to span her hips still with my larger hands about her. I pulled her towards me playfully again, upsetting her centre of balance as she fell easily back onto the bed with a small surprised squeal. She was giggling as I hooked one of her svelte legs over my shoulder, my lips finding the sweet heat between her legs.

Kelly gasped in a small moan and stretched apparently delighted, arching her back as my fingers dipped into the pool formed in our pleasure. Skating my fingers over the fine skin deep inside her I drew the moist heat to the rim of her body in a gentle rhythmic touch. Teasing her body while my tongue and my mouth danced about the swollen silken lips, tormenting the small, engorged mound I found there.

Caressing and flicking this hard little node with my tongue I suckled softly at the source of her pleasure. Listening for the small sounds of breathless pleasure that could fire my own.

Her groans were growing torrid, lost to all but the sensations sweeping now through her and I loved the taste of her, the sounds she made. They were soft and throaty, and thoroughly female.

Abandoned to her body I doubt she knew she was as vocal as she was but it was for me a pleasure to hear, a delight that encouraged me. It fired my blood, waking my own body again.

I played, my tongue stretching the delicate skin in a lap. My lips teasing her as she wiggled and stretched constrained by my hand and arm wrapped about her hips while I held her body captive. I wasn't going to allow her to escape until I knew she was exhausted with pleasure.

I owed her that after my impatience. Kelly loved and hated it all at the once if the small protests she often made were any indication.

In the end I pulled her to the floor, landing her carefully into my lap and she was impatient beyond care as she reached for my body to guide me back deeply into her own.

This then was her dance. Curling herself about me, her body gripping mine as she gripped about my shoulders and hair savagely. My own body easily answering her need and I happily surrendered to her dance again.

It was a pleasure like no other, once more swifter than we wanted. We were left exhausted, emotionally and physically as we found a torrid release in the height of the fight and the play, frolicking between us.

I eased my back along the floor spent, when her body finally released mine from its waves of passion, leaving her sated as well. Spent in an animal passion she spread herself along my length like a ragged doll giggling softly replete with pleasure.

Neither of us wanted to move, it was warm, our skin slippery with moisture and heat. The scent of our sweat enveloped us as I struggled to gather my strength to find the will to move.

Part of me just wanted to curl up and sleep but I had to remind myself that I was here for a reason, though I had reason enough now to not want to leave her for the moment.

Kelly reached out and stretched, dragging at the bed cover and pulling it roughly from the bed she let it fall, draping about us. She moved little from me, though I knew her body had fully released mine and that she felt as languid as I. Nothing seemed to matter however as we nestled together, nothing mattered much at all.

Eventually she slipped from atop of me to curl at my side. Exhausted I wrapped my arm about her as she fussed, irritated with the arrangement of the bedcover and that made me chuckle. I captured her hand in mine stilling her impatience and she settled thankfully.

When I closed my eyes there was still that dull shaded dimness in the room, with small strips of light escaping between the curtains. It was all too easy to slip into the escape that was timeless.

The Scent of a Flower

Tom

It was the noise that disturbed me, a persistent pound at the door that was becoming more impatient. For a moment I had no idea where I was. It was dark, darker than any night and confused I began to ease myself up.

Kelly was still asleep at my side on the bare floor and it had grown uncomfortable. I nudged her gently, then slowly tried to ease to my knees in the darkness. I was attempting to reach for the long curtain that I knew was there, as crouching I gained my balance, still disoriented.

The knock at the door became an impatient pounding sound. I frowned as my head throbbed uncomfortably in response to the noisy intrusion.

"Kelly! Come on open up!" A male voice demanded curtly. I felt her sudden start and she began to struggle some as I clambered about her, stretching ahead of me. I was searching for the window curtains, still in some confusion. I wanted to flick them open and let some light into the dim shadows of the room. It was way too dark to see properly.

"Shit!" She whispered drunk with sleep, though now alarmed. "It's Pete! What time is it?"

"Night I think." I whispered back still confused, taking her lead from the quiet and frightened tone of her voice.

"Oh Shit! You have to go!"

"What?"

Finally reaching the window I switched the curtain aside, flooding the room with dim starlight as I glanced across at her. Kelly was scrambling for her clothes. I wasn't sure why she was so alarmed, even though her boyfriend was at the door. Couldn't she just tell him she was busy, or perhaps had someone with her now?

"Here! For Chrise-sake get dressed." She spat in a furious whisper, tossing my jeans at me wildly. "Hang on." She yelled louder towards the door putting an end to the pounding. "I can't find my bloody gear."

"Well hurry up fuck-it! I have someone here... I'll be downstairs! An' make an effort! I told you to be bloody ready."

Kelly glanced across at me as I stood up in the dim light from the window attempting to climb into my gear. She looked desperate almost and that had me frowning. Pulling my jeans up with some difficulty I watched her oddly, wondering what this was all about and where I might find my shirt and shoes in all this confusion.

"Oh Shit, shit, shit, shit... shit..." she mumbled furious for some reason while she tossed clothes about, flinging them out of her way while she picked up a mix of garments and tossed them to the bed.

The cupboard doors were flung open and she quickly scoured through the clothes hanging there, choosing a few with little thought. Tossing them on the bed to join the others while she began to climb into those things she had set aside, seemingly with little care.

"You gotta get out of here!" she demanded suddenly in a furious whisper. "You can't go out the front... maybe the window?"

"What! You're kidding?" I questioned surprised as I fixed my jeans.

"No damn it! Pete will kill you," she spat back in a louder whisper.

"I thought you said he didn't care?"

"Yeah... well I lied."

"For chrise-sake Kelly!" Indignant I glared across at her then turned back to the window sweeping the curtain fully aside. It wasn't good, the sill was narrow but at least it overlooked a back lean-too with a sloping tin roof of a sort. I just hoped that it was solid enough to take my weight and I didn't much like the angle of the rusty tin.

Kelly was scrambling behind me and I stuck my head through the window to make a better assessment of a way down from here, when I felt her hand on my back shoving me out.

"What...!" I tried to turn back but her intent was insistent.

"You gotta' go. Now!"

As though on cue there was another hard pound at the door. "Move it Kelly. He won't wait all day!"

"Keep your pants on!" Kelly yelled back annoyed. "I'm nearly ready."

Then swinging back to me she gave me a determined shove. "Go for goodness-sake will you!"

"OK...OK I'm going." I protested furiously now myself, as I reluctantly lifted my leg through the window. "If I break my bloody neck then you can explain it!"

Scrambling I got through the window. I wasn't at all sure of the footing that I found. It shifted uneasily beneath me on the heavy slope as I slipped some, and glared back at Kelly while she determinedly shut the window on me, twitching the curtain back at my look of angry disbelief.

I tried to gain a decent hold on the ramshackle wall to counter the uneasy foothold I had when I heard the door open and an angry exchange. But I couldn't concentrate on that. I was too busy trying not to end up in the back yard in an inglorious heap. Maybe even breaking my neck on the way down.

Looking up, searching for a hold or any escape I was surprised to see Jep balanced above me wearing a wide grin. It had to be the very last thing I expected.

"Up here Tomtom… quick, mind the pipe." He whispered in a gleeful undertone, indicating the drainage pipe off to the side that would have been easy enough to trip up on.

My eyes though sort an easier route, one down to the ground and impatiently I heard him whisper again somewhat annoyed. "Up here, down there is too busy for the moment, you gotta wait a-times!"

Conceding that he just might know what was best I edged out along the uncertain footing of the slippery, sloped roof until I reached the cross junction and then eased myself up unsteadily over the gutter to the upper most rooftop. Finding a sound grip wasn't easy, but I made it to where Jep was crouched and he indicated the small attic dormer window that served as a vent and window in one.

"You'll fit through there I think, it would be best an we can wait… wait till it is quiet."

"I can't get through that!" I protested. Eyeing the small dormer window with serious doubt.

"Cause you can… cause you can Tomtom. Come on."

We inched along slowly towards the small window casing and when Jep reached it he was able to push at it easily, clambering through without a thought. For me though it was a squeeze, one that had me twisting and turning into an uncertain space before I finally managed to get my wider shoulders and the rest of me through the small opening.

My skin was scraped and stung in places where I was sure I would find a splinter or two. It had been a really tight fit; a struggle and not having my shirt to protect me or even ease me through had not helped.

The air was stifling inside the small dark space that was actually the high central cavity between the ceiling below and the tin roof above. Someone had laid out rough floorboards though, as unstable as they felt and there seemed to be a trap door of sort over at the edge, which no doubt allowed access through a ceiling somewhere.

But what truly surprised me was the crumpled mattress tucked up against the edge of the roof in the corner and somewhat in disbelief I recognised the curled shape of a child, one wrapped tightly in a ball with only the gleam and movement of a child's eyes peeping out through the tightly held blanket.

Jep seemed not to care, but I froze at the sight. He shuffled over towards the tightly cocooned bundle while I looked on stunned.

"It's OK. I'm her special friend aren't I?" He said softly, in complete confidence. "She doesn't like it up here much... she doesn't. I told you so I did," he whispered as he turned to reassure me.

Then turning back to the child he grinned in confidence, squatting even though he fitted easily under the roofing struts. "He's good... good for you. Don't worry they won't be back tonight. I heard him... heard him say this week sometime but not tonight... not tonight."

The child barely unfurled the blanket she had wrapped herself in, revealing a mussed mop of dark hair as she looked across at me, flicking her eyes between Jep and I.

"He won't hurt me?" she asked Jep timidly.

"No... nono...no. Not Tomtom. He is a good man. He has come to help he has. You'll see... you'll see. He won't let them hurt you." Jep reassured her gently.

"She can see you?" I whispered surprised.

"Of course she can." He reacted scolding me. "A child she is... a child still and her fear opens her eyes. While she's afraid... that is why... she will see me."

I nodded, something else new I realised. Then it dawned on me that this was likely why my sister Debbie could no longer see Jep, had indeed stopped seeing him years ago now. She had no longer been afraid. I was amazed that I hadn't known that and a great deal fell into place.

"Hi." I said softly trying to appear confident and safe in the eyes of the still balled figure. "Call me Tom if you like. What's your name?"

"Iris."

"That's a pretty name. You don't hear it much. It's a flower isn't it?"

The child nodded timidly. She was still afraid and it seemed that this wasn't going to change anytime soon so I settled carefully cross-legged fashion onto the floorboards where I was. I couldn't have stood in any comfort as there was barely enough height in the apex of the roof and none for me at the sides.

"Why are you hiding up here for goodness sake. Its so dark isn't it?"

The child shook her head as though in disagreement but then said in a whisper. "They don't like me downstairs. They will hurt me if I go down there. He said they would and it's true too."

"It is?"

Nodding she looked across at Jep, as though she was looking for reassurance, or maybe confirmation. Then she turned back to me with an uncertain look. "Are you going to take me away?"

"Me?" I thought quickly. "Do you want me too?"

For a moment I thought she was afraid of the idea and she glanced across at Jep again. He however just curled up on the mattress near her as she thought over my question.

My head was throbbing painfully and I suddenly became aware of it more so in the cramped and dark stillness of the roof cavity. There was little I could do about it at the moment but I was glad of the darkness, I had a feeling any light would have made my head ache worse and quietly I cursed Kelly for her impetuousness.

Jep shuffled closer to the kid as though to encourage her. "Where do you wanna go? Is there somewhere you wanna go?" he asked quietly.

"Home."

"Where is home?" I asked carefully.

"Mums place."

"Do you know the address?"

"Smithfield Road."

"Where abouts?"

The girl shrugged. "With my Mum."

Stumped I thought it over while she waited hesitantly.

"Do you know mums phone number?"

"No. I can ring three zero's though if you have a mobile one?"

I reached for my back pocket and pulled out my mobile, then thought about it. "Maybe not yet. We have to get out of here first. I think there are people downstairs and I don't want them to know I am here."

"We're going tonight... tonight Tomtom. They are coming soon, but not tonight." Jep said suddenly under the scrutiny of her wide eyes.

"Do you know where they're taking you?" I suddenly asked, curious.

"The man said it was a ship, a big ship where it would be nicer. They said Mum can't have me anymore, she doesn't like me anymore."

I watched stunned as the little girl's eyes filled suddenly and she dropped her head, struggling to hide her feelings.

"Did your mum say that to you?"

She shook her head, her whole little figure desolate as it curled tighter into a ball.

"Then why do you believe what they say? Do they know your mum?"

Again she shook her head, but this time she looked up hopeful and that look was one you couldn't release easily. It was full of such hope.

"Then how can they say that? I think they're telling porkies maybe." I whispered looking for anything that might please her.

The small hope reflected in her eyes was heart wrenching. Something for her to cling too I decided before I added, "It would help if you knew a phone number. I wish we could ring someone to come and get you."

The look in the little ones eyes was tragic and I searched around for something, anything that might ease her silent pain.

"OK. Instead lets see if we can get outa' here." I added as I shuffled over towards the cover to the mantrap near the corner.

It was easy to prise open. Using the struts that held the small cover I carefully lifted the square of wood. Directly below us was a bedroom. It was in a shaded darkness, tidy even, though there seemed to be no access ladder of any kind that I could see.

I didn't give that a second thought, knowing that I could easily drop the distance, instead I listened for a moment and then glanced across at my Jongorrie who waited patiently with the little girl.

"Can you get around the house?" I asked suddenly.

"Sure can... sure can Tomtom. What do ya wanna know?"

Sitting up I glanced across at him helplessly frustrated at his attitude. "Well I need to know who is about for one. We need to know when we can get through the house easily."

Jep nodded, and then I realized he was nodding at the window exit. An easy exit for him but not for me, I hadn't even considered it an option.

"No. It's too dangerous with a kid. We go down and out through the front door Jep. Go an' check who is about and don't be so damn lazy. Come back when the way is clear."

Climbing to his feet he sighed. "You make it more difficult Tomtom... more difficult than it is," he complained wearily but he shifted through the dark light and he was gone in the next moment.

"I like the way he does that." I said softly to the little girl after a starkly quiet moment. "Wouldn't that be neat if we all could do that?"

Iris nodded, but the small smile peeped out as she further relaxed the blanket about her.

"Are you cold? Hungry maybe?"

Again she nodded. "I didn't like the sandwich." She explained, though I couldn't see any food around.

"How old are you sweetie?"

"I don't like that name. He calls me that name." Whispering she again pulled the blanket tighter and just for a second I wondered if I really wanted to know what her worst fears were, those same fears I could see reflected in her eyes.

"Sorry. OK Iris, can you tell me your age?"

"Eight. I'm nearly nine. I'll be grown soon, it doesn't take long really."

"Well we'll see if we can get you back to your mum. It might take the night though. Hang in there kid. I promise you we will get out of here."

It did seem to take forever too, as the wait for Jep stretched from minutes into seemingly hours and we both became restless. Thankfully Iris curled up to sleep on the crumpled mattress, the long night taking its toll.

I began to wish that I hadn't so summarily dismissed Jep on his errand but it was a relief when he turned up again. It would have been about 2ish, or 3ish in the early morning if the stillness and light outside were anything to go by.

"Where the hell have you been?" I whispered annoyed, trying not to disturb the little girl still curled up and sleeping soundly now.

"I had to wait... wait I did Tomtom... like you said! I've been busy... too busy. You have no idea... no idea." He whined annoyed. "They've gone to bed... all gone now down there an' its quiet. Took their time they did, I knew they would. Busy... busy I've been."

"There is no one about?" I whispered, moving towards the little girl.

Jep shook his head annoyed that I would even ask again.

"Iris... wake up swee... Iris."

Blinking confused she emerged slowly from sleep and she sat up rubbing her eyes. She was wearing a scrap of what was a summery outfit. Something you would wear to the beach on a fine day. No wonder she had kept the blanket wrapped around her slim figure.

I wondered for just a moment what she might have been up to when she had been bought here. There was no time to conjecture though as I reached for her, taking her with me over to the mantrap.

"OK. No one is down there. It's quiet and we want it to stay that way so be very, very quiet baby. I'll go first and Jep can help you."

Lifting the mantrap I peered down, checking that all was clear. The bedroom door was closed which was a relief to see and as I eased myself down into the tight hole, I flashed the little girl a reassuring smile.

The ceiling was highset and dangling with a grip on the high mantrap I looked about for a soft landing. The room was sparsely furnished and I was grateful that I wasn't wearing my shoes for the first time that night.

Without much more thought I dropped the few feet to the floor conscious of being as quiet as I could, landing on all fours trying to cushion my landing and then I froze there, listening intently. It had been a dull thud and hopefully one no one would think much of.

All was quiet about me.

Looking around quickly, I saw the high stepladder leaning up against the wall. It wouldn't reach the ceiling but it was enough to get me back up and enough to get Iris down. Jep could take care of himself.

Once we were both on the floor I set the ladder back against the wall soundlessly and moved to look out through the door. It was locked and I swore softly to myself.

It had to be locked on the outside, the old fashioned keyhole was blocked and I hoped that it was with the key. It only took a glance at Jep before I heard him about fiddling on the other side as he turned a key and the sound in a bolt slipping, which was higher up the door. The playful grin I sent the little girl had her grinning back at me happily, her smile was a delight and a relief to see.

"OK let's go." I whispered taking her hand in my own and leading her through when the door swung open. The two of us stepping out into the dark hallway as I signalled the little waif with a thumbs-up, hoping to make this all seem like a game.

We reached the ground floor easily but the front door had a deadlock on it with no key in sight. Annoyed I glanced towards the back of the house searching down the long, dark hallway as I quietly turned us to head down that way.

In the kitchen at the very end of the hall it was dark and all was quiet. With a glance at the central kitchen table, messy with the remains of a meal, I quickly picked out some of the roast chicken scraps left there on someone's plate. Without further thought I handed them to Iris as we passed through towards the door.

Testing the locks on the back door I was relieved when I found the key had been left in the thing. I knew Iris was gnawing on the chicken bone by the way she had released my hand and the soft hungry sounds she made.

The kid was starving and that made me angrier than anything else around us. I felt the urge to kill this bloke and it was an urge that sent a searing heat through my gut stirring the Moogie Eye.

It was the noise in the kitchen that startled me though, the clatter of plates hitting the floor. As I tossed my glance back to find out what the hell it was, I saw Jep move like lightening and knew immediately he had knocked something off the table.

The sound was deafening as it rattled around the kitchen and I reached for the little girl. A sudden rousing noise and confusion in the room nearest to the kitchen had me working hard at the door.

Someone shouted and then there was another scramble of footsteps along with a shout of enquiry from the hallway. Then the sounds in the pounding of feet reached the front landing from the stairs.

"Jep! Damn it!" I spat furiously angry with him as I wrestled with the aged lock and then realized there was a high deadlock here as well, but at least they had left the key in the door.

It took a second to get it open and I knew Jep had joined us as we scrambled through the door to hear the noise of yet others descending the stairs along with the clatter of doors banging against walls. Calls and confusion seemed to erupt everywhere.

Swinging Iris into my arms, barely thinking about it I bolted into the small closed back yard and looked around wildly for an escape. I knew the layout of the yards around me from the day earlier, when I had looked out from Kelly's window. It took little thought to choose the most open path, the one I remembered only vaguely.

I all but tossed the child high when I reached the fence, launching her towards the top of the high brick wall. Leaving her to grip at the top of it shakily crying in abject fear. I vaulted the thing fairly easily using the pile of wood and scrap leaning against it as leverage.

Iris screamed however, in confusion and terror as she watched me go over the top leaving her seemingly perched there high on the wall. I think she felt I had abandoned her to whatever was making the racket in the house.

I wasn't sure if she was falling, or if it was a jump into my upheld arms, one driven by fear because of those who had now reached the back yard. Perhaps it was a bit of both I told myself as I caught her up when she fell into my hold on the other side of the fence. Both of us landed heavily in a clumsy tangle of legs, arms and feet. For a moment we scrambled around the small, grassed patch of yard next door.

Half dragging her, half carrying the now sobbing child we raced around the far side of the neighbouring house, we fled down a narrow drain-like easement and spilling clumsily out onto the still quiet street.

Iris was sobbing softly, terribly afraid of what was happening to her but I wasn't about to stop and check if she was scratched or scared. There was no time to reassure her when I heard someone emerge through what had to be the front door of the house. My look was wild as I tried to decide what would be the easiest path out of here, deciding on the most direct.

I grabbed at her hand again when I had just barely steadied her fully and I urged her to run into the darkness with me. Thankfully she obeyed and with her hand securely in mine we raced down the road together, though she was way too slow to gain any ground.

I heard a shout but didn't stop. This was followed by a few foul words and the race of footsteps well behind us as we swung around the far corner. Grabbing at Iris once more, I swung her firmly up into my arms and wondered quickly if I could run carrying her at the same time.

It seemed hopeless suddenly, a small kid like her couldn't outrun a man and I struggled with that as I looked feverishly for an escape route in the few seconds we had.

Jep emerged from around the next corner and seeing him I took off towards him. Having gained some ground I dropped her to her feet, quickly swinging her to a halt before me in a mix of urgency and desperation.

"See Jep!" I demanded roughly and was relieved to see her nod, though she was still very much afraid. "Right! Go to him, run as fast as you can and tell him to look for a cop... up at the Cross... look for the big fountain thing. A water circle up the hill with lots of water and find a cop... with blue and white checkers on his hat... an... and all in dark blue. Go to him, no-one else you hear?" I demanded tersely.

Then I let her go with a small shove and watched her falter then turn and race off down the lane towards Jep. He waited at the corner turn, dancing from foot to foot impatiently for all the world as though he had somewhere else to be.

Drawing deep breaths I turned to face the beat of the on-coming footsteps. Everything in me screamed to draw forward the death stone, to use its power and fearful strength. But I didn't know who was coming around the corner. For all I knew it could have been Kelly. Was I prepared to take the risk though I argued harshly with myself?

Unsure of using the Moogie Eye against anyone who wasn't of the Spirit world, I faltered. In the next moment two guys swung suddenly around the corner and I fought the temptation to glance back towards my Jongorrie and the little girl. I wanted to give them no clue where to look next so instead I braced myself firmly in a defensive stand, attracting all their attention as I tried to look as threatening and as confident as I could.

A third bloke swung around the building following the others and I took the time to mark him well in my mind, knowing that a bully always put his minions ahead of him in a full on confrontation.

He was a finer build and slower than the others and I figured him to be Kelly's boyfriend. He eased up almost immediately when he saw me standing there. It gave me a good chance to take in his face and the frustrated anger of his body. Braced as I was, I waited for the other men to reach me.

There were no women following them, but by the time I realised it the first two had reached me and were screaming something about the child, demanding to know where she was.

I felt the wild clout of a hard fist connect to the side of my head unexpectedly as I was scuttled to the ground, staggering under the blow. Then as I gained my feet again, preparing to draw the death stone forward something struck me hard on the back of the head causing me to reel. I knew I was falling into a sinking blackness. I attempted to curl into a defensive ball, knowing I had left any attack too late and this was not going to be pleasant.

Too Late – A Lesson

Tom

Waking up with no idea where you are is never pleasant. When I went to move the pain that hit me was unbelievable. For a time I froze, not wanting to move and with difficulty I lifted my arm to shade my eyes from the brilliant glare that was as painful as it was uncomfortable.

The ground beneath me was rough and cold. Then I realized I wasn't wearing my shirt, or shoes for that matter and my jeans felt damp and cold. It just didn't make sense to me at all.

I tried to turn and attempted to open my eyes again but once more the pain hit me and I knew my eyes were swollen partly shut, it hurt even to feel my face. I went to shift about but the pain of it stopped me again, leaving me to groan in the acute discomfit.

"Tomtom... you awake. Are you...? Tomtom."

The noise was insistent and I knew it was my Jongorrie. Turning to the sound I strained to see, though I could only see through a slit in my left eye. I found the sullen shape of him after a moment of adjustment. He was sitting near my head waiting expectantly.

"Where am I?" I mumbled through swollen lips, a difficult task even to talk.

"In the bush. Not the bush... the city bush. In the city still and it's a bad place to be Tomtom, too many people about ... too many eyes. I dragged you here under the bushes when it started to rain. I couldn't stay with you... couldn't stay all the time but you were sleeping, not really here. That was when I found you... and here was better than out there and you're heavy! Heavy you are... heavy Tomtom."

Jep was making no sense to me, though I remembered something of the efforts of the little forest man. The pain of it was a memory I hadn't lost. I recalled times when I had swept through consciousness and chosen oblivion instead. Then others when I had chosen to sleep, letting myself slip away. It didn't hurt as much when I was lost to time.

I tried to roll onto my back but even with that, the pain stopped me. I didn't think anything was broken, it wasn't a sharp bite of pain but the bruising and swelling kept me still. It was much easier to be still enough to ignore the stiffness in my swollen skin.

Through the dappled shade of the bush above me I noticed the stream of bright daylight through my squinting eye. It was blinding but it took me a moment to realise that it was the sun that was overhead, almost directly overhead. It must be near midday or after I rationalised and then the memories began to return.

"The girl...?"

"We found the cops... the blue ones you wanted me to find. I like the tops they have. Checks is good... good it is, easy to find and she is gone with them. I told her to tell them what happened just like you wanted, her mother should come she should. Who would have checks on their head?" He added absently as though having just thought of it. "They will lookout for her won't they?" He demanded irreverent of my present discomfit.

"Jep!"

"She is with them, I left her there hours ago Tomtom, you've been here for a while sleeping. You shouldn't be 'ere, you should have used the Moogie Eye Tomtom. You failed... you failed you did. I heard them say it and I couldn't stay!"

I groaned impatiently not understanding his gabble at all. Then I struggled to reach for my phone hoping it was still in my hip pocket where I usually left it. At least his rambling prompts had given me that idea.

I was wrestling at the same time with his words and trying to figure out just what the hell he was on about, it just seemed all too confusing.

I winced with the movement of it as I then tossed the phone over in front of him, my head aching and the glare of the day was too much. It was then that I noticed that even the screen looked strange. It registered in that same instant, that it too was shattered.

"There... ring it will you." I whispered between swollen lips.

Jep looked at the phone like it was something alive, then poked at it before he ventured to pick it up. "You want me to what?"

I groaned again. "Ring someone on the damn thing."

Confused he looked over at me.

"Damn Jep! Give it here!" I demanded through stiff lips, impatient with him and growing steadily angry as I struggled with the pain racking my body.

I moved to take the phone off him, rolling over as I stretched for the thing but my head swam sickeningly. I couldn't have found a number but once I managed to at least unlock it I just pressed the emergency numbers 000, dropping the phone near my head while I waited inert with the thing on speaker.

I couldn't tell them much, it was an exercise in frustration and it took a while for them to find me. In all it was an excruciatingly painful experience dealing with anyone, both mentally and physically.

When the ambulance arrived finally, Jep had taken off again but they gave me something to kill the pain. I think they at first they thought I was a drunk, or maybe that I was someone who had been mixed up in a street fight of some kind but I didn't care either way. I just wanted the pain and discomfort that was even now part of my breathing, to stop.

When I next woke up properly it was dark and I was in a bed where everything looked white and anaesthetic. I figured that they had given me something to sleep and that this was a clinic of some kind.

At the very first movement I wished that I hadn't bothered. I had been in fights and scrapes before but nothing like this. It seemed every part of me ached, my gut, my legs, especially my face and even my arms.

There had been times when I had been awake and chosen not to stir, times when I knew what was being said but I had chosen not to speak because of the pain and discomfort of even moving. But now my mind was reeling with the need to know what was going on.

I moved slowly to test my face, which didn't really feel as though it was a part of me anymore. Then unexpectedly I was surprised at a sudden shift of someone nearby.

Looking over carefully I saw Big Jim. He looked like he had been sleeping in the chair near the head of my high bed, by the ruffled appearance of him.

"Hey... steady on there sport." He whispered softly as he sat up into an easy line of vision, his expression full of concern.

I acknowledged him carefully. It seemed not even my mouth worked properly anymore.

"Don't talk. You're lucky you even have any teeth. You really pissed someone off majorly son. With luck the swelling should start to ease tomorra' maybe. For the time being, just sorta nod maybe?"

I moaned in agreement carefully and then I tried to move testing my limbs. I shifted in the hope of sitting up a little but the movement caused the pain to sweep along my gut and back.

"Don't move either," he warned. "They figure someone took to you with some type of rubber bludgeon, a pipe maybe. You are black and blue, or maybe black and blacker from head to foot," he chuckled amused at his own joke. "A couple of cracked ribs too but not too bad."

"Where...?" I could barely manage the word before I gave up and it didn't even come out right.

"You're at Saint Vincent's in Darlinghurst. They found you at Rushcutters near the harbour there in the garden. Looks like you've been in a fight. They also found junk in your system son so you have some explaining to do. You shouldn't be anywhere near that shit."

Again I moaned and tried to shake my head but it was all too difficult so I just closed my eyes.

"Well get some sleep, the cops want to talk to you later. I'll be right here when you wake up and then you can talk to me first…"

Big Jim's words just faded from that point and so did I, as once more I decided I much preferred sleep. It seemed it was deep into the night and the effort was just all too hard.

When I woke fully the next time my head seemed clearer and they had taken the drip out of my hand. I still felt like crap though and I still hurt in all the wrong places but I could think more lucidly. That kept me awake and ready to deal more with the world again if only remotely.

There was a day tray near the bed with a drink and covered plate on it. It tempted me hugely, though I wondered if it would be worth the effort it was going to cost me.

I was cravingly thirsty, though I remembered the early lessons of trying to move so I attempted it with caution. It hurt like the buggery but there seemed to be no one about to help aside from the voices I could hear indistinctly. Those on the other side of the still drawn bed curtains that surrounded me. I just wanted a drink, nothing more, no conversation, just that damn drink.

It was a painful struggle but my body seemed more able to move. Even if it hurt in parts, I felt better for the effort and I managed the drink in the end. My hands weren't so damaged it seemed, as was the rest of me but my face still felt like it was twice the size it should have been and my back ached mercilessly.

What I could see of my body was knocked about and bruised, the bruises were a deeper shade of dark and that meant heavy bruising. My midriff was tightly taped, nursing an injury at my side if the pain was any indicator.

Setting the seemingly heavy cup aside I eased myself back as someone twitched the curtain aside. Big Jim stepped in followed by two police in uniform. The blue and white chequered ribbon on the caps made me smile initially as I recalled Jep's description, but it was again all too painful.

"Tom. Your awake I see, these are the officers I mentioned and they want to hear what you can tell them. Is that right?" he added turning back to them.

"Yes. We need to do a report. Can you tell us what happened son?"

After the initial struggle to ease myself up, which I managed in the end, I kept it simple. It seemed that they were ready to believe me, or at least the version of events I related. A night out, a pill or two, pretty girl and a missing wallet, shoes and I couldn't think what else. Yes I got into a fight with three guys, no I didn't know them and they were done with me. I think the officers were pleased to have it all dealt with so plainly and Big Jim agreed with not pursuing it further. There was no point really.

Once they had gone Big Jim took to the chair again. He settled back and waiting until I too had settled, relieved.

He then looked across at me squarely. "OK, now you tell me about it." He demanded quietly in no uncertain terms, though he kept his voice low at barely a murmur.

It was much harder dealing with Big Jim. He brooked in my own words no simple explanations. He wanted to know what had happened. What was more he knew about Kelly, if not quite the exact details, he knew I had gone to see her. He also knew about Iris but he didn't know her name or anything much other than she was a child. Jep had been busy I realized.

"So you knew this bloke... Pete had a kid in the house?" I asked with strain as the realization came to me.

"I found out just before you did. Your Jongorrie has been told to keep me informed. I've spoken to some of the local mob too and it seems this bloke is into all sort's of things. He has a finger in lots of pies, mostly bad business involving kids too. Messing with a Kadaitcha initiate though is going to be his undoing. The local Elders are angry an' there is talk of payback. A matter of Lore now with the business of the little kids."

"Jep! That little ...! He could have told me all this." I struggled with the words while my growing impatience was making my head ache again.

"No. He tells you only what you ask of him and he's been busy these last few days. Apari has been asking for his help as well which is an odd business. Your Jongorrie needs to keep me informed when he feels it is necessary and that is a good thing son. He has no choice in the matter. It's not just the Elders involved in this now, they have the ear of the Kadaitcha ... big business it's becoming. There is talk of corroboree and there has not been such talk as this in ... well a long time. It's a good thing to hear."

"My Grandfather knows all of this too?"

Big Jim shook his head. "Not all of it but he will hear. Your Grandfathers only interest in this is you. You were doing well, he had confidence you would deal with it or he would have got word to me. Talking of which..."

"Apari is here?" I asked not sure if I was pleased or wary.

"No. He won't leave the caverns of the Kadaitcha Tom, not until it is time and he has good reason," he said quietly. "He stays there most of the time now with the others. You know that. However they aren't happy that you didn't use the tools you were given to deal with this." His words were barely a whisper, not wanting others to overhear this business that was ours alone. "In the old way Ariaka … you should have used the weapons given you. Even against the whitefella', our world has changed … it is time."

"Many remaining of the tribes, our mob too, are as white as the whitefellas. Light skinned we're becoming now Ariaka, lighter like you and others of our clans. Our blood has been mixed, the tribes have been mixed and the ways of the Lore belong to the land, to Country, not only to the Blackfella. Those who belong to this Country are subject to its Lore. Things must be put right. Blackfellas or Whitefellas... colour is nothing to the Lore."

"How do you mean 'in the old way'?" I whispered back uncertain.

"Well to begin with, you could have involved Kintji-iruka. Jeremy could have helped manage this and it would now have been done with. Between the two of you it would have been quite easy. You could have waited until he got back. There are things he could tell you even though he is young. You also ignored your most valuable tool, the Moogie Eye. That is a grave mistake, one that has put you where you are now. You do not do these things on your own son, that is not the way of the Kadaitcha. It is not our way," he warned, his voice urgent and soft.

"I didn't want Jeremy involved, I didn't know... he wasn't there."

"Your dealing with an evil thing Tom, something beyond yourself. You need all the tools you have been given to deal with this in a right way, in the old way, within the Lore. You need to uphold the Lore in your Country for blackfellas and whitefellas, for all-fellas. If you want the Lore to look out for you then you gotta' obey it son."

"I did... I swear!"

"No. You did what you did for yourself... for a woman." Big Jim huffed in a light-hearted disgust. "I can see this and you can't it seems. Your Grandfather was right. Maybe you are not yet ready. Because of that, you are now sore and sorry and you are in here! It was the wrong way you did this thing."

"The little girl, she is OK now. I did the right thing Badjimala, truly!" I struggled not only with the words but with the disappointment in his look. A disappointment that had found it's expression in his words.

"And what of the next child? What of them? Do you think you have dealt with that? What this man does is against the Lore, against his own mob. He has not been dealt with Ariaka. From what Jep has said he traffics in kids and likely women too, though it is the kids that will bring the Lore down on his head."

"The next kid?" I repeated hesitant at the thought, as his words sunk in and then I remembered something. I remembered that Kelly had said she was going overseas on a holiday and all I could think of was the word, trafficking … the man trafficked in women and children.

"Yes. He is as bad as the Numereji serpent that preys on the Spirit Children and yet he walks free. Like a serpent that steals and still he walks free amongst others to steal what isn't his right. He is worse than that because he does these things for something that is of no worth and he destroys many lives. For this, the old Lore would judge him Ariaka and you are the tool the Lore has chosen to do this thing."

"What should I have done then? I can't see how…?"

"You should have prepared, waited, taken the time to prepare yourself and your tools, your weapons. Planned in what way you would do this thing."

"Then I will do that if it is what I should do." I agreed determined.

Big Jim nodded. "Then you have a great deal to do. I know Apari has bought you another chance, but the Kadaitcha will be involved now. This is what I am here to tell you young Ariaka and this time you will do this the right way. The Kadaitcha will call on the world that is older than the city or even the whitefella. There is a judgement to be made here … in the old way of things. It is time."

"Jeremy will be back soon and both of you have lessons you need to learn if you are to face the Lore giver. You are as bad as each other and you test me… it is a bad thing!" He finished frustrated.

"Can you advise me?"

Nodding he stood quietly. "First lets get you out of this place. I never liked hospitals. There is a great deal to prepare and you have learnt this now at least Tom."

Glancing across the room he moved closer to speak in a low voice, silent to anyone who may be paying more attention than they should. "Apari has bought you time, another chance. The Wolgaru serpent will demand proof that you have found this wisdom you couldn't find before. Proof that your hate and temper doesn't govern you and the serpent will deal with this thing also. He will demand his due when you face him again Ariaka."

I wasn't at all sure what I should take that to mean but I knew not to question him on this now. He sounded pissed off enough with me as it was. Maybe later, when he was less in a tested mood I would get away with questioning him and hopefully understand what was needed of me. I had to put this thing right, or the cost would be too great.

Often it was best to wait until you were told many things as it is a sacred business that reveals itself when ready and I had to remind myself of this. I had to trust in the Lore and it wasn't an easy thing when you were blinded by life and the costs of living the life I had chosen.

My body still ached when I moved and my head was none too steady when Big Jim bought the old ute up to collect me. It was good to be at last headed back home and I wanted nothing more than to sleep at the moment.

Over the next few days my bruising faded slowly but my body was healing quicker than the disappointment I had in myself. Big Jim helped me with preparations and I wondered why I hadn't done this before.

I had watched my Grandfather doing the like, but he had used different tools and had different ways. The whip was my choice and Big Jim had approved. I would have need of this he said.

It was on the first morning possible that he took me into the surrounding bush to begin the ritual of preparations. Looking for a wallaby for our purpose we found one soon enough. Baking it in our fashion in the coals of the fire, searing away the fur.

It wasn't only for food though. What Jim wanted was a particular bone, which was split to a slither. It was a long slender bone that was then honed to a fine point over the night with song, ceremony and intent.

This fine bone was then dried and slipped into the handle of my whip helping stiffen my grip and giving me a finer control. He schooled me in using it properly and I came to understand its purpose. All the time Badjimala spoke of the stories in our Lore, teaching me the code of the Kadaitcha. It was a code as ancient as the song.

He was right, I should have prepared and not gone in so sure of myself. This was not a business that was light to deal with, nor easy to contend with in its implications and consequence. I knew this now. It wasn't a lesson I was going to forget easily.

We were away for a number of days in all and I knew that Badjimala had called a council of men for early the following week. We were headed back to the cottage when the weekend arrived while we waited for the men to gather. Big Jim wanted to check-up on Jeremy and it was good to hear he was to be a part of this over the coming ceremony.

He hadn't asked what we had been doing in our comings and goings. He didn't need to know as we usually never kept tabs on each other anyways and I decided it was just as well.

He did however seem more curious about other things when we had a chance to catch up.

"Kelly was asking if I had seen you. I think she has something going for you. She seemed really curious, even worried." He commented as we were poking about the kitchen both looking for a feed of a sort.

"When did you see her?" I asked indifferently, hoping I was pulling it off as I rummaged in the fridge for something for my sandwich.

"Last week at TAFE. I said you had been off camping with others. She wanted to know when you would be back."

"I'll see if I can catch up with her next week, maybe Tuesday. I have to go and see my boss anyway. Big Jim has organized a gathering next week and I will be part of it all. The men, the local Elders have something on the go. I might be in ceremony soon I think from what has been said. I'm still learning what it is all about... you know what they're like." I added smiling.

I knew that Jeremy would understand that dealing with the Elders and with the Kadaitcha involved, it was never a clear business. Not for initiates especially.

Jeremy just nodded, but his look told me he wasn't finished. "So do you two have something going on? Kelly and you?"

"Would it worry you if we did?" I countered.

"Nup. It would be nice to know though. She is still seeing this other bloke Pete. You realize that don't you?"

I nodded. "Yeah I know. But it's not serious or anything between us Jeremy, we're just friends... an' this Pete bloke. He's a real bastard, stay right out of that business. It's not good."

For a time we tossed banter about. His mood slowly lightened when he joined me out on the balcony with a bowl of breakfast cereal despite the late hour. Curious about what had been going on in Jeremy's world, I added to the conversation. "Been up to anything lately?"

"I was up at Nimbin, in the community while you were away."

"Yeah? What got you up that way then? Who did you catch up with?"

"Andrew took me up last weekend. Didn't find out about you being in hospital till you were almost out. It was only a few days though, just hanging around mostly. Met a nice girl, you should meet her sometime. She would be just your type."

"From the Community?" I queried surprised. "It will be a wonder if the girls there haven't warned her about having anything to do with me."

"It's not that bad you know. They still talk about you but," Jeremy added on a chuckle. "I think Alex and Aine have been putting a stop to a lot of the worst gossip. Maybe they've moved on to someone else to talk about."

"That would be a nice change. Yeah, I guess it has been a while since I've been back. But Alex?" I grinned. "She is still pissed with me I'm sure."

"Alex? Why Alex... I mean Andrews girl...?"

"Yeah. She... we were sort of an item at one time but... well it never worked out. I think I mentioned it before. Andrew is right for her though, they have a good thing going those two and I would never mess with that.

I don't think I want to take Andrew on." I added laughing lightly.

Thinking back to when I had done just that once before and how at the time he had scared the crap out of me. I realized just how young I had been and that was too bloody young for some of the things I had got up to in some ways. About as young as Jeremy is now I realised and it hadn't even been me Andrew was pissed with at the time, it had been with one of the girls from the community, Carley.

Jeremy just laughed and sat back. "Like you have a chance with Alex." He warned on a chuckle. "Next to Buckley's I think."

I just grinned enjoying a world of small secrets about which he knew nothing. "You're right, no chance there."

"So do you still talk to any of the other girls there? I mean… is there anyone special in the crowd that you keep under wraps?" Jeremy asked.

Curious about why he would ask I measured his words. "Nah… why would I do that?"

"Just wondered. Your name came up once or twice."

I shook my head, surprised. Even a little curious then I shrugged. "Nup. Maybe I have more friends than I figured?"

"Yeah seems."

At that I chuffed softly, enjoying the idea.

My thoughts suddenly turned to Kelly and I wondered just how firm I had been with her, or just how right we were for each other. I suddenly had the horrible realization that she held all the cards in our relationship.

It was she who called the tune at the moment and I wondered if I was really happy with that. Did I really have the right to have any expectations at all in our relationship?

With this other business too, this bloke of hers, Pete, it was looking to be a bad business. If Kelly was mixed up in all that then I didn't think there would be much I could do. I might be able to influence things some, where the Lore was concerned, though with Kelly in with that bloke, she was sure to feel the consequences.

Big Jim had mentioned it and it seemed that there had been consequences already to the business with little Iris, all while I had been recovering. The little girl had been returned to her mother I knew now, and there was a deep satisfaction in that for me. The local Elders were still looking into the business with Pete though. They had resources and contacts that I couldn't even imagine.

Kelly was considered a woman grown and as with women she would need to find her own way out of this mess. There was not a lot I could do to help her, she would make her own choices in the end.

Maybe I should rein it in a bit with Kelly I decided. I was getting in quite deep and quite fast, never a good thing. Then the thought occurred to me that I might not even welcome the type of relationship she was offering. Was I even that serious about Kelly or was she just a conquest? Or even a game I was playing at?

Part of me didn't thinks so. Yet I knew that there was no future for us, not while there were other things in her life that were more important to her. Money for starters, seemed to be her biggest motivation and while it was nice to have some, it wasn't my motivation in life.

Then for the first time I realized that I didn't like what she did, not at all. It was like the edge of everything I worked against and that was the thought that unsettled me the most.

With the gathering of the men organized for early in the week we headed out again to prepare for the business of the Kadaitcha. My boss had not been so pleased about my erratic absences and we had come to an amicable agreement in letting me go. Amicable for me that was, he was less than impressed but I wasn't about to explain anything. There were just some things that you couldn't explain to some of the whitefellas.

We were deep in the bush and it was Wednesday night when I unexpectedly got a call from Kelly. I hadn't seen her at all since my beating. I had been too busy with Badjimala as we prepared to deal with this boyfriend of hers. Though I refused to think of him along those lines as a friend of anyone's.

He was a man who had broken the Lore, both his and ours ... the Lore of the land, upsetting the balance between what was right and what was wrong business. To him people were something to be used. Friends just didn't exist in any context other than as a commodity.

I knew Big Jim had been in contact with Elders amongst the mobs in the city and there was a great deal going on. We had been preparing for days, slowly and meticulously. While I wasn't quite sure of what it was that was afoot, I knew unreservedly that it was the business of the Kadaitcha. It had become payback. The men had been coming and going for the entire time we had been bush preparing for ceremony.

When I took the call that night from Kelly we were still in the preparation for ceremony but it was near time to head out, back to the city. Near all was prepared and I could feel the weight of the Moogie Eye stirring restlessly within me.

"Yo... who is it?"

"Tom? It's Kelly... who did you think it was?"

"Kelly. What is it babe, I'm busy." I responded as I looked around at those of the Kadaitcha who were sharing the bush night with me, preparing for the corroboree ahead.

"I was just hoping we could catch up. I haven't seen you in ages and ... and well I am going away on Sunday. You know ..."

"Sunday? That's a bit outa the blue isn't it?" I asked surprised.

"Well yes ... I just found out. I'll be away for a while, overseas... with a client on a business thing. Pete set it up for me ... it's like a holiday. The..."

"Pete set it up?" I queried alarmed as once more I glanced around. "Babe ... look ... are you sure this is legit?"

"Of course it is. He is sorting out all the stuff ... the passport and stuff and he even gave me some spending money. I met the bloke two weeks ago. I've got enough money to get some travelling things, more than enough." She finished on a small delighted giggle. "I just wanted to catch up and let you know really. I mean if you're busy ...?"

"Kelly, look Babe ... I don't know about this guy of yours, Pete. Are you sure about all this?" I asked sceptically, as I moved away from the other men. "This boyfriend of yours is up to no good and this is all a bit 'under the table'. Where is it that you're going...?"

"Dubai, its all legit. Why would he give me money if it isn't...?"

"Babe, Dubai... It's part of the Arab emirates isn't it? That's a bit dangerous particularly for women? Why not Bali or ... or Fiji ... Dubai is ... is a strictly Muslim country Kelly. Have you thought about that? It's not like Australia, they treat their women very differently there."

"Oh you're being silly! It's just a holiday with a client." I could hear the humoured frustration in her voice. "You're nearly as bad as Jeremy sometimes. I can't tell him I'm going overseas ... besides, one of the girls wants me to move down to Melbourne. If anything is said ... that is what I am telling Jeremy ... Not that it would make much difference."

"Yeah well this friend of yours. I'm hearing all sorts of things about him." I said softly. My mind whirling, how did I say this ... warn her? "Kelly ... look Babe. I don't think it is a good idea ... this trip. I thought you were going to Kalgoorlie...? Tom said something about a group of youse..."

"He told you about that? Anyway I can do that later, when I get back."

"If you get back?"

"What do you mean? ... if I get back? Of course I will."

"It's all rather hurried isn't it? I mean this business. Kelly I don't like the sound of it."

"Oh what could happen for Christ sake!" she complained, the frustration there in her voice again as I drew a reluctant breath.

"This Pete, Babe he's a trafficker. He could be a trafficker, he's into all sorts of stuff."

"Oh don't be ridiculous! What do you mean a trafficker?" Kelly demanded surprised and even angry, the threads of disbelief winding through her voice. "In what! Drugs? It's not like I've been asked to carry anything... it's not like that!"

"Surely you've heard of this, you're the freight Babe. Blokes like this traffic in women, in ... in kids even. For all we know he could have even sold you to this business bloke Kelly."

"What! Now you are being stupid... that's .. that's just dumb. Dumb! I thought you'd be happy for me. It's a holiday for Christ sake! You can ... you can just go to hell!"

As the phone went dead I knew she had hung up on me and for a second I just stared at it in frustration. "Shit!"

I looked about at the others from the shelter of the bush, wondering how I could deal with this. On one hand I was out here preparing to put a stop to the bastard and on the other there was Kelly falling right into his plans.

The girl had no idea! She would never understand what it was that we had learnt in these last two weeks, why it was that we were even out here. It was just a different world to the one she understood and the frustration of it was unbelievable.

Pete's reputation around Kings Cross, and within the communities of those who moved through the night was a growing threat. The Elders had decided that it was time to act.

After my experiences with him, the Kadaitcha too had felt that it was before time that he was dealt with. The scars he had left across the lives of other people were too many. But it was the child, the innocent kids who had paid the highest price.

We didn't know how he went about his business and in this we didn't care. It wasn't us who would judge. We knew enough to understand that he stole and traded in children and that was enough. He had broken the Lore and he would be held to account. Others would judge. We only needed to bring him before the keepers of the Lore.

That was going to happen soon, this weekend. As it had happened many times down through time, all throughout this land of ours. A timeless era since the Dreamtime where the Lore ruled the people, it was an ancient and just Lore.

Since the Lore that governed this land had been given, it was that men such as he would be judged. His account on the lives he had taken and the things he had done settled. There was nothing I could do that would change this. He had come to the attention of the Lore keepers, those that I hoped to join when they deemed me ready.

Now he would face the givers of the Lore. Drawing breath I tried to clear my mind. Directing my thoughts into the path even now being prepared. Slipping the phone back into my pocket I stepped back into the ring of men.

Kelly was a grown woman, responsible to herself. There was nothing I could do to stop her and she had made her choices. All I could do was to try and warn her and she would have none of that.

Perhaps this business though would put an end to her plans too I could only hope. We would be heading back after tomorrow and I knew that the council of Elders would be gathering this weekend.

The ceremony would begin this Friday, tomorrow night. Within the shrouds of darkness Pete was going to account for himself. Though he knew nothing of what was prepared. Even I knew only that he was to be bought to judgement in a time honoured way.

For me it was a second chance to prove my strength, the chance Apari had bought me. I knew in some way that I was to again face Wolgaru. We had been preparing all week for this and I was ready to face whatever trial it was that Wolgaru serpent would throw in my path.

All had been prepared and it was now time.

The Djaranin

Tom

All was in readiness. The night was quiet as I waited, though this was not quite how it was supposed to go but there was little for it. When we had returned from the bush we had found that Jeremy had taken off with the ute and Big Jim was less than pleased about that.

My mate didn't even have a licence and Badjimala was ropable. Big Jims own mates were using his vehicle and we had been counting on using my ute, aside from other considerations.

In the end we had come into the city by train and I had left Big Jim to meet the others down at The Domain. I would meet up with them again at the gate into the gardens near the head of Woolloomooloo Bay as soon as I could. I knew that Badjimala would be waiting patiently for me there, likely along with others and standing around here was getting on my nerves.

The Kadaitcha were on the hunt and I had been sent on to meet up with Jeremy. We were both to be in on this and I was impatient for my mate to get his arse down to where we were supposed to gather. We had a few hours yet but there was a lot to be done and we needed to be doing it now.

The house across the road where Kelly stayed had been quiet mostly. Pete had gone inside earlier. I wondered if Kelly had even made it home.

Pete's arrival had surprised me at first but then I had felt the movement of shadows about this place. My skin had tightened and the Moogie Eye, the stone of the Kadaitcha had begun to burn slightly within me.

I had recognized and sensed then the swift shadows of the Djaranin as they flicked through the evening earlier and I had realized that they too were on the hunt; they too had found their likely quarry in Pete.

I hadn't known that they would be hunting throughout the city and it had bought home to me the strengths of the Djaranin, even in this modern world. My worlds were beginning to collide.

That knowledge sent a shiver and anticipation through me. It was all going as the men had planned and I was growing impatient with Jeremy. Badjimala had reminded me to take my churinga, my whip, and I had thought little of it as I had wound it around me concealing it under my shirt, but now I was glad that I had it with me.

This business was all coming together and I wanted to make sure I pulled my weight this time. At the very least I knew that my Grandfather expected it of me.

When Jeremy turned the corner at last, I looked about carefully. I stilled for a minute trying to feel the presence of the Djaranin, wondering where they would be.

They were still nearby; I could feel it and I had guessed that they would be following wherever it was Pete went.

Then I noticed Kelly was still in company with Jeremy and in part I was relieved. I had wondered if she was perhaps inside with Pete. It was a relief to know that this wasn't the case for certain now. That left me wondering how to get her out of the way of all this.

I stepped out from the shadows and carefully made my way across to intercept the two of them.

"Hey you two. So where is the ute?"

"Its back a few blocks, parking wasn't easy to find. You know how the city is. Have you been waiting long?"

"Nope. What did you two have planned?" I asked quietly trying to think of anyway we could get Kelly out of the city for tonight at least.

"Well… nuthin' Kelly is headed back and I guess… I was going home."

"Big Jim wants to meet us down the Domain way." I said, wondering if I should try and get Jeremy to take Kelly all the way back to Cronulla… would she even go though? She looked as though she was still angry with me.

My thoughts were then unexpectedly cut-off. It was a sound that silenced the three of us. It grew to a racket coming from the tenement where Kelly stayed. We had all stopped for a moment hearing its growing volume, each of us trying to work out what was going on.

Frowning over the increasing raucous noise I tried to reach out with my other senses towards the Dark Dogs, trying to discover where they were, wondering just what the hell was happening.

"That's Sandra yelling…?" Kelly whispered in recognition.

Swinging quickly she moved off with a pace in her step, turning towards the sound of the argument while both Jeremy and I stepped up to follow her with our own sense of urgency.

It was a building racket, an argument coming from the tenement building and as we got closer we realised that it involved more than one, maybe two or three people. They were all yelling at someone and thankfully I realized that there was no low agitated growl. The dogs were not involved in this ruckus at least.

Kelly swung quickly in through the gate and trying the closed door through which the din was growing more harsh, she pushed it open and burst in, slamming it back on its hinges, leaving us to follow her lead.

It wasn't hard to find the room the fight was coming from. Sandra was screaming in a harsh and protesting bellow as we first heard the angry tones of a male voice arguing with her.

By the time we both reached the door, Kelly was in the thick of it and screeching at Pete who had the other woman by the hair.

I knew instantly who it was. It was the same bloke that had rounded the corner, following the two who had beaten me to a pulp two weeks ago, the same bloke who had arrived earlier. He was dark haired and wiry and my first thought was to beat the crap out of him and return the favour he had shown me.

"Let go of her! You bastard... let go...!" Kelly demanded as she launched herself at the guy with her fists flaying high.

Pete was standing over Sandra, his own fist curled viciously into her dishevelled hair, forcing her to her knees as he spat his contempt over something she had done. In the moment he had swung wildly out at Kelly as she had flown at him.

"You bloody bitch!" he spat as Kelly collected the blow. "So you think you can just leave!" he demanded of her.

I had seen enough, struggling to keep a tight rein on my anger I gathered a fist and swung into the fray, launching my weight at the scrawny bastard.

Pete, saw my punch coming and lurched back, dragging Sandra with him by the hair and then he released her unexpectedly.

The punch went wide but I had known that was likely. Swinging quickly I grabbed at the finer built man gripping him by the shirt, angry beyond words as I lifted him easily, slamming him up against the wall. My other fist moved in neat and I buried the weight of the blow into his gut.

Having winded him I then let him drop to the floor, watching him crumple to the ground with some satisfaction.

He struggled to gain his feet as he fumbled amongst his jacket folds. I thought at first he was going to pull a gun. Instead I saw the flash of a blade and the relief swept through me as he scrambled back onto his feet pointing it my way ... then dithering over even that choice.

His look was wild like a trapped animal and we all stood frozen, facing each other. Then I moved to brace up to the blade, knowing that I could take him on. I was fast on my feet and a knife had never scared me.

Taller and broader than he I stood a better chance in a scuffle than the animal in front of me. Seeing my stand the mongrel began to show all the signs of a coward he was. His eye's slipping about in desperation while he searched for what I was sure was an escape.

Something in me was enjoying this, the thrill of the fight or perhaps the glory of the moment. The man was a coward and he dithered like a trapped animal. He knew that he was up against more than he could handle with the two of us, Jeremy and I, both marking him as though he was prey.

Kelly suddenly screamed and it shattered the moment as the high sound echoed wildly through the house.

Staggering for just a second the animal's glance flicked wildly again still looking for that escape. Then in a quick movement he faltered and dived for the door when Kelly screamed yet again, seemingly spurring him on.

In disbelief I watched as Jeremy suddenly dived out after him and immediately I followed trying to stop the kid. Didn't he know that the Djaranin were out there waiting!

"Let him go." I ground out as I caught my mate in the hall and hauled him to a halt. "We aren't done with him yet. Leave him!" I repeated in urgent warning. "Let the Djaranin round him up we have a place to be at."

"What!" he demanded. "He's a shit! You saw what he did to the girls … he doesn't give a shit about anyone but himself." Then he paused as though hearing me suddenly. "The Djaranin?"

I just nodded at last satisfied he had realized what I had said.

"Can't you feel them about?"

"The Djaranin?" he repeated still unbelieving.

Again I nodded "They're on the hunt. I could feel them before but I wasn't sure. Now I am. That is what this is all about. Jeremy … mate, you just don't know the half of it."

Quickly I moved ahead of him, I had to keep up … I couldn't let this go without being in on the hunt.

"But he'll get away. He'll come back for Kelly!" Jeremy said desperately and with all seriousness.

I glanced back at him once and felt the heat of the Moogie Eye urging me on, I was not meant to be here. I had to follow.

"No he won't." I whispered, then I noted the women moving up behind Jeremy. They were frightened but I couldn't have them follow us either.

"Look stay with Kelly, see her safe I have to go."

"But… but what about the ute?"

"It's not going anywhere. You better go and collect your whip if you want to be around for this… it's in the ute I think, leastways it was when we left. I'll meet you down near Mrs Macquarie's Chair when you're done. An' loose that distemper of yours… rein your anger in a bit. It won't help you, or Kelly for that matter."

"The Botanical Gardens?" He repeated confused.

Impatiently I reached for the whip, tugging it from about my shoulders, hidden beneath my shirt as it was. I coiled it tightly into my hand in an attempt to keep it from the eyes of the women. I was preparing to step into the night. I couldn't wait any longer.

"Yes. We'll be there in the gardens... don't be long."

I took off into the night then, Jeremy would have to deal with the women, I had things to do. More important things, those that I'd been preparing for all week and I was now running out of time. If Jeremy didn't make it then there was nothing for it. He would miss the ceremony and for him there would be another time surely. This business was just too important for me not to be a part of it.

I knew the dogs would be pressuring their quarry towards where they meant it to be. Although I couldn't feel them about me anymore they had to be headed down towards the Botanical Gardens for sure. That was where the Kadaitcha were gathering and as I ran through the night I recalled the stories the Elders had recounted during our time in the bush.

It was an old Bora ring, a ceremonial ground where the serpents would dance in times past. This same place was now in the heart of the Royal Botanical Gardens and although the gardens were gated and locked during the night hours, I understood well that they were locked for reason that was ours.

Out of respect for the Lore, the first Governors of Sydney Town had decreed that they be locked to protect farm cove from the raids of hungry convicts and ticketed men, but also to protect the sanctuary of the Lore. It was the ancient Bora Ring, which sat below the gardens. Sitting even out of sight of the Governors House.

Bennelong, a warrior of the Cadigal had been given a camp and then a cottage nearby to help guard the secrets of the Bora Ring. Only he and the remnant of the Eora mob, along with the Governor had been the keepers of the secrets of Farm Cove.

In return the mobs of the Eora, and the Cadigal mob had protected the fertility of the grounds in their ceremony. Ensuring the survival in the provision of food for the first settlement in Sydney Cove.

At first it had been hard for the Cadigal to watch the whitefellas struggle to survive, to watch the hunger and starvation of the settlement in those first years two centuries ago.

The blackfellas could see the food all around them that they could have eaten but the Spirits of the cove had made the whitefellas blind, payback for their stealing the land of the Cadigal.

Then the Dreamtime Spirits had punished the mobs too for not sharing as within the Lore. Many of the Eora people and others had died when terrible diseases had arrived to punish them in those first years of the settlement.

We had known the Lore, unlike the whitefellas who hadn't known these things. The whitefellas had been like ignorant children but the Eora had known the Lore. The punishment for the mobs had been harsh.

After the deaths the Spirit men had wrought. That of diseases which had decimated the Eora people, the balance of the Country had shifted. The Eora people were the water people of the harbour and it had been this mob that had suffered the most in those days. It was clear that their world and ours had changed.

Those left of the water mob would not war with the settlers. They needed to ensure the balance of things and not further anger the Spirit creatures of the Lore who lived around the secret places in this, their harbour. The Governor had granted protection for this sacred place of the Cadigal then. It had been a mutual agreement of benefit to both people.

Even if the whitefellas had now forgotten these things, the Lore protects its own, and the mobs had not forgotten.

Today it was still respected and the ceremonies of the Bora Ring were still favoured. They were held in secret in the heart of the city, safe from prying eyes of those who should not see. The ceremonies were held secret from the intrusion of those that had no understanding.

Wolgaru still danced in the stillness of the night and she would dance again tonight. This was something that I was not going to miss.

As a Kadaitcha initiate, I would dance within the ancient rings with her as I had done once before. I would take my place amongst the men of the Kadaitcha and begin my journey as a keeper of the Lore. It was what I had been trained for, what I wanted more than anything in my life.

Badjimala was waiting for me at the gate as I ran down through the Domain and we moved out, finding the path along the shore towards Mrs Macquarie Chair where I searched for the other men.

The Botanical Gardens were well gated and fenced but our whips serve many purposes. It was easy to scale the fence with their help and once Badjimala had shown me how, it was a simple thing that bought me much satisfaction.

Once within the sanctuary of the gardens we moved down through the paths quickly, cutting through the gardens. It was only as I approached the rolling lawns near the ponds that I realised just how many others were involved in this rite of passage. I was not the only one in ceremony.

Amongst them was my Grandfather who stood waiting quietly within the shadows of the old-man boab. The only sound that broke apart the silence of the gardens was the soft rhythmic beat of the sticks, muted so as not to disturb the city.

Immediately when we reached them, those who were gathered there, Apari began to dress Badjimala and I in a coating of dark charcoal ash, as they were dressed. This dark ash silenced the dark gleam of our skin as we stripped off our city clothes preparing for the arrival of the Lore giver. My hair belt was fixed around my body in the manner of a warrior of old and I fixed my knife into its holds and secured my whip once more.

"The Djaranin are near, the hour was growing late and the ceremony will begin soon." Grandfather said in all seriousness as he took up the white down feathers of the Kadaitcha and dipped his hand to the blood mixed in the small wooden bowl.

I was surprised when he swept the blood about my skin, making a design within the fine ash on my chest. He spread the blood about me in wide circles over my upper chest and then began to carefully pat it down with fine down feathers, as well as with other more delicate designs and a great deal of pride.

"Others should know Ariaka, that you have been blooded before." Tossing a glance across to Badjimala who also was being attended by men of the Kadaitcha, I noted the satisfaction spread between the two men. He too accepted the touch of the men painting wide circles in blood on his skin and dressing them delicately with the same white down.

Grandfather had painted two circles on me, each side of my chest, pressing the down onto them carefully he continued in is low chant. Then he marked me across the bridge of the nose so that Wolgaru should know me and recognize me as a warrior of the Lore.

"The judgement has been made, you have missed this but the hunt is yours Ariaka. Badjimala will call you to the task, this when the Serpent is ready to dance with you and the moment of judgement will be yours. I shall attend with you, also as your hand. Badjimala tells me that the churinga is prepared."

Within the gentle light of the stars I looked around me as I tried to discern the movement of men in the shadows, then my eyes stretched beyond the shadows to the spill of light across the lawns while my Grandfather continued to attend to the designs of my ceremony.

There in the soft moonlight I notice movement across the smooth lawns and I realized these were the slither of snakes, no... eel's they were, because they seem to make the ponds their home.

They were serpents of the harbour dancing in a path across the rolling lawns of the gardens and it was a truly wondrous sight.

They seemed to gather in form, making their way between the harbour and the ponds as though seeking out that which should not be present. It was a dance all of their own and speechless I watched them.

Grandfather laughed as he noted my expression and my amazement. "Yes, it's their dance as the Serpent prepares. The Djaranin are on the edge of the harbour with their prey, they will be here soon. They have not yet bought him over the gates and he has found no place to hide from the things he has done to others and those against the Lore of the land. The sorrow and pain he has bought to others in the breaking of the Lore is a price that he now meets. Listen for the snapping of their teeth and low growl of their anger."

Having completed his task Badjimala and I were led to the edge of the shadow to mark the passage of time and I noticed that there were others too, who sat on the very edge in the nightshade under the trees waiting for the light to shift over them in turn. They were difficult to see, given away only by movement and you had to concentrate carefully on this movement.

The charcoal ash hid the sheen of their skin and all was black wherever I looked as I settled beside Badjimala and Apari, our voices low.

"Ariaka, it is your ceremony also and you are ready. As is shown by the design of the Kadaitcha your Grandfather has painted, you have killed twice. This time you will also kill, sparing the Shade of this man from the torment of the Djaranin. As I have taught you, you will use your churinga to take his life and grant him release from what he has done. Wolgaru will hold him to account in her own time."

"Where is he?"

"He deals with his judgement and soon the Dogs of Death will be finished with him. They will drive him near the Bora grounds and when you hear the summons of my whip... it is for you to prove you are a Kadaitcha. Without fear, anger or hate you must do this thing while Wolgaru is busy with the other initiates."

Seeing the younger men gathered elsewhere in the shade of the night I noted their own preparations and realized there were ceremonies other than mine happening around me. "I'm ready."

"Then we will wait."

It seemed forever that we waited while men attended to other initiates. The night shadow shifted slowly, so it must have been over the hours of the deep night.

A few of the men moved, the shadow of the Kadaitcha and Sorcerer's, coming with stealth across the lawns. Always they were careful in their movements so as not to disturb the dance of the eels as they prepared the way for Wolgaru.

Some took up their own churinga, whips and the other tools of the hunter, moving towards the gate near Mrs Macquarie's chair and I wished that I knew what was happening there.

Badjimala was silent, as were many of the men but for the quiet clap of the sticks and the deep drone of the song on the lips of the Elders. We were still and quiet until a moment when he too took up his whip, the churinga of his choice and moved outside of the shadows.

The low growl of the Djaranin cut across the sound around us as the coil of Badjimala's whip snapped against the ground, herald to the Djaranin. Two others move up to join him in his push towards the movement and shadows now crossing the lawn.

They moved in unison across the smooth lawn and as they began their dance at the approach of the Dark Dogs. I too noticed another dark form moving across the lawn also.

The initiates had gathered within the ancient Bora Ring now marked by the seat of Elders in the form of the ancient circle of rite. The rings of the Bora had been buried long ago, but the power of them still marked the place well and the Elders could feel its strength, even as I had felt it before in the hours of the daylight.

My eyes were torn between the sights of those who danced with ceremony in the Bora and the approach of the Wolgaru Serpent. She came from the harbour as though having arrived at the old Man of War Wharf, though she had emerged from the waters of the harbour and I wondered at her path.

Wolgaru was larger than I remembered her and then it came to me that she was really one of many, a mob of her own and this Serpent was an ancient and noble spirit creature of her own tribe.

Her movement across the lawns was guarded by the harbour of the eels as though preparing her path. At first she kept low slithering along the ground as she approached the circle of young men, intent on their trials.

Apari touched my arm, drawing my attention again to the dance of the dogs as they left off from what had amused them earlier. They moved to attend Wolgaru, tamed and smarting only at the shift in the whips of the serpent killers amongst the Kadaitcha.

"Come, it is time." Grandfather said softly.

Climbing to our feet we moved over towards the crouching heap the Death Dogs had left. It was a strange sight and it wasn't until I approached that I realized the motionless mound on the ground was the Dodger. I knew by the sound of his breath, the rasp of air drawn over the teeth and as we approached the sight of him became clearer.

He could barely see us, dusted as we were in the dull darkness of charcoal and hidden in the shadow of night. Quietly we crept closer like ghosts marked only by the white down of our dressing, leaving the others to their dances.

Apari crouched low, wary of what had once been the man but was now reduced to a rabid creature of the night. The Dodger lifted his head and for the first time I saw the sweating glean on his skin, streaked with blood and dirt though his eyes were dulled by pain.

His clothing was tattered and he was almost naked like we, only scraps clung to his hide of what had been the neat dress of the night. It was plain that his arms were savaged by the teeth of the Dark Dogs and that his legs so badly gnawed and torn, that he could hardly have stood the pain of using them in a lucid state.

I felt no fear in our approach, though he fought to steady the sickened sway of his body as he attempted to face what he could not clearly see of us. Anger no longer touched me at what he had done to others and to the children. I was touched by only a sense of justice having been done.

There was no hate in my move towards him only a sense of need to bring an end to his trial. Acceptance in the judgement that had been bought against him consumed me and now, there was my part in this to play.

Apari moved with stealth up beside him and in the darkness raised a cudgel, a threat that the man sensed as he tried to move his head. Perhaps in the hope of finding what little sense he may have had in that moment he tried to shuffle back and out of the way.

The strike was quick and the deafening thud solid as the cudgel knocked the sense from the man's last moves. It sent him crumpling back to the ground from where he had struggled to rise.

Silently Apari stepped back and I knew this was my time. The way had been prepared.

Stepping up I bent over the form before me and carefully raised the body of him to rest against my legs, as one would hold a sheep for the shearing. He was a lamb now, bought to the slaughter and gripping my whip handle in my teeth I carefully drew from it the long splinter of bone, which had stiffened the handle.

It was an age-old way... a way bought to us by the givers of our Lore, the Serpents. I knew the place, I had been instructed well and as Apari looked on I positioned the sharpened point of the slither into the well of the neck, a place behind the bone. Then carefully and silently I slid the slither to its purpose.

He stiffened, as though the slight spear served to bring him to life and then I felt the last of his life slip from his grasp. Pete died in those seconds as the fine bone slipped through his heart.

Withdrawing the slither carefully I handed it to Apari and let the carcass of the man fall to the ground. It was done and there were only a few who had even noticed it, as the ceremony of the initiates had gone on around us.

Wolgaru though, was one of them who had noticed.

It wasn't long after that when Badjimala once more cracked the whip to the air calling attention to the distraction of Wolgaru. The Djaranin too stalled and swayed carefully in their dance outside the ring of Elders. They marked those with their churinga's balanced in their hands, protecting the initiates.

All watched on carefully, between the dogs and the Lore giver to see what path of the serpent would take. Wolgaru was once more on the move and her shift was now towards where Apari and I stood.

Then I understood, it was then that the realization came to me when I stepped back smartly with my Grandfather, leaving the way open for the giver of judgement and Lore, Wolgaru.

Slipping stealthily, her path quickened towards us. She poised and coiled suddenly, measuring her prey. Then like a lightening strike she whipped in towards the offering of the Kadaitcha and struck.

Wolgaru chanced at the carcass of meat, that which had once been a man. Taking him up in a fierce grip she coiled rapidly about her prey, her fangs grabbing as her coils crushed the form that had been prostrate on the ground.

The glistening length of her was wrapped in a grip of death as she squeezed the carcass beyond recognition. Then waiting, watching carefully she checked on the attendance of the Djaranin to protect her in her vulnerable moment as she stretched and exercised her jaws, consuming him whole.

The Djaranin moved up protectively as she coiled about him, moulding his body, squeezing it to a form and position better able to accommodate the rhythm of her powerful jaws. They waited, poised to pounce should anyone try to disturb her in her meal.

It was time then to spill my blood in payback for what I had done. No other would pay the price for my deeds as I now knew Alex had done when she had been my woman, one bound to me. I had learnt my lessons well and as such I knelt to the ground.

Taking my knife from my belt I ran the blade recklessly, slashing a path down my arms. My blood spilling to the ground in a quick flow, returning to the spirits of the Country the life I had taken in my course.

I then watch silently, fascinated as Wolgaru consumed the offering we had given her and waited for the Spirits to take their due and settle the account.

Swallowing slowly … and with delicate deliberation what was the carcass, Pete vanished. Squeezed in past the constraints of her jaws and after a time, long and deliberated, he was barely a bulge in her belly. She then moved off with the slithering motion of the serpent, shifting the weight of her meal along her body. These things were all bought to a balance in those moments and I was satisfied that all was now well.

Many of the initiates had been removed, exhausted and recovering from their dance with Wolgaru. Many had already been taken away to heal and rest after their ceremony but still Apari and I watched attentive as Wolgaru reached the safety of the entrance to her caverns, the hide deep within the now sleeping city.

Badjimala moved up with us, escorting her as we stepped carefully in her wake following her path, ensuring clear leave for the Djaranin and Wolgaru as she silently, finally slipped over the sandstone wall and into the waters of the harbour.

It was a wall built by the convicts near the old Man of War Wharf, that which stood sentinel for more than two centuries alongside where the Sydney Opera House now stood.

Surprised, I watched as she slipped into a purpose-built entrance fashioned in the sandstone wall. An entrance and tunnel that took her into the serpent caverns, those deep beneath the city while she followed in the wake of the Djaranin.

Badjimala clapped his hand on my shoulder as I stood astounded and speechless having watched her path. "Come Ariaka, we must clean up before the city wakes. Others will be making their way over at Mrs Macquarie's Point and we should join them. This thing is now done. There once more is a balance to these things for a time."

Lost Ceremonies

Tom

The water of the harbour was cold but most of us plunged in none the less, it was the only way to deal with the fine charcoal ash that had coated our bodies. It was just off sun-up when I settled high on the rocks beside my Grandfather.

Badjimala had gone with others to ensure that the Bora ring was clear of any sign that we had been in ceremony and that all was wiped away. You didn't tempt the fates by leaving something behind.

We were well outside the gates at the tip of Mrs Macquarie's point. It was a public area here so we had nothing to worry about and soon the public would be bustling about.

We wanted to be gone by then, as the Elders discouraged attracting any attention to our purpose. Our ceremony was not one for public display, particularly for the secretive Kadaitcha amongst us.

Settling beside my Grandfather Apari, I waited for his words. I knew he would be leaving soon and I sorely wanted to seek his approval for how I had conducted myself. He would know this but it took a while for him to speak.

"This thing... I am proud of you Grandson." He said softly, rewarding me with what I sought from him. "It is like the old times when I was a young man like yourself. I remember it, how it felt when I passed through the initiations to be what I am, an old man of the Kadaitcha now."

"Thank you Apari, that means a great deal to me."

He nodded and then continued hesitantly. "The only thing that weighs on me Ariaka is that you have allowed women to crowd your judgement more than once and this weighs heavily. Too many times this has happened and others have seen this too."

Drawing a reluctant breath his glance seemed as restless as the harbour waters rolling over the rocks and still I waited. "When I was a young man there was a ceremony that some of us underwent, an initiation rite that was conducted by the women. The last rite of the young Kadaitcha initiate."

"The women?" I whispered in disbelief wondering if I had truly understood his words.

"Yes. It was an important ceremony for a young warrior like you. A trial by fire and it made you a strong and good man. It has not been done now for many years. It was a rite of the desert mobs mostly... even then. So much has changed in my time."

"Is it an initiation that you want me to take part in Apari?"

The old man nodded, the weight of years on his shoulders now reflecting in his eyes.

"There was a time when you challenged the Kadaitcha Ariaka, and many have not forgotten this. There are those who say you like the women too much, but for such as you there is a ceremony in our histories, in the old way."

"You see there are those amongst the Kadaitcha who are strong but allow the influence of women to change their thinking, because they look good in the eyes of their sweethearts. They are sweet on the women and because of this were not accepted by the Lore keepers easily. Such men as these are seen as undisciplined and the old men who are the Shadow Walkers of the caverns find this a bad thing. Some say you are one like this. But there are no women left who can lead you through such a ceremony that would make you a good man, a strong Kadaitcha with a deep sight Ariaka. I have searched for such a thing and have failed. None amongst the mobs left still practice the rite."

Disappointed in myself in some part, I cast my glance to the harbour as the first rays of a red sunrise danced off the restless water. "Is there no way to discover these things again? If it's truly something you feel that is needed then I would do a great deal to please you. I think that Alex… she would have been able to steady me… Should I…?"

My Grandfather smiled and then laughed in a chuckle, one contained to his memory. "The woman is no longer yours, but she did have the sight you need. There are others Ariaka and this is a rite that would make you a good man. A man that does not seek too much the pleasure men find in women, so much that it crowds his sight. You need a woman of sight, a strong woman to help you and one who understands your world."

Surprised I looked across at him and then grinned at his assessment of me. It was humoured; a humour that showed in his eyes but it was also serious. I preferred the humour to the serious intent.

Apari just nodded, knowing my thoughts. "I have spoken to the Kadaitcha and also the men of the caverns, those who do not seek the light of the day."

"The Oruncha?" I asked surprised.

"Yes. I am closer to these mobs now Grandson. After this time with you, I will not return from the caverns. I have decided that I no longer can live in a place so wanting of the Lore. In my time I have spilt too much blood and I want only to rest now."

"Do they know of this fire ceremony of the women? Maybe where I can find out more about it?"

Apari nodded, as though even the words were too sacred, or too mummoo to speak even. What was needed was the language of the eyes, or the senses and that took courage and wisdom beyond my own.

"The Fire Ceremony, yes I have found the beginnings of this thing." Apari said softly. "But it is not an easy thing to begin again, once more. There is a great deal to be uncertain about and this … it weighs heavy with me. There is danger in the mountain of fire where you need to look for this thing Ariaka."

"If this is what you want me to do, then this is what I would choose to do." I answered solemnly.

Immediately I could see that this bought him peace and some sense of pride. A pleasure that shone in his dark eyes even while they were hesitant with unanswered questions.

"You choose well my Grandson. There's a mountain in the red desert, near what the whitefellas call the Macdonnell Ranges of the Centre. It is the red heart where fire was first bought to the people. It is a Dreamtime history that is not often told. It's a history, one that tells of the Unthippa women of Etuta. It is the fire mountain, as known by the blackfella. I no longer remember the story as I should, it has been a long time, but others do. There the fire ceremony began when it was bought from the Dreamtime. But this is not a place you can go without your woman. This is a woman's ceremony Ariaka, a woman's history."

I drew a deep breath, "But I don't have a woman."

"You can take a wife Ariaka. Is there one you would choose?"

I shook my head grinning. "No."

"It is good then that I have chosen one for you." He answered softly with a smile of pure amusement.

"You found me a wife?" I asked surprised. "When?"

Apari nodded. "I have been very careful in my choice but if you don't want her then it is for you to say. She has been chosen with care and with much trouble. The Kadaitcha approve of this choice, she is a choice from within the Lore, from amongst those who could be your wife and yet could also lead you through the fire mountain, as you would lead her. This would step you through the ceremony that will strengthen you.

"We no longer follow these ways of marriage though." I added smiling.

"In some things we do Ariaka. In some things we do. If you take her to wife you must give her time, enough time to learn. You must treat her well. She doesn't know all our ways. This woman is different, treat her with care for there will not be another like her for you. If you treat her badly then it will be a very bad business you will find yourself in."

"OK. Then when will I meet this woman?" Half believing he was joshing me I looked again for the torment in his eyes. There was glee, amusement but no measure of torment. He meant what he said. "What if I don't like your choice?"

"Then I will send her back to her people. It has all been arranged and she waits for our decision even now. The choice is hers also, she may not choose you, even though there is a lot now to commend you in the eyes of her people."

"Yeah?" Still I was disbelieving that any woman would be willingly in such a position as this, these days. "When do I meet her then?"

Now there was a measure of torment in his eyes and it made me smile. "In good time my Grandson. She can teach you of the things you will need to know and together you can find out the truth in the fire ceremony. This too has been amongst her people also but this was a long time ago. They too thought they had no need of it anymore and now, they have found a need."

I shook my head not understanding and my brow puckered. "How do you mean...?"

"She can tell you these things, it is not for me to say. It's women's business." He dismissed suddenly.

At that I laughed as it was just like something the wily old man would say. I knew I would get little more out of him so I didn't tax him more on this. It was like a game of wits and it was a game we both enjoyed. It reminded me of when we had hunted together before.

"OK ... I will meet her when I do and not before."

Apari nodded and then settled his glance back out over the waters of the harbour watching the first of the golden light skip over the surface as though lost in another time for a moment. "You still have soot behind your ears Grandson, go and wash it away." He said finally.

Laughing at his tone I climbed to my feet and headed down to the water where it lapped up onto the rocks. Once I was finished at the harbours edge, I turned to head back towards the others.

Jeremy was approaching up by the popular tourist walk. He had missed the ceremony and I knew he would be sour on that. But part of me was glad he had missed watching me take a man's life. He still seemed so young at times.

I turned towards his path and headed off up towards where he now stood, disappointment clear to see even in how he stood.

"Hey ... Jeremy."

"Tom."

"You should have been here earlier mate. It was something you should have been a part of I think. But not to worry, Badjimalla managed it and there were a few others who were able to control the Djaranin."

"Jeezus!" he shook his head feeling the disappointment like a physical blow it seemed.

"I came through good. It wasn't easy though. It is one thing to learn how to do something, another to actually take a life." I answered trying to find a way to console him.

"Take a life? What the hell happened? You didn't... kill someone? What ... what did you do?" he repeated disbelieving.

I was glad that he had asked. There were things he should know of me I decided then. "It's not the first time ... that I have taken a life. But this time it was something different. I had decided that it was needed and that it was what I would do. It was my decision. I wasn't angry or... or unsure even. It was simply something that was to be done. He couldn't be allowed to live... the pain he had bought the young kids. The pain he would continue to bring. To him it was nothing. I didn't know though ... The Wolgaru serpent ... I didn't know about her but the Kadaitcha did. They knew, and now so do I. It is done. I am what I am I guess."

"The Serpent ... was here?"

I nodded. "This is her place, she is here. I didn't know that either but she is here. She lives beneath the city and it is here that she comes to dance. She has family here ... in the gardens and I have watched her dance Jeremy. I'll show you one day ... her dance."

Jeremy settled down on the rocks silent and I felt his disappointment keenly.

"Can you talk about it?" he asked quickly. "I feel I really should have been here but I ... I wasn't."

I turned noticing Big Jim's approach, he had been in the gardens with the men and it was clear that all there, was now in order.

"Yes ... with you, later. We can talk about it later when I'm more settled maybe. Where have you been anyway? I thought you might be here sooner than this." I added.

"I was putting Kelly on the train, she and a couple of friends have headed down to Melbourne I think, or maybe Kalgoorlie. They have work there she says?"

"Yeah. It was on the cards."

"What about this Pete bloke?"

That question surprised me. Why I had thought he wouldn't need to ask it I don't know. "He won't bother her. It is done with ... that part of it."

"It was him you hunted down wasn't it? ... But how? Why?"

"The Death Dogs caught him, that wasn't my part. The Djaranin play their own part in this. There is nothing they don't know when all is said and done. It's as though the Serpent and the Dark Dogs are one really. They are the judges in the evil in man. I made no judgements on that."

"God! What did he do? I mean ... Kelly was afraid of him an... and so was Sandra. She's a he you know?" His amazement made me smile.

"Yeah ... I think there is a lot you don't know. Maybe it's time you knew. Come on. We better go find the car before too much longer. It seems the men are finished in the gardens and they have opened the gates by the look of it, it must all be cleared up."

Big Jim also turned to greet Jeremy after he had released my grip in a handshake, as though we had not met for some time.

"This was a good business. Tonight has been a good night. And where were you while all this was going on young Jeremy?" He demanded suddenly of my mate.

"Tom said ... I was to look after the women so I was. I got the women away; they have left ... down south for good I think. I only just got here."

"Yes I know. It was a hard job to keep the Dark Dogs at bay without your hand in it. There were others to help fortunately," He added softly with some satisfaction.

"I don't understand." Jeremy seemed at a loss to understand what had happened and I realized he didn't know what he had missed really.

"What is it that you don't understand?" Big Jim asked patiently.

"Well what has happened? Jeremy answered ..."

"Lets talk about it then. You need to understand young Jeremy." Big Jim added turning us away from the gardens and back towards the public walkway. "You don't understand what has happened here, is that it?"

"Well yes. Why...? And the Serpent ... what ...?"

"Young Jeremy ..." His tone was serious and patient as he continued softly. "You have to see things through the eyes of others if you are ever going to understand the whole of anything. And that son ... is a talent you need to learn. Now listen up to what Tom can say and you will see what I mean. It's OK ... you're young. It will all be clear to you in time."

We talked as we headed back towards where Jeremy said he had left the ute. Along the way Big Jim excused himself after a time to catch up with some friends who were resting in the bush along the nature walk. Taking time in the quiet of the morning as the men made plans to leave the city.

Something I too should do I had been told, it was merely a precaution but a sound one.

The trip home was slow as I told Jeremy of the things I knew. I let him drive and as he seemed to be handling the ute quite well without my badgering, while I considered if it was time I invested in a new vehicle.

I needed something more suited to rougher country, something like Taipan's forbie perhaps would be better for where it was I wanted to go. I wanted to head into the heart of the continent to discover what I could of this ceremony Apari had mentioned and the ute would not cut it.

I agreed with what Big Jim had said about heading out of Sydney for a time. It was a good time for me to leave the city for a bit and learn more about my country and the scope of the land.

He wasn't the only one who felt that after such a ceremony I would be better off outside of the cities reach. You never knew what the true consequences of what had just been done were.

It certainly was something to hold my thoughts. After all I had chucked the job and if I didn't find something to keep me out of trouble, Taipan was sure to intervene. He still was forever wary of me getting into strife. He still didn't consider me to be a man of my own destiny even if my Grandfather did.

That thought made me smile … it was time to reconsider the arrangement of my life. For the moment though, all that began to occupy my mind was the tempting thought of sleep.

I was truly buggered and when my head finally hit the pillow there was little between oblivion and me that was welcome. It was a great place to be I thought as I slipped easily into my dreams.

Waking to the World

Tom

It was the languid afternoon heat that you could feel late into a day that woke me. It had begun to drift through the glass doors and was now crossing the bed. I could feel it against my skin and it felt good. The doors must have been left open and the slight breeze off the river was tickling my legs and feet, cooling them.

It was a pleasant feeling for a time. So I just let it overtake me as I slowly stretched my senses and my body to waking while I lay on my belly amongst the crumple of sheets and covers.

When I finally opened my eyes I found myself looking straight into a set of bright blue eyes and I wondered if I was still deep in sleep.

These belonged to a young woman who sat cross-legged on the bed barely an arm stretch from me as she watched me silently. Was she a dream or had I missed a day... a night even?

Slowly I realized that I was actually awake and this sight was one that was settled about me.

"Shit!" Jarring suddenly, pushing up off my belly and onto my elbows in shock, I was stunned at her presence. I went to turn about and then realized that I had ditched my gear on the floor. I wasn't wearing a stitch of clothing, as was often my custom at night.

I grabbed at the crumpled folds of the sheet hastily. This young woman looked way too young to be in my bed and it was more to preserve her modesty rather than my own. What the hell this female was doing in my room completely baffled me.

"What the fuck!" I spat, shooting her an annoyed look as I scrambled to cover myself in a struggle to bring my thoughts together.

"No." She said softy. She wore a smile that challenged me and I felt that the humour in her eyes was at my expense. But her words confused me for a moment and I frowned.

It was a frown she answered simply as she continued to watch me, as though expecting me to greet her. "I know that word ... fuck ... Alex told me and there was no fu... "

"Alex!" I spat flummoxed, cutting her words off curtly in shock. What the hell did Alex have to do with this girl?

She echoed my frown and then answered simply. "Alex. Your wife, though she is with Andrew now. She no longer wants you."

I dragged myself around to a sitting position completely disconcerted. I was mentally scrambling to gather my wits while I tried to settle the covers and piece this all together.

I was unable and unwilling to climb out of bed and sort this out in the moment so I struggled with the pillow and sheets as best I could. Dragging the covers across with me, while I tried to calm myself.

Mentally stretching to gather my thoughts together I dismissed the shock of finding her here and began to search my mind for reason for her presence.

In small glances I scanned her expression looking for answers, my eyes running over her restlessly. It was when I noticed the plaited and finely worked woven band around her slim ankle, a band she was absently fiddling with now.

The weave was familiar and it looked to be made of a twine of her long blond hair with what were much darker locks and it was something of a shock as memories drifted to mind. The dark strands of hair were probably mine I realized as I recognized the unusual plait. Having seen the like before around Alex's wrist, I understood its possible meaning.

There was no mistaking that plait, a distinctive twined circle fashioned as it was in its weave. Unless this sort of thing was suddenly coming into fashion, it had a set purpose.

I knew about such a talisman. Once, a lifetime ago Alex had shown me hers. One worked by the women Elders in the Daintree Rainforest. It had bound us together then, along with little Ellie as well, though neither of us had known it at the time.

Frowning I caught her glance. "Did you get that in ceremony?" I asked quietly, hopeful and disbelieving of my thoughts as I used a small gesture of the chin to indicate the ankle band.

"Yes. Apari had it worked for us, to help us."

Immediately I understood why she was here. This had to be the woman my Grandfather had chosen for me I figured quietly. There was no other explanation for it, though I hadn't expected to meet her so soon. I couldn't even think of how she had got in here and what the hell she was doing on my bed.

There was a great deal she needed to explain, the least of which was how she had come to know about Alex. I was suddenly mindful of my Grandfathers words also. How he expected me to treat her with care and consideration and I understood the meaning behind his warning. This woman I reminded myself, I had need to take considerable care of.

For a time it was like a standoff, she watched me carefully, as carefully as I was checking her out. I couldn't believe she was so young. I couldn't believe she was even here and yet there was something about her, something which spoke of a fine and strange intelligence.

She couldn't have been more than seventeen or eighteen at the very most and yet there was little by way of youthful hesitancy in her eyes. It was disconcerting.

The most shocking thing however was that the girl didn't look Aboriginal in any way remarkable. That was plain to see but then maybe, maybe she was. Maybe she was one of the white skinned aboriginal mob, those of aboriginal heritage that had been given the colouring of the whitefellas. Though her colouring was exceptional. Her skin was that soft honey tone that would colour deeper depending on the amount of time she spent in the sun. Now though, it was a very gentle shade. Perhaps she was more islander than aboriginal.

Would Apari have found a match from amongst others than those within the tribes? The only aboriginal feature I could identify in her appearance was the gentle tawny tone of her, which seemed barely touched by the sun. But she did have that unmistakeable even olive colouring along with a small button of a nose. A subtle and gentle shade, but it was an even olive skinned shading none the less.

She looked totally at ease where she was, as though there was nothing unusual in being in my bed. The lightness of her skin wasn't all that was unusual. She also had a tawny colour to her hair that was streaked with a white blond. The length of her hair spilling down around her shoulders in wispy wayward ripples, it almost reached into her lap cloaking her. The temptation to sweep her locks with my fingers was hard one to resist.

Her simple shift outlined her shape, barely grazing her skin. The fabric looked as light as a whisper, almost as weightless as she appeared to be. The girl was small, finer in stature than most girls and almost painfully thin. It wasn't as though you would notice this first about her however. She was like a wisp of a woman and yet she had all the shape and curves that a woman should have and you could see she was smart.

"Who the hell are you?" I asked finally and in an even tone having collected my wits. It was clear to me that she wasn't going to speak unless I spoke to her first.

"I'm your wife Ariaka."

Stunned at her use of the name my Grandfather had given me I looked across at her. She shouldn't be using my name in such a way. "Tom … call me Tom."

She dropped her eyes immediately as though I had chastised her, then strangely enough raised her glance again to challenge me. The look she gave me was beyond her years. "I have only ever known you as Ariaka, but from now on I will call you only Tom."

"Good … Thanks." I added uncomfortably, feeling a little churlish.

With effort I softened my voice. This girl was strange in some way, she wasn't reacting like a normal woman would and it disconcerted me.

"And you are…?"

She frowned. "… your wife."

That made me smile. "No. I mean who are you, your name?"

For a time she just watched me quietly, as though trying to work something out. Then suddenly turning away she climbed off the bed, going over to what was obviously her small bag and began rummaging through the pockets.

I straightened up and settled myself again carefully, more at ease. I couldn't understand why she just didn't answer me. Instead, she simply returned to the bed, climbing up onto it again and handed me a plastic pouch. It was a passport and curious I slipped it from its pouch and opened it.

"Taipan has said that this is what I should use when I am asked who I am, it is an identity book."

"It's a passport." I added frowning. "But I …" Immediately I had opened it I realized what was going on with her. The passport was for Kirri Ariakas and with a small chuckle, and somewhat amazed I understood as the pieces fell into place for me. This was Kirri, the girl Jeremy had spoken of from the inlands. I had questioned him about his experience in the caverns months ago and I had heard that name then.

"You're Jeremy's Kirri!" I exclaimed softly in revelation.

"No. I am your wife Ar.. Tom. Jeremy has only helped me, I have never been his."

"No … I didn't mean…" giving up I shook my head on another smile. It wasn't unlike talking to Jep I decided, talking to this girl from the Inlands. As I considered it, I had to smile at the small ironies. Little complications in the flow of conversations, which I had become accustomed to when speaking with Jep, only now it was somewhat different. "When did you get here? I mean who…?"

"Your little man from the caverns bought me here. After dark last night but it was the Elder, the Kadaitcha man who has … spoken to my people and arranged this thing between our people."

"Apari?"

"Yes. He took great care in this thing arranged between us. My people were pleased of this."

"My Grandfather." I clarified with a smile. It was more to make her aware of the connection more than anything else.

"He is a good man." Kirri added, returning the smile with a small one of her own, as though to reassure me. "Old and wise in many things, perhaps you will be like him in time."

It was an odd thing for her to say and with questions filling my mind I glanced back at the open passport in my hand. She would be eighteen I calculated quickly and then I remembered something Jeremy had said when we had spoken of the Inlanders. They aged much slower than we did.

With a new curiosity I examined her more closely as I stretched an arm to pass her passport back to her.

"Oh... Your arms." She said quickly, having noticed the scoring down my arms from the ceremony in the night before. Reaching to take the passport from my hands she had obviously seen the bloodied lines now dried and well on the way towards healing as far as I was concerned.

Kirri immediately climbed from the bed, intent on a purpose, and frowning I watched her skip along delicately like a fine feminine imp, disappearing into the bathroom.

My arms were fine. They had stopped bleeding some time ago when I had washed myself in the harbour the night before. They were now merely streaks of dried blood over the small irregular gashes, in no way inflamed. Perhaps where the gash had hit a vein it was a bit messy, fresh even, but it was nothing.

Moments later she emerged from the bathroom with a cup of water and a wad of toilet paper. "Here let me clean it. It is serious."

"No it's not. It's healing."

"Ari .. Tom! Please, you will get sick."

"No... no Kirri." I protested as I pulled my arm from her light touch where she was preparing to wash the gashes. "It's fine woman." Laughing I made light of her protest. "It has been washed in salt water and it's nothing. They are nothing." I added flicking my arms over to show her where I had caused them to bleed, a quick movement before her eyes. "They aren't infected, they are fine. It's just a little blood. They are clean cuts and it will heal easily... two or three days at the most. It's nothing."

Watching me intently, frowning still, she took my wrist and pulled the most damaged arm out in front of her as though to inspect it more closely. Then, instead of doing just that, she lightly ran her fingers over the small cuts and grazes and stilled for barely a moment as my skin tightened at her touch. The smile that touched her lips was gentle, caring and I felt like my mother had just rewarded me as she had when I was a kid. It was the oddest of senses.

"You are right Tom. But let me watch these... such as this is dangerous for me."

"For you?" I questioned not understanding.

"Such things as this can easily make you ill, in the warm dampness of the Inlands, it is unlike the dryness here."

"Oh. I see." Shaking my head I denied such a thing was likely to happen here. "Here, it may happen but it isn't serious. I will heal in no time. But the Inlands?" I smiled suddenly seeing the opportunity to learn a great deal about which Jeremy had been unable to answer. "This we must talk about so that I may understand you." I added carefully.

Kirri's smile was sweet and I enjoyed the reflection of it. "I will stay to teach you these things, there is a lot I would learn from you also."

Suddenly on reflection I understood something. It was not only I who was making choices, Kirri had choices to make of her own and I too was on some sort of trial. Apari had said that there were choices we both had to make and this had been what he meant perhaps.

Why she would choose to come to a strange place, or even another world where everything was different, to live with a man she didn't know was still a mystery to me.

"So you have now chosen to stay with me?" I asked confirming my thoughts, surprising even myself.

Kirri nodded her agreement. Then mischief seemed to light her eyes. "You're strong, pleasing to my eyes. Yes."

"I am?" I smiled flattered at her words. "And you as a wife... are pleasing to my eyes too." I added tormenting her playfully.

Instead of smiling though, she sat quietly, her mood taking on a sombre tone. "You are easy to please," She said softly. "Too easy to please, to make a good choice. There is a great deal that we need to understand about each other and you are young, eager."

"Me!" I couldn't believe what she was saying, it seemed so strange coming from her lips. Almost as though I was something of a disappointment. She however just nodded confirming her meaning.

"You are a husband to me while I am amongst your people Tom. I will obey you in many things but you are young, untried in many ways too. This I know, I have been told. This place..." as she looked around I could see the strangeness of the things she saw shadow her thoughts. "... the Edgelands are strange for me, the... city. Your little caveman who helped me... most of these things are strange for me."

Her words were soft and apologetic but in her expression I could see determination beyond my own. "I have seen many things but the Edgelands for me have always been a strange place. I need your protection. Taipan said that I should ask you to help when I'm uncertain or afraid. I am this all the time here. It is very different from what I know."

Her words were in the manner of a confidence and I frowned trying to understand them. "There isn't a great deal to be afraid of here. I mean … there are things you take care with but…?"

"No. There is a great deal that maybe you understand but that I don't. Will you help me understand? Teach me these things and not get angry when I don't know something? Aine said you might get angry with me."

"Me? Angry with you for not understanding?" Smiling I shook my head in an attempt to reassure her, though I was disconcerted at Aine's assessment. I reached as though to run my fingers down the length of her arm wanting to feel the soft warmth of her flushed skin and reassure her. The hesitant flush of her face that was enchanting when you saw the look of doubt and uncertainty.

Instead of relaxing, Kirri jumped, startled at my movement, she was obviously afraid even now. Perhaps that she didn't understand my intention quickly crossed my mind.

"Hey… It's OK. I was just going to reassure you." I stretched my hand open as though to explain its intent.

Kirri shook her head. "This will take time. I am sorry but I will try. Touching … this thing. It isn't a thing I am common to. Your … touch, is a surprise thing, I don't expect it. I understand that the men of the Edgelands are quick in anger and … and eager to touch. I aren't… don't know this well. I'm not sure when you are angry yet."

"Touching? What ever for… You shouldn't be frightened. It's a simple touch, a common gesture. I wouldn't touch you when I am angry Kirri. Is this really something so uncommon that you're so frightened of the threat of anger where you come from?"

"We do not do this. We are … sensitive to touch in my land. Anger, or loudness also is not a common thing for us. We are a peaceful people, so maybe you think we are placid perhaps, others have said this. Where I come from, my place, it is not angry and … and fierce like the Edgelands are. As a people we are quiet, calm and consider many things before we act. It has always been our way… the quiet."

"I thought this was to be your place now. Are you sure that you want to be here?" Again she dropped her eyes and waited expectantly.

"I'm not angry with you. I don't get angry so often." I added carefully.

Gathering my breath I watched her display of meekness but something told me she was not so meek as she wanted me to see.

"OK. How can you be a wife and not accept my touch?" I challenged.

Kirri looked up and smiled. "Alex said you might not understand these things."

"Alex!" I exclaimed ... and sat back into the pillows flummoxed. "Alex has nothing to do with this." I drew an irritated breath and floundered. "You have obviously spent some time at Taipan's?"

Nodding she smiled. "Aine and Alex have been teaching me to help make it easier. The Edgelanders ways are very different to the Inlands and yet we were once the same. I was to have stayed longer but Alex, her baby is near time and Andrew was concerned I believe. Your Mother and Aine will be helping Alex and I didn't want to be a burden for them as their time comes near for the birth."

It was my turn to nod my agreement. "How is Aine?"

"Big ... very big she says and that is true. It is another little boy, they know and your older brother is pleased. I enjoyed my time with them a great deal and I saw a great deal too. They were very kind to me Tom."

"And Alex?"

"Very big also and it is a little boy also. Your people are very lucky; to know these things early is a wonderful thing. That is amazing for me to see. The women are not so ... so at risk in bearing children."

"A son for Andrew." Very happy with that thought, I knew how much Andrew would be concerned for Alex. I doubted he would have got over losing his first wife, knowing how much he had feared for Alex when Ellie was born. Hopefully all would go well and if not... I would hear about it I was sure.

"Look. I will do you a deal, an agreement between us." I added seeing her look of uncertainty. "You will not talk of Alex until I choose too and I ... I will not try to touch you until you choose to allow me, or until you touch me first. Does that suit your sensitivities?"

Kirri smiled her pleasure. "I wish to touch you."

I grinned. "Sure."

Stretching over, Kirri bought her face close to mine. It was an odd gesture but as I sat still she touched her nose lightly against the side of my own, running the gentle touch as though a light caress between us. One where our noses caressed against each other and then completely satisfied she sat back.

I chuckled suddenly, "What was that?"

Kirri smiled unsure and flicked her fingers as though answering me.

Shaking my head I watched her. "I don't understand the silent language of the fingers Kirri."

Frowning she thought for a moment. "I don't know how to say it. There is no word..."

"What you just did. What were you doing?"

For a moment Kirri thought about it. "I was sharing a breath with you. Together we breathe as one. Didn't you feel this breath between us?"

I smiled, that sounded quite neat. "We do it differently. It's a kiss I think. You kiss like a Kiwi."

"A Kiwi?"

"Hmm... an islander, one who knows the old way. Let me show you how we kiss." I grinned at the thought as I went to move in towards her but Kelly shook her head surprisingly shocked. "What's wrong?"

"My old mother told me of this. This thing ... a touch with the mouth. I don't...?"

"Your old mother?"

Kirri nodded. "She also was given the tasks that bought her to the Edgelands. They would trade also then and the men of the Edgelands would ask for many things. They would meet them, as I met Jeremy, in the caverns and the serpent men would take them through the caverns of the Serpent."

"Many things?" I repeated encouraging her. I knew well the terms of trade between the mobs or tribes of different people and wondered if it was the same thing.

In our history the common trade before colonisation was for women and food, as well as even later in the colonial era when the whitefellas would trade for women. Exceptions were for tools, and weapons but they were ceremonial trades. Stories as well and dance could be exchanged but women were the most common terms of trade. Access to women was an important part of traditional trade, long since passed now.

Then remembering Kelly and Pete, I wondered if it really had changed when you looked at it with fresh eyes. With Kirri... would she see the difference I wondered?

Kirri had no hesitation. "The women would trade for food, food that was different... sweet and crisp. Good foods." Her smile touched her again as her look became conspiring and amused. "They did not take all this food back to the Domina, there was a special food that they liked to trade. There was a new food and the men of the Inlands were never told of this I don't think. My old mother would tell me not to say... it was a secret thing that would have angered the men."

"Food? So the women traded se ... a kiss for food."

"Yes of course. A kiss, that is what it was said but also… other things."

Chuckling I nodded. "I understand other things. Other things that would go with the kiss."

"You did not always do this thing. The… kiss."

"We didn't?" I asked, having never really thought about it.

Kirri shook her head. "Some of the women did not like this kiss. But it was like the new food. We thought they were both new and to like one and not the other was perhaps wrong. Perhaps it was a special trade thing, we did not know and the women wanted this new food. It was sweet and nice."

"Hmm … I like this kiss of ours you know." I added chuckling again. "This other thing… the breath thing is not the same."

Kirri sighed softly in deliberation. "I am not sure of this. It is not our way, it is new to me."

"OK. Would you trade with me?" I said chuckling. Enjoying the game.

Her look was sharp. "Trade? … in what?"

I grinned. I could stretch this I knew but the game was enjoyable. "A kiss. Just a kiss, I could show you this and you can decide."

Kirri smiled gently. "For what?"

I shrugged. "What would you like?"

Pursing her lips she thought about it. "A food. It is the favourite food of my old mother and she spoke of it often when I was younger, I would listen to her stories and loved to hear them. I always wondered what it would taste like. She said she missed this food when the men from the Edgelands never returned."

"What was it?"

Shrugging she attempted to answer as best she could. "It was yellow, golden yellow like your sun but soft centres." With her fingers she pinched the air indicating a size and I searched my thoughts to understand her. "Juicy I think you say. With crush… crunch… Um… sweet… and long like a banana, those we have, but it was straight."

"Like a cob?"

"Cob? No… like that though."

"Corn. A cob of corn… long and slender, wrapped up in green leaf and fine vegetable silk." I measured the size of a cob in my hands and looked hopeful.

"Yes. Corn. That is it I think but different. Maybe a little different."

I grinned. "We can go to the shop and you can find it. It's a deal?"

Sitting back pleased with herself she shrugged. "Yes I think so. This is a good trade, something I would like."

"Good."

Without thought I climbed out of bed, the bathroom called and I was in no mind to give it a thought. It wasn't until I reached the door that I remembered Kirri still sitting quietly on the bed.

Pausing at the door, facing away from her I grinned unrepentant as I glanced back around the jamb and noted her small smile as her eyes had followed me. At least she wasn't shy. It would make this all a lot easier I realized appreciating the candour, the knowledge and small pleasure in her eyes.

I understood that just because she was a wife to me, didn't mean that I could take liberties without her invitation. Not in the old way of things and this was from where the measure of these things was drawn for the both of us. These things were by mutual consent, I was not an Elder and therefore I had no right of certain expectations. My Grandfathers warning again echoed around my thoughts.

I hadn't even observed the responsibilities to be found in the old arrangements. Responsibilities to her family, which were impossible to meet under the circumstances but then these obligation's were no longer values we held either. Apari would have understood this.

Still she was a wife given to me and what is more it had been obviously arranged and settled with. She was here, she had agreed. Beginning with a trade of some kind was a good start for us as we tried to make a success of this arrangement.

There were expectations of each other that she would understand as well as I, clearly cut from our traditions. It was a marriage of the traditions from her world, as well as mine it appeared.

Then again now was not a time where the old traditions were commonly observed. I did have leeway here, as did we both. We could make our own rules to a degree and the thought teased me. Just what were the rules in her world?

Under the shower I thought about how this could possibly work out. It was easier these days, no expectations and not a lot of responsibility. At least most of the time, then again did any relationship come without some responsibility?

Thinking of little Ellie suddenly I wondered if she had met Kirri, or even if Alex had told her about my little girl. Kirri had obviously spent time with Taipan, Aine and definitely Alex but who else and what had others told her of my life?

Remembering what Jeremy had said about a girl up in the community and the thought struck me. Had he known about Kirri's place in all this even then? Had he even known she was to be my wife I wondered.

The questions wound around my thoughts as I pieced it all together and there were things about all this that I wasn't too sure I liked. Things that had been held from me and I hated that.

With my Grandfather I expected it, even with Taipan. They had my welfare at the forefront and there was always the right time and place to tell me things, even though I was a man. But Jeremy...? I was going to have words with my mate I decided.

New Beginnings

Tom

When I emerged from the shower, Kirri was nowhere to be found in the bedroom. However I found her busy in the kitchen cutting up fruit, seemingly quite happy and remarkably settled.

Jeremy too was settled at the dining table over near the large glass doors that faced the river, opening onto the high verandah. It was clear to see they had been talking together quietly and neither was a stranger to the other.

"Morning." I tossed his way as I moved over into the kitchen for a strong coffee. It wasn't something I drank often, but today I needed it.

"Morning?" My mate said. "Bit late?" A smile threaded his voice.

I threw him a glance that was not without question. He didn't look as though he had been up much longer than me so his comment was a little misplaced I thought. Once I had my coffee sorted, I left Kirri to her meal prep' in the kitchen area, joining Jeremy at the table as he watched us smiling in a strange knowing way.

"You knew about Kirri?" I asked quietly.

Jeremy just grinned unrepentant. "Your Grandfather told me not to say anything. Sorry. I didn't know when she would arrive though, but it was mentioned. We met up when I went up to the community last week and... like it isn't like we've had much chance to catch up you know."

"Hmph. Thanks."

"I did mention..."

"Yeah. I guess you did." I added distracted.

Kirri moved over to join us, a bowl of fruit in each hand. I was surprised when she placed one of these in front of me. It was an amazingly small amount and I looked up catching her eyes."

"For me? Thanks ... Um." I picked up the spoon hesitantly.

"You don't like this? It's good!" she protested at my glance.

"Yes. Thanks... but Umm... I need some more than just this." I explained with humour.

Surprised she immediately went to pass me hers but I stopped her. "No. You eat yours, I will just get some more." Her look was uncertain as she watched me curiously.

There was plenty of muesli at hand and despite the later hour I headed to the cupboard and taking a much larger bowl I filled it, as was my habit.

Emptying the fresh cut fruit she had prepared I added a further tub of yoghurt from the fridge and returned to the table, smiling now content with what was my breakfast.

The look of amazement on Kirri's face was worth a chuckle.

"So much? And … what is that, the white pudding?"

"Yoghurt. You don't know that?"

"No."

"Not surprised if that is all you eat for a meal… you eat too little woman. No wonder you are so small." I said gently. "You need to beef it up a bit. Here try some."

Taking a small measure of yoghurt on my spoon I held it out offering it to her. Kirri just looked at it doubtful at first, questioning me with her eyes.

"What is it again?"

"Yoghurt. It won't hurt you, it's nice … milky and smooth. Great with fruit, honest." I answered chuckling.

Hesitantly she stretched forward to taste just a small amount from the spoon, frowning over the texture. Then she nodded surprised. "It's sour milk? Like Aine gave me once, only she makes it in a big bowl. Not in that cup thing?"

"Tub… it's a tub not a cup. Yes, it's set milk stuff. Try it with your fruit."

"Maybe tomorrow. I don't want beef with my fruit though," she added oddly enough."

Jeremy chuckled and just looked over at me expectantly, as I frowned. It took a moment to dawn on me that she was referring to my earlier comment.

"No. I didn't mean to eat meat with your fruit." I clarified smiling. "I mean you could but … it's more a sauce or garnish or something like that. Though you could fry a banana I suppose," shaking my head I thought I understood her reluctance.

"You didn't mean that… Then why did you say it?"

"I didn't… I mean it is just a saying. You need more food, there is so little in your bowl."

Looking down at her helping of cut fruit she shook her head. "No this is enough. Thank you. I cannot believe that you eat such a big amount." She added in a small voice. "Then I am not accustomed to feeding men, they can eat so much."

"You don't feed the men in your family?" I asked curious.

"No. I live with the women. The men have their own place. It is our way?"

Interested at her explanation I thought about it for a moment, even

Jeremy was looking up curious. "Men and women don't live together?" I commented curious.

Kirri smiled. "Sometimes, but mostly we have separate places ... camps you would say. It is our way. It will take time for me to learn your way of things. I am not accustomed to this." Waving her spoon around she looked at us both. "I knew that it would be different and I will become accustomed, I will soon learn these things."

Grinning I shook my head, my glance taking in Jeremy's own amusement. "This is going to be hard going." I said on a chuckle.

"Tell me about it." My mate commented as he chuckled too, although we both shared a grin at Kirri's subtle look of confusion.

As I made my way through my meal I considered how I was going to get out of Sydney for a time, as both Apari and Big Jim had suggested I do. I guess I should have expected that but it was something I hadn't considered too deeply.

I could go up to the community, but if anyone wanted to find me that would have to be one of the early places they would look. It was a hard decision and I wasn't too keen on heading into the Daintree in Northern Queensland either, with the wet season fast approaching.

As I listened to Jeremy and Kirri exchange light conversation, mostly about cows surprisingly enough, it occurred to me that I might need to include some arrangements for her. Having the responsibility of another person, a wife no less was new and put an entirely different light on anything I might do.

"Kirri, did you have any plans? I guess I should ask you, but we should work out what we're doing. I need to get out of Sydney for a time." I tossed into the flow of conversation easily. Picking up at the same time that Kirri had never actually seen a cow or any sort of hoofed animal.

"I will stay with you. Where you go I will go also," she answered easily.

I pursed my lips, seeing all sorts of problems here. "That might not be practical. Perhaps it would be best if you returned to help Aine, to help settle in some more or... or maybe you would like to do some studies in the new year. That might help you?"

"No. I will stay with you," she persisted stubbornly. Her look was one that was very determined.

"I don't have a house, a place for you to stay if I leave here. Maybe Jeremy... can stay with you while you go to college or even school?" Looking across at my mate I raised my brow in question.

"Oh no... not me." He answered easily, a wide grin as he enjoyed our dilemma. "I am headed north with Big Jim once my studies are finished.

There is a job up there for me, they're looking for a bush guide in the Territory and I'm going to be helping Big Jim as a side-kick, till I find my way. We were talking about it the other week... been arranging it for a while. I'm going to take him up on it and I won't even be here. Besides she's your wife ... seems she should stay with you."

"I'm not sure that's practical!"

Jeremy shrugged. "I'm sure there is a way. Where were you planning on going?"

With a shrug of my own I thought quickly. "Maybe some travelling, I have an idea to head out into the heart of Aus' the Macdonnell Ranges, down south of the Rock. There's some things I need to look into. Stuff that Apari has suggested."

"Well then take Kirri. I'm sure she wouldn't mind, she might even enjoy the experience. See some of the country."

Looking across to her I considered the possibilities. Apari had also said something about that. She was on her own journey or ceremony I recalled. Maybe I needed to take the time to talk to her about it.

Kirri was quiet, silently watching me as she waited for me to speak.

"You been camping before? It's a long way, a lot to plan and adjust too. I don't know if you'd like it?" I asked quietly.

She shook her head. "I will go with you Tom. I can learn this thing if you would teach me."

I grinned. "It's not just teaching or learning, you may not even like this way of living. It... it's difficult sometimes but it is a... a thing that I like."

"I will do this too then." She said softly.

"But...?" I stopped myself. What was I doing here? "Look, give me a minute to work this through but we have to get out of here soon. You may not like camping, travelling... it can be a difficult life style."

"I will stay with you Tom. I will learn this easily I think. If it is something you enjoy then I need to understand this. Your Grandfather said that we should journey together and help each other."

Flicking my brow I gave up. "OK ... give me a while I need to make some phone calls."

I rang Taipan, taking my phone outside as there were a few other things I wanted to talk to him about concerning Kirri. I needed to clarify just what had been her experience back at the community. My brother on the other hand was expecting me to ring it seems.

When I explained what we had been talking about he seemed to understand surprisingly enough and agreed that I needed to vacate Sydney as soon as arrangements could be made.

He also mentioned that Kirri was recovering from some medical transitional stuff to do with her travel through the caverns and that I should treat her carefully, give her time to recover. It was hard to draw him out about it and I gave up in the end. It seemed it was nothing serious that I need to worry about but just to watch what she ate for a time as it could make her sick.

"If you're headed up into the Centre Tom, then I think you need to look at that vehicle of yours too?"

"Yeah… that was something I was going to look into. I think it's time for a new vehicle and I have my mind on a Prado, something with a bit of guts." I answered though a cruiser was out of my reach and that would have been ideal. "You up for a brotherly loan?" I ventured hopefully. "I have some money saved, but not near enough."

The phone was quiet for a time and I held my breath as I waited.

"I'll tell you what. Go an' find a vehicle, second hand and have it checked over. I'll send you the number of a friend who might be able to help. He knows the market but I think it would be a good idea to think about how you're going to travel. You need to accommodate Kirri if she is set on staying with you. We have a small camper trailer down there in storage. She is a few years old now but you can borrow that. She's quite comfortable, it's the one Aine and I used up north."

"Hey… yeah I remember it. Has it still got the fridge with it?"

"Yes… it's all together. How about you organize that car and you can pick it up. Have you thought about what you want to do with the ute too?"

"Well yeah. Maybe a trade…?"

"You won't get much. I might arrange for it to be garaged and it can stay down in Sydney if you can't think of anyone who might want it. It would be handy to have a vehicle available down there. Would that suit you?"

"Yeah sure."

"Good. Get back to me with details on the car and I'll send on the address where you can pick up the camper and store the ute as well. May as well use the same place."

"Thanks Ty. I owe you."

Taipan laughed. "Yeah you do. Live cheap and we can carry the costs."

"You're on. Thanks."

I knew Ty didn't mean that literally as I rarely taxed the accounts. Then I knew he would organize it on the business side. All this was shuffled to the back of my mind however as I considered my new vehicle when a phone number came through on contacts. It was the guy who would be able to help me with finding just the right vehicle I would need.

It only took a quick phone call and to explain who I was before Ty's mate was talking vehicle options. He was a dealer it seemed, or had contacts as he said he would immediately get onto finding just the right forbie for me.

I couldn't have been happier when I stepped back into the cottage. "It's all settled. I've got someone looking for the right car and Taipan has offered us the camper trailer."

"Geeze … half you luck!" I could see Jeremy was pleased for me, but clearly also seeing our departure as not something he would personally celebrate. "I guess I get your room for the rest of term hey?" He added as an on-thought, which was perhaps the only good thing in the arrangement for him.

"Yeah … I tell you what, get your driving licence and you can take on the ute too. You don't seem to mind driving it about."

"No joking?"

"Sure … she's yours. Just look after it. I'll give Big Jim the keys though 'cause I don't trust you not to drive it without a licence! It can stay in storage until you sort it out, then she is all your problem."

Later that afternoon at my insistence I took Kirri out shopping with me for the first time. We needed to build up a traveling tucker box and there were other considerations in travelling into the remote areas we were heading if we were to travel easily together.

I avoided Miranda Fair Shopping Centre as it was too big, too noisy and too crowded. I opted instead for the local village atmosphere of the smaller shopping centre nearby. I didn't think Kirri was up to much more, all at once.

Kirri was all eyes when we parked. I tried to guide her through the few small shops gathered in the centre, she on the other hand, just wanted to watch and see everything all at once.

"So much!"

Laughing I enjoyed the delight in her face. "This is nuthin' Kirri. This is just one of the smaller centres. I thought you might find the big centres too overwhelming."

As I settled the gear I had bought from the hardware, into the ute, I pointed us towards the small supermarket for food supplies.

"Aine took me to a place that had a few store rooms, but here there is so much…"

"Store rooms? Don't you have these shops Inland?"

Kirri shook her head. "We don't have trade money like you have, we have no need for it."

Puzzled I thought about that. "No money… but how do you earn things, or even get things?"

"What we have is for everyone. If you need something you get it from the others, or from where the things are stored or made."

"But who supplies the supply stores then. Without money ..."

Surprised by the question she just looked up at me confused. "We do, everyone does ... what needs to be done, is done, or ... or made. It is needed then someone will make it because they can."

"What if you want something that isn't at this store of yours?"

Shaking her head she still looked confused. "If there is something I need and it is not to be found then I find it, and find out what others want in exchange. I get it from them."

"What if they don't want to give it to you?'

Kirri frowned and then looked away as though disturbed before her eyes returned to me. "Then you must find it elsewhere. What if someone doesn't want your money, it is the same I think. Mostly it can be arranged but there are times where others ... will help you arrange what you need."

"Sounds idealistic, but I guess if it works for you."

Nodding she seemed however in some way distracted. This prompted me; there was something that was disturbing her thoughts and not for the first time I wished that I could read her mind.

"Is there something that you ... are you annoyed at something?"

Startled she looked up, and then her smile was full of contrition. "I am not angry ... just ... just confused I guess. Do you have money for these stores? You will need to give this to them for the things we need? It seems a bad arrangement to me, this money thing. What if you don't have enough?"

With a grin, I reached for my wallet and flicked out the credit card. "This is better than money, with this we can get what we need."

Picking the card from my fingers she examined it. "Then we should use this. You give this to them? But you can only get one thing, and then this is gone?"

I laughed. "No it's ... like a passport. I give it to a store only for them to process. They give it back ... they don't keep it. Like I did at the hardware it just counts up how much money I have spent and then takes it out of my account."

"Like the bank Taipan mentioned, where they count up this money that you use. They keep and count your money there and give you a token... this card? So you don't have this money anyway... I don't understand this, it doesn't make much sense."

"Taipan has spoken to you about this then? He might explain it better than me but it is just the way it is. You need money here to do most things."

"Yes. He tried to explain to me the money that you use to trade. It seems silly to me to trade like this. Why not just use what you need? If it is there then why would you not use it?"

"It's more complicated than that." I laughed hesitantly, not wanting to upset her.

"It doesn't need to be. If everyone can use only what they need then why... why do you need this thing. It is better without it I think. It is alike a child that eats too much, they get sick. You take only what you need, this is better. Why would you need more?"

Giving up on trying to explain the need for money I just chuckled. "This argument could go on all day, lets just get what we need before the shops close."

"They close? What if you need something?" Kirri asked surprised.

Laughing, I shook my head indicating that the discussion was over. I then just shuffled her ahead of me, giving her a chance to look in the window displays. This was something, which clearly entertained her, and me, as I watched the fascination in her face.

The small clothing shops had her interested the most, it was as though she had no thought for food, whereas I was determined to pick up at least the basics for a tucker box supply for when we finally were on our way.

Kirri on the other hand seemed to have forgotten all about the corn I had promised her and was more intent on the things she found in the shop. It all seemed to her to be large selections of goods, as she carefully and quietly watched the people around her.

I could see that she noted what people wore and how they interacted with each other. She was comparing things particularly clothes with what she saw in the shops I figured. Prompting her question's, helped me see how hard this must be for her at times, this adjusting to a different way of things in my world.

"I need new things, clothes like those." She pointed out as a group of boys and girls ambled past the window unconcerned.

"Clothes? Didn't Aine and Alex take you shopping or something?"

"Only the once. It was too difficult for her and I would not let them go so far in the heat. It was too difficult for both Alex and Aine I thought."

"Oh... Um... OK. Then lets try here and we can sort out what you need." I suggested as we paused across from a small clothing shop that seemed to carry a line for the younger women.

Anything would have done. I just wasn't into it at all but Kirri seemed to know what she liked and was fascinated by the whole business. The only thing I insisted on was that whatever she chose, it had to be durable and easy wear. Something the like suited to travelling and camping.

The assistant was a middle-aged woman and she seemed to know what we wanted. The range of things she bought out were practical for camping, a selection of shorts, tops and jacket type things that made the top of the counter as Kirri sorted through them.

It was fascinating as I watched her compare the pieces of clothing, she tested the texture and feel comparing this with others. She was taken with the bright summery colours with a number of things. It made me wonder about the Inland and just what life had been like there, or even what type of things had filled her life in just the day-to-day living.

The few clothes which she had with her had been light and strangely durable looking, but they were all solid plain or earthy colours mostly cream or white. They mostly had a texture like silk and I had thought that they suited her well.

We ended up with a number of bags and I insisted on hunting out a couple of pairs of jeans as well as some more durable cargo type pants. She preferred a fit looser than I would have thought, but it was when we reached the fruit and veg' shop that she looked on with a seriously amazed expression.

"What is this?" she demanded of more than one display. It was entertaining to see her select and carefully smell some of the vegetables and fruits as I tried to help her. Even the shop assistant, a young boy normally concerned more with the arrangement and stock of things got wholly involved in her persistent questions.

I explained that she was from a remote community and the guy seemed to buy that readily, but it was when we got to the display of corn that her eyes really lit up.

"This is the cob isn't it," she asked fascinated.

"Yep, and we'll have a few of those." I said, collecting up a prepack with a playful grin.

"Can I try?"

"They need to be cooked first, just a few minutes."

"Why?"

I shrugged, handing her the bag. "To soften them I guess, I don't know? We just always cook them in boiling water."

"You can't eat them like this while they are new?"

"Well yes you can but cooking is best."

"I want to try them first, before you soften them … can I?"

"Yeah sure. Wait till we get home though, it will be easier then and you can compare. Most of this stuff is cooked before you eat it, except the fruit."

Kirri just shook her head and went on to the next display with the overeager puppy of an assistant who was hovering in the background irritating me.

When we got home it took a couple of trips down the path to get all our shopping into the house and Kirri immediately gathered up her loot from the clothing shop and vanished into my bedroom. It was just like a woman to do that I thought and I found in it something really amusing.

Jeremy was nowhere to be found and I figured he had maybe headed out to a friends place, given that it was still the weekend. I didn't expect him home really so it was of no concern.

While I packed the large plastic tub we would use for a tucker box, with a selection of dry and tinned foods and other non-perishables, these meant for the camper trailer, my mind skittled over small practicalities.

Kirri obviously felt she would be staying with me in the bedroom but I wondered if it was the most practical arrangement. Perhaps I should suggest she stay in the lounge room on the sedan until she felt more confident with me, or I even wondered if I should. We hadn't even discussed it and this completely filled my thoughts as I contemplated the implications.

I had no idea what her expectations were, aside from what we had talked about. I knew, on the other hand that I would easily fall into any arrangements she might have in mind. Perhaps this should be something we also could discuss soon.

With the travelling stocks put aside I set about boiling the water for the corn and lightly fried up some thin steaks for dinner. When it was plated, I spread the corn thickly with butter letting it melt and ooze down over the cobs. Taking the plates out to the verandah I set them so we could sit overlooking the river feeling this would allow us to enjoy the evening.

Moments later, still occupied with her purchases I found Kirri examining her reflection in the large bathroom mirror. She was wearing one of the many loose shirts over simple leggings with a stretch top thing underneath and they rather suited her fine frame. She looked delighted with it, as I leaned up against the bathroom doorjamb watching her.

"Looks good." I commented when she swung about, surprised at my presence reflected in the mirror.

"You frightened me?" she warned with humour, then she turned back to her reflection. "The colours are lovely, and the feel of this." Running her fingers down the flowing fabric of the top she smiled. "Our clothes are very simple, we don't have so much difference in things."

"Yeah well come on, dinner is getting cold outside on the verandah."

Swinging about she danced happily off into the small storage room off the bathroom, as though to change.

Surprised that she had chosen there I realized this was where she had now settled her gear. Kirri was pulling at the over-shirt as though to change when I put my head around the doorway of this anteroom off the ensuite. The room that Kiahan, Aine and Taipans young son had used which was now mostly a junk room for me.

"No leave that, come and eat." I insisted, still taking in that she had left the bedroom to me and not too sure I was happy about that. Then again, what had I expected I asked myself as she stepped up to follow me. The small sedan in there would fit her, she was small after all and I guess she was more comfortable in her own space.

Out on the verandah she settled down to her plate curious. "What is this?"

"Meat. I bought the thin ones though they are nowhere as good as the thick ones..."

"And this is fat?" Running her finger along the cob she had lifted it to her lips tasting it. "I have had this before, but not like this. This is runny like ... like sauce."

"It's butter, it's good for the corn, it makes it moist."

Picking up the cob Kirri licked it, then frowning she bit into the cob tasting the corn appreciatively. "Is there more without the heat?"

"Yeah, I kept some that isn't cooked but there is more in the kitchen if you like."

"I like it. I don't think I like the sauce."

"Its butter, not sauce and you can have the rest later if you want."

"Must I eat this?"

"What? The meat ... sure. Have you tried it before?"

"Yes and I don't like it much."

"But it's steak ... It's good for you. You can't live on what you eat Kirri, you will get sick."

"No, I don't like carrion. Meat, Aine would give me eggs and Alex was showing me beans ... or lentils she called them."

"Well try it ... it won't kill you and it's not carrion." I encouraged her, but I was a little put out.

Dropping her eyes carefully, Kirri picked up the corn and tapping the melted butter from it as much as she was able, she went on to munch her way through it silently before she said softly. "Your meat is dead and decaying. What is it you call it, if it isn't carrion? That is the word I was told."

"Look OK. If you don't like the meat then give it here and go and get something else."

Quietly she stood, taking up her plate as she slipped the meat onto mine, somewhat relieved. Then she headed off back into the kitchen. When she returned she had the remainder of the corn on her plate, both cooked and uncooked and sitting quietly, began to eat it contented.

Occasionally she would look across at me, but each time I caught her glance she would quickly look away. It was driving me slowly to annoyance I realized.

"What is it?" I demanded softly in the end before it drove me to saying something I might regret.

Kirri shook her head. "You are right, I should eat what it is you prepare for me but I am sorry. I can't ... eat that."

"The meat?"

"Yes ... I have tried but it ... it makes me ill."

"Ill?" I repeated surprised. Remembering what Taipan had said about some foods not agreeing with Kirri's stomach. I realized then that I was maybe being unreasonable. "I didn't realize, sorry. OK ..." Taking up the last mouthful of the meat I popped it into my mouth and watched her, observing her subtle distaste which she tried to hide.

Kirri looked away contrite as I chewed and swallowed, that was when I came to a decision. "If you do the cooking then, I will look after the camp and the gear while we're travelling. That way you can cook what you will eat for both of us and occasionally I can do my own cooking. When I want to eat dead and decaying stuff, since you don't like some things and I do. Does that suit you?"

Kirri nodded, unapologetic yet apparently happy to reach a place of agreement.

"Do you like the corn?" I offered, as an olive branch.

Her smile was like the sunshine in the shadow of the night. "Yes, without the sauce."

I chuckled at that but stopped myself from correcting her.

Our talk returned to what impressions she had of her day and my taciturn mood eased. It was getting late into the evening but I was still fairly fresh from the late start to the day I had enjoyed.

Settling down after a time I tried to work out the character of this strange woman who was my wife and I found myself enjoying it more than I had thought I would.

Listening to her I came to realize that she was a person with strong views and strength of character not often seen in such a young woman. Then again she was an Inlander and her age and experience was likely a lot more than my own. What did she make of me I wondered?

"What really bought you to the surface Kirri, to the Edgelands? Why did you agree to this ... this arrangement?" I ventured curious after a time. "I must seem young to you I think, you age slowly don't you? I must be very different to what you are accustomed to."

I watched her carefully trying to read the things in her expression that she was not likely to volunteer.

Startled at my question, Kirri suddenly stopped in the moment, looking across at me with such depth that it was disconcerting and it was a moment before she answered.

"You are very different, it is true."

"Then why did you choose to come here?"

"Because I needed to come. It was time that we understood the differences we have. Time is valuable and should be used wisely"

"I don't buy it." I said challenging her quietly, sitting back crossing my arms annoyed that she seemed to be fobbing me off with the reasons Apari, my Grandfather had used. I felt however that there was more to it.

I knew with Apari there was. He hoped I would grow from the experience in some way. But what was it for Kirri? What would bring a woman to agree to a partnership other than for the grand good of all, as she had suggested.

Kirri just watched me and then continued hesitantly. "Yes, there is more in this arrangement for me Ariaka, and for many others."

"Tom." I corrected her, but she just smiled a small apology.

"Tom. I am sorry ... I forget. There is more, you are right. That you see this is a surprise to me, I had not thought that you would. It is not important for you."

"Then tell me what it is if it's not important."

"It is ... for me most what I need, what I want the most amongst everything. Long ago this thing was lent to the tribes of the Edgelands and now it is time for it to be returned to us. This is what I am looking for Tom, it is a secret thing amongst the women. The business of women, I cannot talk of this thing with you. But you can help me retrieve it from the old tribes."

"A churinga?" I asked surprised. "This cannot be found, or replaced. It is not in your own stores, this thing you want?" I asked, returning to a light teasing tone.

"No." She answered simply, her eyes levelling at me in all seriousness.

"You would perhaps call it such, but to us it simply belongs to my people and we would have it returned."

This was a serious business for her and I recognised it now. I knew that many of our old churinga had been stored in secret caches known to the old tribal people and wondered if this is perhaps what she meant.

It was not unknown for spirit items to be lent as a special favour but to hear that these had been exchanged between the Inlanders and the Edgelanders was a new and different concept for me. It left me curious.

Most of the churinga items had never been handed on to younger Kadaitcha, if indeed anyone could have been found in the "Killing Times" for the tribes. They had been hidden, or returned to their spirit place as the tribal people had left their country.

I wondered if there would even be any people left who would know of these storehouses, or even of what may be found there. These things had been lost to the tribes generations ago, amongst my own people and certainly amongst most of the tribes, if not all of them.

"Then tell me what manner of thing this is. Why was it given in the first place?" I challenged her. I needed more information to help her find what it was she was looking for and I doubted she would understand the upheaval and displacement our tribal people had faced with the coming of the whitefellas and the arrival of a different civilization to our lands.

Reflecting the tone she was using I continued. "I can't help you if I don't understand what it is your looking for. Or I might even stop you without realizing it. Have you thought of that?"

Kirri, thought about it momentarily. "But you look to find the same thing also."

"I do?" Confused I frowned. "I want ... nothing that I don't already have. What I want is ceremony, as you already know. Maybe ... maybe a woman to help me would be nice." I offered with a smile.

"I will help you, Tom. This is what I can do and in doing this, I can help myself."

"Explain it to me." I said after a time, persistently. "All of it ... Explain to me how we can help each other."

I had decided that in being totally candid about what I wanted was perhaps the best way to go here. I was also going to force the same candid truth out of her one way or another.

"Kirri, you are my wife and that's great." I began in trying to reassure her. "I like that but you can also help me find out more about something ... something that is close to me, which I want to achieve. This is all about what my Grandfather told me when I found out that he had arranged a wife for me. I also need to understand what it is that you want out of this arrangement of ours. You know I never thought I would take a wife, I had accepted that as a choice in my life."

Nodding she took a breath. "You are looking for the secrets or the ceremonies of the Fire Mountain. You need the ceremony. It is your Grandfathers wish, the wish of the Kadaitcha also. It is an important thing for the men of the caverns I think, for you to reach this ceremony. That which was born in the Fire Mountain of your histories."

"Yes. This is what my Grandfather believes. And you are looking for...?" I prompted, refusing to be drawn into what was the business of the Kadaitcha.

"I am looking also for Fire Mountain. It is there I will find where the dark firestone is stored. It is a churinga amongst our women, an old and precious thing that should be returned to us. This is my purpose and this too is found in the Fire Mountain of our histories. It is a stone like none other and it has the gift of sight, for those who can see. It also has the gift of death if it is used in this way, it can be sharp like none other. I know this thing was once used by the Kadaitcha of your world, as it was used in my world by our old people."

That perplexed me some and as I thought it over I tried to piece together the things she said, marrying these with my own knowledge.

"The churinga are usually forbidden to women in our Lore." I questioned softly, not wanting to upset her. I didn't understand why it was a woman now seeking this sacred item.

"In our Lore, it is not so."

"You have the sight of women, this Apari has told me. This is why he has chosen you to be my wife. You can also help me find what I want but I don't need this stone, I have other tools. What I need is a ceremony given to women, not men. It is a ceremony for men though, so yes... I do need you Kirri. Why do you need me?"

Startled she looked across at me. "But ... but for the same reasons always."

"Which are...?"

"This thing belongs to the women, it is forbidden the men but it is the men who guard these things on the Edgelands. I understand this. This is why I need you to help me, as you need me to help you. I cannot find my way through these caverns Ar... Tom. I need a man of the emu, who can take me where I need to go, who can protect me. A man strong in these things who has the knowledge of the caverns, who can control the serpents and ... and the other creatures of the caverns. This is you. There are very few like you now I am told. Not many travel through the ceremony as you have done, to become what you are. You have gifts and my people have been told this thing. You can move through these places, you can protect me."

Sitting back I continued to piece it all together as I considered her words. So we needed each other it seemed and it was for this reason we had been bought together.

I could also see now why Kirri had agreed to be my wife. It was the price of my help. The way of her people in repaying a debt for my help, the help of the Kadaitcha and it bound me to protect her. It would be perhaps a price I wouldn't mind either I decided.

Then I wondered about just what was this dark stone that she had spoken about. I had never heard of the like but maybe it was something I would discover from her in time.

Kirri had said it was a valued churinga for the women, perhaps a sacred thing even to her people, I could understand this.

Were these reasons the only ones that would bring her here, or even for her to agree in coming to the Edgelands to be a wife to me? There was a personal price she was paying and I could see little reward for her. So far I had only heard of the rewards her people would get out of this. There had to be more to it for her personally to take such risks.

She sat before me, silently watching me and I wondered what it was she was thinking. Did she even know how to find this Fire Mountain, had her people told her?

Recalling what Apari had said, I understood he knew where this place was but his understanding was drawn from the Lore, not maps on a page. I understood where the legend or the story of this gift to men was, where fire had first touched the earth when it was given to men.

I knew where this would lead me. It was for me to discover this place in the heart of Australia, somewhere in the Macdonnell Ranges. It would not be impossible but it would be hard enough to discover where the Etuta mountain was and to find the key to the stories which surround the history of fire and man. These mountains no longer bore these ancient names and perhaps these names were no longer even used.

These ceremonies and histories were often no longer celebrated as with the ceremony I was seeking. They had been lost in the "killing times" for our people. Lost through the death following the diseases the whitefellas had bought and the murders of the tribal people by those who took their land.

But the Country still sung the ancient songs if you knew how to listen for them and this I was confident I could do. The Ancient Spirits still ruled their Country, even if men could no longer hear their song easily.

I also understood that the places I had planned to go were a trek into some of the remotest and most beautiful parts of Australia, a place extreme in its seasons and demanding in its isolation.

Big Jim had often spoken of the Macdonnell Ranges, which were his home and his Country. It was a place he loved a great deal and I intended to catch up with him as soon as I could, to find out what he could tell me.

It was no less a challenge I would enjoy. This was why Taipan had been so willing to help. He would understand the challenge and would not allow anything to stand in my way, if it could be helped. He wanted to help me be all that I could be.

Did he know the whole of this I wondered? Likely not, though he would have the whisper of the Spirit Men in his ear guiding him as a Karadji does, who guides his people.

"Do you know where the Fire Mountain is?" I asked challenging her.

Kirri climbed to her feet and moved over to the edge of the verandah, looking deep into the skies as I stood to follow her. She was a small slight figure against the darkness of the evening. "There, the head of the emu," she said as she pointed out the stars. There are stars, which point the way, can you see them. This I know, together we can discover more."

Looking up into the deep night skies, I saw the dark shape of my totem in the bright cluster of the Milky Way. It was easy to pick out the Southern Cross too, at this late hour and the skies were clear. I knew this sat at the head of the emu and it was easy to see. Once you knew the form of the emu it was not hard to find. "I see the emu, but what pointers lead you?"

Kirri flashed me a delighted glance, "I look at the star maps and see the many stories I have learnt well to lead me. It is in those there… see the pointers just over the hill there. That is the way to the Fire Mountain."

I didn't need to look, I knew where we were going and I knew now that she too knew this. She hadn't lied to me or tried to mislead me. Moving closer behind her I stretched my arms about her without touching her, capturing her within the circle of my arms and the verandah rail.

Conscious of her aversion to touch, I moved carefully. Holding her captive against the railing of the verandah. She was going to have to deal with me I had decided.

Kirri baulked at my closeness as I whispered softly. "You are going to have to get over this no touch stuff Kirri. It is not our way and you need to become accustomed to me touching you. You are my wife and you have chosen this too."

Gripping the railing for support she answered me equally as softly. "It is not something I can overcome easily. To touch … is to expose me."

Confused I waited, trying to understand. "In what way?" I demanded softly whispering into her ear beneath my lips.

Kirri drew a breath. "I have the sight of women, but … but in touch I see too much, often."

I frowned. "How can you see too much?"

"In touch, I see things. Our people are sensitive, we do not touch often as it reveals too much, like sharing, becoming a part of the other. It exposes us to others."

"I don't understand." I offered, not seeing her meaning.

Kirri took a moment and then carefully turned to me as I eased myself back, giving her room but still holding her captive against the railing as I tried to find the meaning in her eyes.

"Today, this morning when I touched your arm. I could see what was to become of your wounds. They were nothing and you were right."

"You knew they would heal easily?"

"Yes. I knew that. I knew also that these things … these wounds were something that you did. Something that made you stronger in some way."

Somewhat confused by that, I tried to find in her words their meaning, but the scent of her reminded me of other things, those that had me smiling, somewhat irreverently.

I was reminded of a promise as I watched her lips move, watched the light reflected in her eyes. "You owe me something." I said softly.

For a moment she frowned and then, her frown cleared. "Your kiss?" she asked. Leaving me to nod with a simple smile.

Kirri swallowed. It was as though she was not looking forward to the prospect and I drew a breath patiently.

"You are going to have to get over this other aversion of yours." I suggested patiently.

Nodding, she rested her weight back against the rail. "Show me then," She invited. "I am ready I think."

Chuckling at the look of resignation in her eyes I moved in closer, though not touching her, but for a soft caress of my lips against her own. It was a gentle gesture, not a kiss. It was just a caress of the lips as though we were sharing a breath together in my way, not hers.

Kirri stayed perfectly still and accepted my caress though I could sense her frown. I didn't move back though. I was enjoying this and teasing her was fun. I caressed her lips again with my own, drawing from her an involuntary response. Her lips moved with mine in a gentle dance.

I felt her small upturn smile against mine also, so again, our lips touched in a teasing brush. I could feel the relaxing of her mood. Her wariness was dissipating and being replaced by curiosity but it was enough.

Carefully I moved in towards her, my lips claiming her own gently. Showing her, teaching her and her response was a small victory for me. As I deepened the kiss I felt Kirri's hands move up to my chest, resting there then uncertainly gripping the fabric of my shirt as my arms moved around her bringing her gently into my body.

She was small, lost in my arms. Such a fine body of a woman like she, was like a promise against me. When I heard her small involuntary moan I suddenly released her. I didn't want to frighten her at all and I had taken more than I had intended.

Kirri staggered slightly, leaning back against the railing, still gripping my shirt as my hands found the support of the railing again in releasing her. Watching as she drew deep steadying breaths I wondered if she knew to breathe through her nose. She looked scattered, her expression lost to her sensations.

"You're supposed to breathe woman." I teased chuckling, "... through the nose. You don't hold your breath, you relax." I said teasing her gently, trying to contain the humour I felt.

Shaking her head she just looked up at me with a scattered expression. Drawing a deep breath she shook her head as though to clear it and then as though noticing for the first time she was gripping at my shirt she suddenly let go, stretching her fingers deliberately.

Easing them, then placing them behind her she gripped onto the rail. Remaining still captured within the prison of my arms as she was.

Again she shook her head as though clearing it. "That was strange."

"Strange nice or strange bad?"

"Yes... nice. Strange I think," nodding she continued. "Strange but ... but nice somehow."

"I liked it." I chuckled watching her reaction carefully.

Standing back I moved to the solid table and shifting aside the cutlery I perched my weight against the table top, folding my arms as I watched the thoughts shift across her face. "I didn't mean to hold, or to touch you quite like that." I added shaking my head.

"No. It is fine, I didn't ... see, feel it was wrong ... it was, it didn't ..."

"You didn't see or sense anything? I mean... I don't know how this works for you?"

Shaking her head she just looked at me. "It was different, somehow it was not like touching does."

"You'll have to tell me how you mean. I don't understand this touching stuff, the problem you have. Maybe you can blind yourself to ... this other stuff."

Kirri was looking at me oddly, it was a strange expression as though she was seeking to explore my mind, my thoughts and yet couldn't.

"I don't understand what it was ... between us."

"It was a kiss." I answered suddenly grinning. "It always feels nice, particularly the first times. That is different, it's nice and it sorta gets nicer when mixed with other stuff."

Kirri shook her head again. "I need to rest, my thoughts are not clear and I need to ... rest."

"OK. Are you all right in the little room? I noticed you have all your gear in there. We can share the big bedroom if you want." I offered magnanimously as I stood up, but making the offer with a smile that should have been easy for her to read.

Shaking her head Kirri just moved off slowly. "I need to rest, I won't disturb you."

"You've already done that." I tormented her as she passed me, looking back as she slipped through the large glass doors of the bedroom down from where I stood. Her look was confused to say the least and for some reason that made me grin.

Picking up the plates and gear still sitting sentinel on the table I headed for the kitchen, my own thoughts distracted.

At least I won't have to do much cooking I thought absently. That had to be a plus though I was going to miss my meat. I enjoyed a steak occasionally and I had just got back into eating the way I liked after the constraints of our training.

Oh well, it was just something else to adjust too I guess. There was gunna be a lot of adjustments to make, it was just another of many.

Stacking the dishes I could hear Kirri moving about in the other room but it was as I swung to make my way to my own room that I noticed the shadow shift on the verandah, through the glass.

I was still for a moment, suspecting it might be Jep and I was suddenly impatient with the thought. But it wasn't, it was too tall, too slight to be my Jongorrie and I frowned realizing it.

Unsure if it was my imagination, perhaps even a shift of the starlight shaded by a cloud or a shadow of the spirit lands. I waited silently as my eyes adjusted.

I was accustomed to seeing shadows of past times, past worlds as they merged with ours. It had been a part of my childhood, a part of my initiations and a part of my life.

The shadow, a soft grey form shifted again, seemingly drifting towards the other end of the verandah and I carefully moved with it. Wanting to see if it was a reflection from the bedroom or a shift of the light. I knew if it was a shape from the spirit world that it would not necessarily realize that I had the sight to see them, they were sometimes as blind as us.

There was no sign of it again though and restlessly I tested the world around me. The Moggie Eye was calm within me, my senses were quiet and I was reassured. But the memory of that faint shift of light, of silent slip of motion, stayed with me.

Shades of Things

Tom

Waking the next morning I had a strange sense of déjà vu as I blinked at the strong morning light. I was looking once more, straight into a pair of sky blue eyes watching me.

I couldn't help the smile as I carefully rolled onto my back, relaxed, no longer perturbed by Kirri's presence. She was sitting as before on the bed covers as though she had scarcely moved from the morning before.

"You gunna make a habit of this?" I questioned softly with irony as I stretched, hauling the covers carefully.

She just looked at me, curiosity in her glance while she waited as though expecting me to continue?

"Can't you sleep or sumthin'?" I queried again softly.

Kirri shook her head in disagreement. "I sleep when I am tired and I am not tired now."

"Is there nothing you would rather be doing than watching me sleep?"

Again she shook her head after a moment, leaving me confounded. It was meant to be an irony but somehow she hadn't seen it.

"OK. So what is so fascinating? Do I snore or something?"

Kirri shook her head yet again, silently.

"Hmm ... Don't you find your bed comfortable then?" I tried again in an attempt to get her to talk.

Frowning she seemed to consider the question with all seriousness. "It is comfortable."

Frustrated at her non-commitment to the conversation I rolled over to my side and propping my head on my hand. I watched her then with the same intent she was watching me. I wondered also just who was gunna give in first.

Kirri did, she dropped her eyes for barely a moment before she raised them to mine again. "You don't like me watching you?" she responded after a moment.

I grinned. "I don't care either way. But I would like to know why?"

"You confuse me sometimes and I want to understand why also?"

"I confuse you?" I muttered in disbelief. "Am I so hard to understand?"

Kirri nodded solemnly. "Yes."

"In what way? I thought I was pretty simple to understand. Though I guess ... a lot of things might confuse you and that can worry a guy. Tell me what is so confusing and we might figure this out?"

This was a small game for me and I smile as I was settling in to enjoying the play. I waited while she obviously thought about it.

"You are very different from the men of the Inland. They … they are more independent I think."

"Is that good or bad?" I chuckled, not really understanding the explanation much at all.

Kirri shook her head as though she too didn't know the answer.

"OK. Different how? There can't be that much difference surely?" I teased her.

"There is. You are …" waving her hand about she attempted to elaborate but seemed to find difficulty in finding the words.

"That doesn't look like finger language, and if it was … I wouldn't understand it." I chuckled.

"No. I am … it is hard to explain. You are different in every way I think."

"OK." I thought about it. "Name some ways." I grinned across at her, encouraging her, enjoying the exchange.

"You are tall, much taller. We are smaller people I realize that now and you are all colours. Yesterday I saw that you are many shades but that is your sun I think. You also are very strong, just you. Not everyone maybe. This I noticed and yet you are gentle at times. Careful with me, and not others around you always."

"Not everyone. It would be a mistake to think I am soft with everyone. I am a Kadaitcha Kirri and this means I have a place in this world. One that demands things of me and these things aren't often gentle. But you're right in that I am trying to be careful with you. My Grandfather has asked that I take care. So I try."

Frowning she nodded. "Yes, but I have only heard of this from amongst your people the things you do. I have not seen it but it is there. That is maybe what is the strength you have, that I can feel within you. We also have people of the Kadaitcha but we call them by a different name and they are … different too. So I understand this."

"I am also a man who likes being a man Kirri. You are my wife and that too has demands that are between us. Have you thought of that?" I challenged softly, grinning at the direction this game was taking.

Kirri nodded with a flush reaching up through her skin. "Since last night I have thought of that."

"Only since last night?" I asked, chuckling.

Again she nodded. "In the Inland, it is not like … like last night. When you kissed me. It is not like that. These things between men and women are much slower, more considered."

"What is it like then if what we felt…, what you felt was not familiar to you?"

Her glance caught my own and strangely held it, plumbing the depth of my thoughts, it reached to the point that I wanted it to stop for some reason.

"You felt this too. Is this something you feel when … when you do this?" She asked after a moment.

"Kiss?" I queried not sure of her meaning. When she nodded I could only smile. "Yeah … sure. It is something that I have learnt to want as a man. To me a woman, one who I hold in my arms, is enjoyable at the least." Then shaking my own head I wondered. "This is unfamiliar to you? You don't understand the needs a man and a woman have?"

Kirri nodded slowly. "This is something of our histories, stories and song but it is not something that we find now that … that urges us. Touching is not something that we do often and this feeling…" Pressing her hands to her stomach Kirri frowned. "Do you understand what …?"

Uncertain I sat up slowly and watched the play of expression in her eyes. "You don't have this … drive for each other in the Inland?"

"Yes, but it is different, we are different. We want different things. These things are important to us too but it is different. What I feel with you… what you make me feel is different. The Edgelanders, you… are more … physically expressive in these things. For us there is ceremony, a binding and bond when two people choose to mate and you do not have this I am told. Your ceremony is not of this thing we have. Aine has said that you also mate without ceremony. It is something you do. For us ceremony is always a part of the mating."

I raised my brow in surprise and contemplated her stumbling description. "Do you think the Edgelanders are more basic in this Kirri or perhaps more demonstrative? We sometimes have ceremony too, it is probably akin to yours surely?"

I was surprised at her assumptions, if not her complacency. I didn't think that the worlds could be so different in these things. Men and women were the same all over the world I had thought and perhaps likely within it as well.

Nodding slowly she agreed, as though it was clear to her. To me however it was barely short of an insult for some reason. Her comparisons seemed to reflect badly on the Edgelanders as she called us. It seemed that I came off in a primitive light, unappreciative of ceremony. Even as she went on to explain.

"Our ceremony is very different, Aine and I spoke of this. It is maybe a bit of both I think but for when a man and woman come together there is particular ceremony and this you do not have. Men and women live very different lives in my world and companionship, mating together is a choice. You give of yourself, when you kiss. This we do not do, we do not take, nor give."

"OK I can see how you would think without ceremony we might be … negligent. If you don't touch much or even feel the need to touch, to be close to someone would be the same though I am sure."

"Not like it is for you. Mating is personal for us. We do not share what we feel. It is ours alone. Last night you gave of yourself with your lips on mine, you offered me something and I didn't understand. I was almost an abandonment of the things around you that I am not accustomed to. I am not sure of what to do with this thing you give me, this feeling."

"You didn't like this?"

"You are angry?"

"You just said I, my world was … base. That can't be good? You think us too uncaring, or careless maybe is a better word for what you find between a man and woman, between us. You don't like this?"

"No… that is not like what I meant in a bad way. You… you have a different way. It just surprises me that we are so different in this thing. My old mother never explained this."

I drew a deep breath, slowly. I was going to get to the bottom of this I decided. This was not a light issue to have between us.

"You are my wife Kirri, and while I know there are … is a certain understanding between us, there is also expectations. If you don't like me to touch you, then you should return to your people. I will touch you in time, it is my way, our way."

Considering my words she nodded. "I wish to stay here, on the Edgelands Tom, but I am familiar only with our ceremony, our way and in this I do not understand you. You seek only women, not the strong companionship of your kind, that of men. Those ties are the strongest of bonds in my world."

Her words confronted me for a moment and then I ventured. "In your world it is common for people … for men to seek men in this… this companionship? So women seek out women only as life companions? I can understand that you lived in a women's camp, but I didn't realize…?"

"Yes. Companionship is something between two people who are the same sex, men or women. Mating is something between a man and woman who choose to mate, to have children. But it is not a big part of our lives. It does not control our choices like it does in your world. It is a transitory thing... it changes. What is important is what is the good thing for all, for everyone."

Further confronted by her explanation I ventured. "You prefer the company of women?"

Kirri nodded. "I live only with women, the women of my family. I understand these things between women."

"But ... no I mean sex. Mating as you put it?"

Kirri frowned. "I prefer the company of men in this as you say. But I live with women. I do not live with men. They live in their own company, in their own ... camps mostly. It is our way."

Relieved for some reason I drew a steadying breath. "Well that is a good thing."

"Why would it be different? I would not choose to come to the Edgelands if it was other than this for me. I would not choose to be your wife during my time here."

I grinned. "In my world, sometimes women ... choose these things and it makes for unhappiness, it is... confronting for many. Men also, they are not always sure of this stuff. Relationships are seen as best between a man and woman so they stay together, live together. It's seen as a balance of things."

"Why would they do this?"

I shrugged. "We maybe are less ambivalent in this."

"I am not ... ambivalent. That meaning is ... unsure?"

"Yes. Then you accept this though ... in my world, that we live together and mate together. That we stay together."

"Yes. I knew this thing when I came from the Inlands. I knew there would be many differences, but it surprised me. This giving between us."

Stretching over carefully she slowly and deliberately brushed her nose against mine in the same soft way she had, the way in which she shared a breath with me. In her own way it was her concession.

I was at first surprised at the gentle touch but then my pride flared and I reached for her. My hand wound with determination into the hair falling loose at the nape of her neck, pushing her gently back into the pillow. Holding her half beneath my weight as I moved to kiss her deeply.

Kirri's hands immediately went to my shoulders as though to push me away but instead they danced with indecision as my hand slipped down over her body and I deepened our kiss in a gentle passion. The feel of her body beneath my hand was sweet, but my actions unnerved her.

When my lips released hers she was breathless. My lips sank easily to the rapid pulse at her neck as I tasted her skin carefully. The path my lips were taking surprised her, as much as my growing desire for her was now surprising me.

Kirri's skin had a sweet musky taste, her body warm and freshly flushed as I moved down over her, pinning her to my bed easily. My hand slid down over the shape of her, settling on her hip appreciating the warmth of her body through the light fabric of her clothes. I nudged aside the loose neckline of her night shift seeking her breast with my lips.

It was a strange fabric, as light as a whisper and when I reached up to pull it aside touching her, Kirri shuddered within the weight of her drawn breath as though surprised at my actions.

The heat of my lips dropped to her breast tasting the delicate skin there, teasing it softly. Responding as women do I could see that she felt this thrill, her nipple hardened under my touch. Chilling and teasing the now damp skin with a soft blow of breath I nuzzled at the delicate rose of her skin as I felt it tighten in her response.

It was the small groan, the thread of surprise woven within it as she shivered under my touch, which distracted me. A response to the gentle torture of my mouth as I played with the rose of her nipple, this was what stopped me.

At first it was with pleasure that I stopped and looked up curious at the sound. Then confusion flooded through me at what I saw. It was in the tension in how she held herself.

This was like a torture for her I thought for a moment given the fast pace of her breath and the sweep of emotions she was apparently feeling. Fascinated and a little curious I pulled back to better see her face and more easily read her expression.

Her eyes were closed as though in pain, her brow puckered but she had surrendered to this. Her head was arched back into the pillow as though offering her breast to my touch but she was removing what was herself from the experience. I could feel the tight tension of her body under my hand as she lay beneath my balanced weight.

"Kirri?"

She drew a ragged breath, not moving. Waiting silently it seemed.

"Kirri!" Pulling away from her I sank almost reluctantly back into the bed after a moment, watching her. The arch of her body collapsed slowly as she finally looked up at me with a frown across her brow. "This is … you are too tense." I said steadily, curious. "You don't like this?"

"I … I am tense?" she whispered as though surprised. "It is just … your way. I did not think … you surprised me."

"Yes. I can see that." Easing myself up and away from her carefully I slipped over to the edge of the bed to leave her. It was the only way that I could trust myself to stop at this point.

Taking a minute to gather myself I threw my eyes over her, noting the confusion, the tension still present in her expression. "You don't look as though your enjoying this much you know?"

I waited, but there was no response and I guessed she was perhaps merely tolerating what was going on. The thought was a bit like a burning ache, one building in my belly. Physically I was not unaffected by what had just happened between us. But mentally, mentally I was slapping myself. She was not ready for this and I was forcing my own needs onto her.

The minute the thought came to me I stood and headed straight to the bathroom. This was not what I wanted between us. We had a long way to go in this journey and we had barely begun. There would be enough time for this when she was more prepared to accept me and it now seemed it was going to take time for her to adjust. I was rushing her I felt and this was the problem here.

The spill of the water in the shower cooled down my body. It was soothing at least as I dealt with the consequences of my actions in my mind. I heard nothing of Kirri in the next room, although I half expected her to follow me for some reason. Though that was more hopeful than rational.

Would she be angry I wondered? Confused even? I wasn't sure how to go about dealing with this woman and I knew I was bloody confused. I couldn't have taken her though, not while she was suffering my touch rather than being part of what our coming together should be. It seemed to me that perhaps our worlds, our ways were very different and I would have to consider those differences.

Kirri had spoken of ceremony and I wondered just what that meant to her? Was this something that I would need to consider and just what was it all about. I had assumed it was akin to some kind of marriage thing but maybe it wasn't, maybe it was more complex than that and maybe she needed this ceremony for her to accept me?

Why had I stopped! This I demanded of myself and yet I had stopped instinctively. Every sense in my body had baulked at continuing... I was unsure, uncertain of her and how she felt.

This was to be a long-term relationship we were building and suffering each other was not going to be part of it I decided with determination. I needed to understand more of what Kirri expected, or even required of me.

How the hell did I get into this place in our relationship I demanded of myself? What the hell was it that Kirri wanted or needed of me, or of us as a couple?

By the time I stepped out of the shower I had settled down some and with a cold determination I dried myself, tossing the towel about me as I returned to the bedroom.

KIrri was still in the bed; strangely enough I hadn't thought she would still be there. When I entered she eased herself up, still watching me with curiosity. It seemed as though I was some puzzle to her.

"You OK?" I asked roughly as I moved over to rat through the clothing in my draws.

Kirri took a moment to answer, but at least she did answer me. "Yes... Are you ... OK?"

It was unexpected and I looked up frowning as I pulled on my gear. "Yeah ... sure. Look I'm sorry about ... you aren't ready for that and I knew it before I even started." I said slowly, apologizing.

"I don't think I understand you." She said softly, seemingly confused.

Straightening I frowned across at her as she watched me boldly. "What I meant is that it all was perhaps too early a thing, we need to get to know each other more. We need to understand our expectations of each other perhaps."

Kirri said nothing, however she nodded in agreement. Not wanting to stay under the scrutiny of her eyes I turned to leave her, stepping out to organize some breakfast. I was hoping that by the time she joined me what happened would be forgotten or maybe she would have forgiven me my impatience even.

Big Jim had turned up sometime during the night and I was surprised to find him in the kitchen as I stepped through from the bedroom. His eyes were sharp, searching mine and I felt myself evading them.

"You're up early?" He tossed at me as I reached the cupboard, he was amused I could see and I wondered if he even knew that Kirri was here.

Ignoring the question I turned to him. "I have a woman here, Kirri, do you know about this?"

My mood was still taciturn and I think he saw that quickly. "Yes. I had heard, how's it going?"

I dropped my glance. This was a caring question he had asked I reminded myself. He was sincerely concerned about how we were getting on together.

"OK I guess. I spoke to Taipan yesterday too." I added hoping to avoid further comment on Kirri. "I'm taking the camper trailer inland. Taking Kirri with me as well. I wanted to ask you some stuff about a place called Fire Mountain or Etuta in the Macdonnell Rangers. Have you heard of it before?"

"Yes, I have. So you are going to find this fire ceremony then. It's an old thing that you are looking for you know. I knew about it, there has been talk the other night between the Kadaitcha but I was unsure if it was what you would do? The men didn't know of your decision."

I grinned suddenly. "I should have known you would know all about it."

"Yeah … well we should talk about this and perhaps I can help you. It is in my Country and if you are going into this region there is a great deal you should understand. When are you leaving…? It should be soon. It isn't safe for you to hang about now."

"I hope to get away soon. Apari has warned me about that. Likely nothing will come of what has been done but you just never know."

"There are a people there in the Macdonnell Ranges who can help you with what you're looking for, those who can touch the Dreaming in their own way. The Iruntarina people, they are a spirit people of the caverns in the heart of the Country. They are very close to the Oruncha. They are a sacred mob. These people guard the ancient stores of the churinga there. The tools and shields of the old Kadaitcha and they keep many secrets."

"I haven't heard of this mob?"

"No you wouldn't have. There is little known of them and it is the way it is, the best way. Many years ago when our traditions began to die, when the old Kadaitcha were passing, the Elders had no initiates to pass on these things of Lore so many took the churinga back to where it was first gifted. Much was given to those people in these mountains. They thought it was safest there, away from the eyes of those who would steal such things. The Iruntarina people guard these sacred things even today."

"Can I arrange to meet up with them?"

Big Jim flashed a smile. "They will know of your coming, you will not need to tell them this. If they choose to meet with you then it will happen. If they choose not too, then there is little you can do about it. They are a very powerful people of the spirit in those mountains. They do not suffer fools and the curiosities of others gladly. They have many ancient ways which they once shared with the mobs, but no more."

"Could they tell me of the fire ceremony do you think?"

"This is not their ceremony, it's the ceremony of women. It's only the Unthippa women who can tell you of this and there may be some amongst them. Those of Etuta, or Fire Mountain as you say and they too are in the heart of this Country. They will be easy to find if they choose to be found, they hide in plain sight."

"Tell me of them." I asked curious as Kirri trailed into the room, making her way over to the kitchen area where we stood.

Looking over at her I smiled a welcome, although my thoughts flashed to what had happened earlier between us. "Kirri, have you heard of these women, the Unthippa mob?"

Her curious glance flashed between us. "Yes, the women of Etuta. I have heard the stories of how their Elders bought ceremony to the Edgelanders and to the Inlanders as well. It was a long time ago that this thing happened. It is the men's ceremony they bought though we no longer practice these things, but do you not know this?"

Big Jim interrupted quietly. "The ceremony the Unthippa women brought is now practiced by the Kadaitcha of the Edgeland's Kirri. It is not as common a thing as it once was. It is also no longer the domain of the Unthippa women. It was given to the Kadaitcha and Tom's rite is now held by the men." Big Jim then turned to me in all seriousness. "Kirri talks of your subincission, this also was once a ceremony of the women which they gave over to the Kadaitcha."

Surprised, I suddenly realized that Kirri would perhaps be more familiar with my body than I had thought. She had perhaps seen the cuts I had received as a full Kadaitcha, this while I slept. I had not thought much about it, but that she should so easily speak of such a thing and to another man truly surprised me.

"And you know of these things?" I asked her still somewhat surprised.

"Yes." With full candour Kirri looked up at me expectantly, having helped herself to a cool drink of water.

I shook my head. "You surprise me." I said softly.

"You have underestimated your woman." Big Jim commented with a grin. "You need to take more care Tom."

"So it is the Unthippa mob, the women that I need to find?" I added, hoping to gloss over my ignorance of Kirri's knowledge. Something that I would have to adjust to I thought. I needed to talk more and act less and the idea was new to me.

That I could learn something of so much value from a woman was also new to me and I could see how my ignorance was apparent to both of them.

Big Jim however considered my question. "Perhaps. This mob would know of the ceremony and maybe Kirri can help you there."

My wife nodded content. "They are the mob that I look for too, they too can help me, so maybe we can both do this thing together," she said softly.

"They would share this ceremony with Kirri, as a woman, more so than with you Tom. Perhaps this is your Grandfathers intent."

His suggestion seemed to me sound, then Big Jim added quietly. "There is a book that was written in the last century which was recorded by a white man, an anthropologist who made small record of these things. It has in the last pages a map and it also tells the story of the Unthippa women. I will get this for you both and it will guide you to where you might find the women in the mountains. Etuta is not a name known today, but the map will help you."

"You have this here?" I asked.

"No. But I know where I can get the copy. It's mine but it's with someone else. I can get it maybe tomorrow. It would be good for you to read about the old things, the stories. The map will also be helpful as it has many of the song lines actually recorded, the travel routes of the old stories and the storylines where once told to this whitefella'."

"Thanks, it will give us a start. That region is filled with mountains and gorges and I had wondered how to go about this, finding Etuta. I looked it up on the internet but ..." I shrugged.

"OK. I will get it then tomorrow. Now, about this camper trailer..."

Big Jim was meticulous in going over what he felt we needed as we planned our venture into the red centre of Australia. That afternoon he arranged to pick up the camper trailer with me, taking it down onto the low flats, which were at times used for parking. This made the trailer easier to access while we climbed over the thing, pulling the storage boxes apart. We checked their contents as we also checked over the trailer itself.

It was late afternoon when Kirri joined us, having stayed back at the cottage to wait for us, packing up the bedrooms and attending to other things for most of the day. I noted also how she seemed to deal with Big Jim with a confidence that I was beginning to envy.

Kirri had walked around to the flats via the road and access track and I had noticed her sitting up above the flats, on the track earlier as she quietly watched us.

It wasn't until we'd begun to open out the tent of the trailer that she joined us. Jumping in easily to help while she watched for any nod or direction from Big Jim about where she could best be of assistance. It was as though they understood each other with more ease than she and I had managed to achieve so far. Their silent finger talk hadn't escaped me either and not for the first time did I wish that I understood it.

I guess it was her deference towards Big Jim that started my line of thought. The way she watched for his instruction with raising the tent from the trailer. That I had done this a dozen times held little weight with either of them, even though it was the first time Big Jim had handled such a thing. I could see he was struggling with the concept of how the trailer unfolded and it really began to irritate me that neither of them seemed to think that I knew what I was doing.

It was a simple process really, made easier by an understanding of what was going to happen when you finally pulled up the floor, which was at present a top lid. It flipped into position quite easily but raising the weight the right way was the key to it all. It was about pulling the tag ropes, rather than pushing the frame.

Jim however had Kirri standing up on the armoured toolbox at the front, albeit the best place for someone of her small weight. But he was asking her to push the frame up rather than guide it forward. This was not really helping the process much at all and I knew from experience that she would be unable to handle the weight.

It took one good well-positioned pull on the guide ropes for me to flip it out. Yet when Big Jim took the credit, having ineffectually pushed at the frame my irritation hit its limits.

"OK, down from there." I said as I left the ropes and stepped up to Kirri. Stretching my hands up to take her by the waist offering to lift her to the ground.

Looking at me nonplussed she frowned. I was certain she had heard the irritation in my voice but I was not up for discussion as she braced herself against my shoulders for a bare few seconds and I lifted her easily.

"If you get around to the other side we can flip out the support struts and stabilize her, then she only needs the cross bars."

"It's a girl?" Kirri asked surprised.

For a minute I just looked down at her, as my irritation quietly dissolved. "Yes it's a bloody girl!" I said after barely a moment. "What else would she be?"

"A boy." She added as she stepped up behind me and I could hear Big Jim chuckle when she continued. "But the trailer is not alive, it can be none of these things."

Bending to adjust the support struts I found myself grinning none the less. "It's not about being alive, it is about being bloody difficult at times."

Kirri frowned. "Difficult? It wasn't difficult was it?"

I shook my head grinning, wondering how to answer her as Big Jim stepped up behind us.

"He's kidding you Kirri. Don't listen to the boy."

With in a second my humour changed, flashing back to irritation. A breath eased it but as I stood, it was with ill humour again.

"Look, how about you get back to the house and start on dinner, this is mostly done. You will get enough practice with it in the next few weeks anyway." Short and sharp my voice raised her frown but without a word she turned to do as I had said.

We both watched her go, as she swung silently towards the track and immediately I was sorry for my taciturn tone.

"That was a bit rough." Big Jim commented in an undertone as he turned back to check on the final struts being at hand. "You should take more care of your woman."

Once more my irritation hit overdrive. "Why? You seem to take enough interest in her."

It stopped him in his tracks as he turned back, his look searching my face and I had the grace to hear in my own words, my evident ill temper.

"OK, that was uncalled for." I said in a small apology offered under the scrutiny of his look.

The man nodded. "It certainly was. And disrespectful of your wife and to me."

He was right and I knew it. My temper was my own and it was uncalled for but how was I supposed to deal with a wife that I knew so little about?

"Yeah you're right and I know it, but … I don't know what I am doing here. It isn't like I chose this Jim and I don't know if I am as ready for a wife, as my Grandfather seems to think."

"So what's the problem?"

Drawing a refreshing breath I looked about me for an answer. The river was a good place to settle the eyes, it moved like my life. It breathed slowly but it was as restless as I at times. It too was swept along beyond its own control.

Shaking my head, I could only hope Big Jim could see in me, my thoughts as I tried to gather together the words. "I don't know her at all … Kirri. She is not like … a choice I have made."

I could see the flash of anger in his eyes and I stepped up folding my arms defensively and settling my weight up against the car. Waiting patiently for his condemnation.

The weight I was carrying seemed overly awkward as I added. "I know why though … and, I have to trust in the judgement of others don't I?"

"She's a good woman and you don't know how much she has come through to get here. You need to appreciate that."

"Yes. I can see that … "

"No. I think you can't. That is the problem. You see only a woman Ariaka."

At the use of my name I baulked as though slapped. I had not expected it and I considered the import of Big Jims words. "What am I missing then?"

"You need to look past the fact that she is a woman and look to the future, your future and hers. She is a woman that is hard to find the like of. She is like no other you would find easily."

"Because she is from the Inlands?"

"Not entirely." Big Jim added, still angry. "She understands things. It is her way and she has allowed you a great deal of rope Tom. Don't go and hang yourself with it! You need to appreciate that. Take some time to get to know her, understand her and learn her ways. These things just might surprise you. Some of the Kadaitcha feared you would jump right in and make a hash of the whole thing boy … prove them wrong. There are those among the men who think you are arrogant and foolish. You have made some bad enemies son."

I wasn't so keen on the way Big Jim dressed me down, but he was right in some things. I didn't really know much of Kirri and maybe I was going about this all the wrong way.

That I had those amongst the Kadaitcha who I had angered was no news. I still recalled easily the discontent of some of the men deep in the rainforest of Far North Queensland. It was a time when I had challenged their own actions, or rather pointed out their neglect.

Right or wrong, I knew I had those who thought I was a bad choice as an initiate and that would likely follow me for years until I had proven myself.

Later that afternoon after we had packed up the camper trailer again I found myself seeking Kirri out. She had done exactly as I had asked and dinner had been ready without another word. She had even cooked eggs to go with the salad, four of them for each of us and I didn't mind that they were quite undercooked. It was like a dressing really when it was all mixed together and I had enjoyed it even.

After having helped with the cleanup I found Kirri out on the verandah where Big Jim had sent her. Appreciative of the meal he had insisted that we would clean up. Kirri had been quiet during the meal though and I wondered if she was still wary of my earlier bad temper.

"Hey… there you are. Enjoying the quiet?"

Smiling softly she turned to me. "It is the night, it is peaceful but … in some way it is a secret time and I am growing to enjoy it."

The balcony rail offered a good place to lean as I joined her overlooking the flow of the river.

"Yes, it is sometimes like that. Look I am sorry about this afternoon, I had no call to snap at you like that."

"You were angry, I understood that."

"No, angry wasn't it. It is just temper and I was wrong."

Looking up at me she studied my face, then slowly smiled again. "It is strange for me to hear you are sorry, I had not expected that."

"Yeah well I am sorry." I said agreeing with her calmly. "Big Jim chewed me out over how I behaved. I had no cause to be like that with you."

For a moment we watched one another and I waited for her to say something, anything, but after a time it was apparent there was nothing she wanted to say. So my words tumbled into the silence between us.

"It seems everyone knows more about my wife than I do. I'm not so sure I like that very much and I guess it makes me tetchy some."

"Is there anything that you would like to know? I will tell you anything you ask. You are my husband, I would not keep things from you."

I released a small sigh... sending it off into the night as I looked out over the fathomless river flowing past us. Kirri was like that I thought, deep and full of so much that couldn't be seen. I had no idea where to begin in getting to know this woman properly.

"Tell me about your world. The Inland... the differences you speak of."

"That is not so easy, there is so much that is different."

"Well then what is the same, or nearly the same. Perhaps we should begin there."

For a moment she thought about it and then turned to me. "Our histories, they are the same."

"Our histories?" I chuckled softly, surprised somewhat. "I didn't think our histories were connected much."

"But they are, only you have no account. Aine was telling me how your memories go back only a short way. The histories go back much further than she could tell me and they are something which we have in common, between our people."

Turning towards her I felt my frown, one she also noticed as she went on. "Our histories have a common beginning, it is us who have changed this thing. We no longer share our worlds."

"How do you mean?"

"We were once one people, but there were wars that divided us. Our histories are tens of thousands of your years in time though you only account from when the Edgelanders began a record in script. You discount most of your own history."

"When you say we ... you talk of the Inlanders and the Edgelanders?"

"There are others who also have chosen a world apart."

"The Mimi people, like them?" I suggested.

"Yes, and others. We all now move in different directions, towards different futures and our ways are different but we were the same once."

I shrugged. Did Kirri know of Sean and Jenna I wondered? Had Taipan told her of their life now with the Mimi, deep in the plateau lands of Kakadu and other places. How much could I reveal to this woman?

"What can you tell me of the others?"

"There are many," she said softly in a simple explanation. There are the Oruncha, the Mimi, those of the caverns and the islands. There are many others who remain hidden from the eyes of the Edgelanders. You are a violent people and this concerns many. The tall people of the mountains and others beneath the lands." She said softly as though in a confidence.

"The islands? So many other places?" I asked, almost disbelieving her.

Turning to me she seemed to look deep into my thoughts before she answered. "Yes, the cloaking lands. You have not heard of these people?"

"No. I mean... we have stories of those who come from the seas. They are the spirit people. The old people call them the Inapertwa, people who are both animal and human, these are in our stories too. Is this who you mean as well?"

"They are different again." Kirri added quietly. "Such spirit people are of many histories, it is an old Lore we share."

I shook my head, wondering just what Taipan or Sean, both shape-shifters, would make of such a statement and smiled in my knowledge. "And these things we have in common you say?"

"We do." Kirri answered simply. "The wars divided us from each other and in many ways we have become very different from each other."

"Like you and I." I added.

Grinning Kirri quipped. "Not so different I think. Except your life is so short, and mine is less ... umm... how do you say it?"

"Less primitive?"

She looked away keeping her thoughts to herself, hiding her eyes from me. "Maybe. But instead of these ... instincts you have, we have sensitivities I think. They are the same but very different."

"And what do these sensitivities tell you?" I asked curious.

Still for just a moment, she collected her thoughts. "That you are difficult, but I trust you I think. I believe you will help me and together we will do well. We can learn a great deal from each other before it is time for us to part."

It was a type of compliment I guessed. After all it was no simple thing to be trusted.

Then she asked. "And what do your instincts tell you of me?"

Surprised I straightened and considered the question. "That you are honest, I trust you. Also that you're trouble..." I added chuckling.

"Trouble?"

"Yes. You test me. You make me think of what I do and why I do it. You're a woman... women can be trouble in their own way. It's a good way mostly."

For a moment she just watched me. "It's a good way," she reiterated and as though content she turned towards the rooms behind us. "I need to sleep, I think I will leave you now."

"OK then. Goodnight Kirri." Reaching suddenly for her hand I took it in my own stalling her. "In my world, a wife would kiss her husband goodnight before she left him."

Surprised, she thought for a bare moment and then taking my hand that held her back, she wrapped her small hands around mine and stretched up towards me.

Instead of the kiss I was expecting though, she grazed her nose against mine sharing a breath as I bent down towards her. It made me laugh in surrender as I accepted her light touch graciously.

"That is not quite what I meant." I said softly.

"Goodnight Tom." In a light step she left me and I watched as she slipped through the glass doors into our room.

It felt good to turn back to the deep night above the flow of the river, my world felt suddenly very good and I was glad we had spoken. Somehow life had taken on a soft edge. It was something I would enjoy I decided.

Shadows

Tom

Déjà vu. I expected it and I would have been disappointed if I hadn't found those quiet blue eyes waiting patiently for me to wake. For a moment I just watched her as she watched me, all while I roused myself properly.

"Still having trouble sleeping?" I asked softly after a time.

"No. I slept well, you though were restless."

"I was? I can't recall."

"Yes."

It wasn't a literal question but I should have known she would think it was. Smiling to myself I turned fully towards her. "I had a strange dream is all, we really should get away soon."

"Yes we should." Kirri answered quietly, then added. "Your little cave man is here."

I frowned, not sure of her meaning and then as I heard a shuffle at the open verandah door I looked over to see Jep standing there, fidgeting in his own way.

"Jongorrie! What the hell?" Sitting up I glanced between the two of them in confused silence.

"Yes she can see me. She can… she can. You should know that by now Tomtom. Smart one she is." Jep mumbled as he fidgeted about on his feet. "Coming in I am. I am … can I?"

"What's stopping you?" I demanded impatient with him. He never asked permission for anything and I couldn't understand why he did now.

"Apari … Apari said I shouldn't disturb you for a time. Not now… not anymore."

"He did?" Surprised I met Kirri's eyes with a touch of laughter.

"Yes he did. But I couldna' wait anymore."

"Why?" I demanded patiently as I swung out to the edge of the bed and stretched. It was a stretch that bought to my attention the warmth in my belly. It was a heat given off by the Moogie Eye and I frowned.

"Yep Tomtom… Yep… you shoulda' noticed it. Ya can feel it can't ya?"

Rubbing my stomach, easing the warm tension in my gut I grew impatient with his chatter. Something was up obviously. Something was happening and this beating around the bush was exhausting. "Spit it out." I demanded with a sudden impatience, grabbing at my jeans still on the floor where I had left them.

"It's the Djaranin... the Djaranin Tomtom, they are hunting again."

"What? So soon? It makes no sense."

"Oh it does... it does!" The wizened little figure protested as he danced into the room in his peculiar gait with his eyes twitching between Kirri and I. "It's you... you it is. You threaten the serpent. You do Tomtom. With time... the time you are taking to leave the city."

"What the hell are you talking about? I don't have a clue Jep... speak plainly for once." I protested as I stood, carelessly naked to the morning.

Making my way into the bathroom with impatience I swung the door with a bang. Then realizing it ... I turned to open it again impatiently. "Get in here!"

Jep obeyed with a flash of resentment, but his glance to Kirri held a certain triumph. For some reason there seemed to be a contest of some sort between them I thought, as I closed the door again on the bedroom.

I didn't know how much Kirri understood and this was men's business anyway, not for the ears of women.

"It's her... she is delaying you and the Dark Dogs are hunting now." He mumbled with an uncertain resentment.

"Why the hell are they hunting me! You make no sense." I demanded again as I went about my business of the morning.

"You risk exposing the Wolgaru Tomtom. They will not put up with that... she is a sacred thing. Secret and sacred and you ... and anyone who remains behind in the city, they risk her exposure."

"How?"

"I don't know! But they are on the hunt. It's those who place her at risk they will hunt Tomtom. It is you! Get out of here... Go today! Before they find you and tear you apart."

I swallowed and considered his words as unpalatable as they were. "Is this the heat I feel, is this why I feel it?"

"It is... it is. It's a warning and the Moogie Eye is gathering its strength to protect you."

"OK. So we will leave. That will resolve this thing?"

"Yes. Yes... leave now. Now, today and it will be good. All done with I think."

"Well today is not possible. Tomorrow, I need to ring a guy about the car but it will be good."

"Today Tomtom... today. Not tomorrow!"

My look was uncertain. I couldn't see that it was an urgent thing for him, but he could be over obsessed with the whole business. Besides there was little I could do under the circumstances.

The camper was ready, that wasn't the issue. But I needed a vehicle to tow it and the only vehicle was Big Jim's. I could chase up the dealer and see if we could hurry up the transfer papers on the forbie he had found for me. At least I was to find out today if it was going to pass the inspections. Surely they would be seeing to the transfer today as well. We could be on our way by tomorrow.

"Not possible. I am waiting on the car, it should be done today though. I will give the sales guy a ring this morning and see if I can hurry him up some."

"Today Tomtom… today!"

Jep didn't hang around after that, it seemed he didn't want to meet up with the Djaranin either, having little to control them with. He left mumbling something about me being distracted enough not to notice him, should it come to a fight.

Kirri was in the kitchen when I got there and Big Jim was with her. He too seemed to know what was going on as he turned to me.

"Your Jongorrie has been here?"

I nodded. "The dogs… it seems they are hunting again. Anyone who is a risk to exposing … stuff." I glanced across at Kirri as I finished the sentence and Big Jim just nodded.

"I'm fine. My business was with the Djaranin. Yours was with the serpent. So it looks like you need to leave as soon as you can. You are too close to the serpent in this business Tom."

"Yeah, so Jep says. I'll chase up the car today, see if we can leave the city as soon as possible. I can't see what has stirred them up though, is there any problem that you know of?"

"No. It was all taken care of but keep your whip at hand. You might just need it if the dogs decide to catch up with you."

I agreed, though I couldn't see it happening. There was no way that I would expose the Wolgaru. It was just such an improbable thing for me to do. There had to be something else going on I was convinced.

The heat in my gut stayed steady throughout the day and that was reassuring. It didn't increase, but then it didn't die down either. Kirri said little but I could see that she had heard much of what had been said and had drawn her own conclusions. About these she said nothing. It was a curious thing for a woman but then Kirri was a curious woman.

The first thing we did was clear out the ute, which gave me the opportunity to bring my whip down to the cottage. Along with other gear that had accumulated in the old ute over time.

Big Jim wanted to put the ute into storage as an incentive for Jeremy to organize his licence. He apparently didn't trust him not to use the vehicle in the mean time.

It was almost therapeutic clearing out the ute as I impatiently waited for news on my new vehicle. By lunchtime we had it washed and clean and taking it over to storage was a simple process with Big Jim's help.

The dealer had been helpful as well and had promised to try and fast track the registration process once the inspections had been done. In the late afternoon I was relieved to get the phone call to say that all the paperwork had gone through. She had passed inspection with flying colours as he had insisted she would. He had told me that I could pick the forbie up anytime.

It was a relief to get the thing down to the flats where the trailer was waiting. To Kirri it seemed the vehicle was like a new toy. She tried every compartment and any nook or cranny she could find. I took the time to stay with her explaining the ins-and-outs of the vehicle as Big Jim and I looked on amused.

"Did you pay for the car with that plastic card from the bank?" She asked after a time, curious.

The question made me smile, but I realized that she was trying to come to grips with money stuff and I guessed that experience was perhaps the best teacher.

"Yep. That is what it's for Kirri."

"The Banks are good then, I can see where it is helpful."

I laughed in the irony of it. "Hardly that, they get their monies worth out of it."

Kirri looked up frowning. "How do you mean?"

"Well we pay interest on money they lend. They give us money and we pay it back, plus some extra in interest."

"Your Banks control your money, they make it? I thought Parliament or the managers ... your government did that?"

"No. The Banks don't make the money, the government does. That is how it works. The Banks just charge to lend you money, it is profit for them."

Kirri frowned. "I will have to think about it. Are you sure they don't make their own money."

I laughed and shook my head as we got back to the business of the camper trailer. Kirri certainly had a different way of looking at things, and a lot to learn still.

As we hooked up the trailer and the car together, we also realized the slow process of figuring out between us just who did what. I wasn't accustomed to working with an off-sider and Big Jim made it an entertaining process with a few witty comments.

Much later that afternoon after Jeremy had got home we were sitting around the table pouring over maps and the like, making plans when a simple comment from him had all our attention.

"We had the cops at TAFE today, asking questions." He threw this into the conversation as though it was of little matter to any of us.

Big Jim on the other hand was suddenly very still. "What?"

"The police." Jeremy added surprised. He was obviously not expecting the reaction he had got. "Called into TAFE, looking for Kelly. They were talking to some of the kids, anyone who knew her. They just asked me a few questions, nothing serious."

"And what did you say?" Jim asked quietly.

Jeremy shrugged. "Just that I knew her. I didn't say much, only that the last I saw her was Friday. I'm not that stupid." He added on a grin. "They just wanted to ask her some questions is all, about … a friend."

My look met Big Jim's. It was hard to know what was going on here. Just why they were chasing Kelly was an unknown, maybe they had linked her to Pete. But then were they even looking for Pete?

Why would they…? We knew nothing was left, no body. No sign that he had been near the ceremony. The Kadaitcha had made sure of that.

"Maybe it's Kelly they are looking for?" I suggested quietly. "Maybe her aunt is looking for her, missing persons or something."

Big Jim nodded. "If she is under eighteen, that could be it."

"She is." Jeremy added. "That's it maybe. Do you think I should say that I got a call from her or something along those lines. I could tell them she's in Melbourne. Maybe she will ring her aunt."

Kirri had been in the kitchen rustling up some dinner when she joined us. Placing a large bowl of salad and chicken in the centre of the table she sat and set smaller bowls with forks nearby obviously for us to help ourselves.

It gave us time to think about what this might mean, but when she too joined in sharing her thoughts, it was then that I began to feel the heat of the death stone warm. Or perhaps it was just that I became more conscious of it.

"I can feel shadows about the house Tom," Kirri added to the disquiet of our thoughts. "A sense of something and I am wondering if it is the guard dogs of the serpent. It is not something I am settled with, it makes me restless."

"What is it you feel?" Big Jim asked quietly.

"A shadow, a sense of something watching, waiting for something. It is disturbing."

"We will be leaving in the morning. It isn't anything to be concerned about. If it is the Djaranin they have no cause to act and all three of us can deal with this. There is no risk here for you Kirri, for any of us while we are together."

I had been considering leaving immediately but I knew the risk would be greater in the dark. Better to stay until morning as the Djaranin liked to hunt mostly at night. With Jeremy and Big Jim here the dogs would not be likely to seek me out, if they wanted me at all.

I understood though the sense that Kirri was feeling. That sense of being watched and it made me wary of shadows and the movement of the bush around us. I was conscious of any sound in the darkness of the night and it kept me from sleep.

Neither Jeremy nor Big Jim could settle either, though Big Jim kept to the boat-shed. I knew he too had his churinga at his side throughout the night and we could call on him in a moment if it was needed.

That night, it seemed at times, was the longest I had spent in an age. Even Kirri was quiet and watchful; she too found it hard to prepare for sleep. Going through our bags kept her busy, along with clearing out the last of my gear from the bedroom and organizing it into storage in the small room she had claimed as her own.

There seemed a lot of excess gear and it was good to be shedding this. I had already picked out what I wanted to travel with aware that we would be away for some months.

It wasn't only getting up into the Macdonnell Ranges that I was looking forward too. I had decided that once we were up into that area I had a mind to catch up with Sean and Jenna who were in the Kakadu region. Only that was going to take some organizing though I figured Taipan or even Andrew could help us in contacting them.

Kirri too was keen to explore something of the Edgelands and while our preparations were touched with anticipation, the whole prospect had an edge of adventure that was very appealing.

We had decided to approach the business that concerned us most first, that of my ceremony. Kirri also wanted to deal with the business of the women though she was very quiet on just what that was.

I was going to have to find out exactly what she meant once we were on the road. It would give us something to talk about in the long hours of driving ahead. First though we had to get out of the city and tomorrow would see us well underway.

We had planned a long run, to get as far out as possible on the first day and I was looking forward to the heat in my gut settling down again. The Moogie Eye, though still steady, told me that the threat was still present and Kirri was as edgy as I it seemed during that night.

I was beginning to appreciate the woman more and that was a good thing. Maybe I was too blasé about how I viewed women in general. Maybe it was time that I stepped back and took note of things I had brushed over before.

Later as I watched the dark motion of the water below me from the verandah where I was happily staying out of Kirri's way, I considered just how I had treated Alex. I could now see the neglect that I had treated her with. I had failed to see it at the time and it was no wonder to me now that Andrew had so easily claimed such a woman as her.

It was there in many of my relationships of the past, but very much so with Alex. I should have taken better care of her I figured and the thought was like the dark skies overhead. I would take more care with Kirri I decided then, I would not make the same mistakes again.

The clouds had drifted in during the afternoon and now the night skies were well behind their cloaking path. This added to my sense of ill ease as I struggled to settle my senses. The Djaranin would be well cloaked in this light and conscious of this I studied the deep bush shadows around us, looking for any hint of movement.

I was on edge, wary of everything and while the heat of the Moogie Eye stayed with me I had reason to be. If I neglected Kirri in any way, or placed her at risk then I would be answering to more than my Grandfather. I had no idea really of what connections she had, or even what her family might do should she be placed in danger. There was a great deal that I didn't know about my own wife.

That too was going to be something I had yet to learn and the prospect of spending time on our own as we travelled around, discovering just who we were together, was beginning to appeal to me.

Kirri's advent in my life surely had its upside, which I was only just beginning to appreciate.

I felt the sudden light touch on my arm as these thoughts swilled around my mind. My wife had moved up behind me and the touch of her fingers on my arm was the last thing I expected. That she didn't remove her touch was also a pleasure. It was as though the contact was more important than the conversation promised in her eyes.

"You gave me a start." I explained readily as I turned my back to the night and welcomed her. "Finished in there already?"

The touch of her fingers slipped down to my forearm in a gentle graze, but remained there. So I moved my hand to cover hers, in some way welcoming her light touch and reassuring her. It was a strange sense of contact between us and I rather liked it.

"Nearly." She agreed softly as my hand weighed over her own. "You are worried still. Will the dogs come do you think?"

"I can't see why they should. I am no threat to the serpent, not that I can see anyway. Perhaps it is something else that has triggered this business. Why...? Does it worry you?"

Shaking her head, she slipped her fingers carefully away from under mine and turned to the cloaked dark of the night. "I see no trouble, not yet, not clearly."

"You see what then?" I asked curious, knowing that she had the sight of women. The ability to sense a path ahead, which was something I couldn't do.

"There is nothing to see yet." Kirri answered swinging her glance back to mine. "The night is a strange one though. It reminds me of the Inlands but it is dark instead of light. We don't have nights such as this, nor even nights." She finished on a small grin.

"Maybe it is that the stars aren't out for you? I can't imagine a night without any stars. All the time being dark with little light to brighten it up."

"We don't have the night." She explained patiently amused. "It is never dark in the Inlands, not in our Domina. In others it is, but ours is always a soft light and it gets misty at times. That is my favourite time, when the mist comes in over the forests. It is very beautiful then and I miss that."

"Mist hey? We will have to find you some then. Perhaps when the weather begins to chill down with winter. We get mist here mostly towards the winter through to the end of autumn. That is a few months off yet."

"Will these clouds bring storms? I am looking forward to that. To seeing your lightening. It sounds like such a wonderful and ... and frightening thing."

"You don't have storms in the inland?"

"Yes we do. But our storms are different. The lightening never reaches for the ground but stays high in the Domina. It lights up the ground sometimes, but never reaches for it. Aine was telling me how the storms in the north of here but up where it is dry and hot, are brilliant and ... and wild to see. She said she loved to watch them with Taipan at her side."

Chuckling I just nodded agreement. "Yes they are that, wait until we get up into the Red Centre and around Kakadu and Arnhem Land. The summer storms there are a force on their own, really something to see as they move across the land like armies of water warriors on the go. The Wet Season is magnificent, hot and crazy scary all in one. The summer storms cool you down and you look forward to them. You have no control over it at all and it just lets loose. It's great stuff."

Grinning at the memories of the wet seasons I recalled from my time in Northern Queensland. I was looking forward to feeling the full force of the monsoons again. I loved the way they lashed the land across the Northern Territory and Far North Queensland.

Kirri seemed to appreciate my description with a certain wonder and I felt the anticipation in being able to show her these things that would be entirely new for her.

It was the sudden shift in the dark shadow, a moment in the night that bought me back to earth again quickly. I couldn't have said what it was that suddenly had my attention, that which had baulked my flow of thought.

It was in the bush around us that this sense of stealth settled about me restlessly. I could feel other eyes settle on us readily, or perhaps it was just my imagination. I wasn't sure.

Straightening quietly I turned back to the slight form of Kirri at my side. "Come on, let's get inside and try and get some sleep. We have a long drive ahead of us tomorrow."

Turning obediently without question she moved ahead of me and for the first time in an age I closed the glass panel doors behind us, shutting out the night. I needed to sleep and I had a feeling that if I left them open, as was my custom, then I wouldn't be getting much sleep at all.

Kirri had headed off to her own small room by the time I turned and I almost called her back. It was a silly thought and she obviously was as tired as I. So instead I climbed out of my gear and stretched out on the bed at last looking for the sleep that had eluded me so far.

I was struggling to settle my sense of wariness about the dark things that moved through the night outside. They were still there I thought, but the heat in my gut was settling as well. Perhaps I was being over imaginative or even over protective.

It didn't take too long really to slip off, settling at last with the knowledge that the Djaranin, if indeed they were around, would have trouble with the door lock at the very least.

The Law vs The Lore

Tom

Of all things it was Jeremy who woke me. I had surprisingly slept like a log in the end. Even Kirri was not there with me when I stirred, which immediately had me on edge for some reason. There was something wrong and I woke up dazed and confused knowing it.

"Hey come on... get up. There are cops at the door wanting to talk to you," he demanded roughly.

"What!"

"Jezzus Tom. Get up will ya'." He demanded again impatiently. "Kirri is out there and I don't know what she's gunna say to them."

As soon as his words sank in I was out of the bed and grabbing for my jeans where I had dropped them. The thought of Kirri dealing with a couple of coppers was not good and I was grateful when Jeremy left me to keep an eye on what was happening, while I scrambled to dress.

I entered the room just in time to catch Kirri answering questions. She looked relaxed and confident, a model wife no less albeit one still in her usual simple sleeping attire. Though I saw that the coppers probably didn't realize what the outfit was.

"I'm Kirri Ariakas, Tom's wife."

"Mr Ariakas?." One of the officers said, greeting me as I emerged from the bedroom. I immediately realized that they had no idea who I was.

I just nodded, with a flashing glance to Kirri.

One of the officers stepped forward handing me a photo from the few he held in his hand. "We are looking for this man, Fida Majeed. He is also known by a few other names. One of his associates said that you were in company with him the other night. Do you recognize him?"

I took up the photo; it was the man I knew as Pete and I studied it with little interest. "Yeah sure, he was at a friends house. I was there too?"

"They said that you had something of an altercation with the man?"

"I did? Well not really, we exchanged words about ... about what was happening."

"... and you left with him?"

"No. Not at all. Listen just what is this all about I mean... I only met the guy for a moment."

The other officer stepped up. "And this girl? Do you know her?"

He handed me a photo of Kelly, it was a particularly bad shot, likely drawn from a surveillance camera from the hazy look of it. It looked like it was taken near Central Station. "I couldn't say. I can't see her features clearly." I offered glancing across at Kirri.

"I see." The officer also glanced across at her. I realized then in that look, that he thought I was evading the answers because of my wife's presence. "Could we have you come down with us to the station for some questions. There are a few things we would like to clear up and you can help us with the enquiries."

"Look I don't know about this. I mean I am leaving today. Me and my wife are moving out of Sydney, headed inland. It is a bit inconvenient."

"We won't keep you long, and it will help us get to the bottom of this."

"What's it all about anyway?"

"It's just an enquiry at this stage but you could assist us."

"Yeah ... what with?"

"We will be happy to answer any questions down at the station...."

The officer went on, though clearly he wasn't going to be asking anymore from me with Kirri being present.

I took the time to dress properly while they waited. Big Jim found me in the bathroom, leaving Jeremy with Kirri while the officers waited. I was inclined to just take off and refuse their suggestion that I go with them to the station. But it was Big Jim who put paid to that idea quickly.

"What's this business about... did they say?" He demanded straight up. He must have had words with Jeremy before he found me.

"They haven't said."

"Well then what the hell are you doing going with them Tom? You need to at least know that!"

"Some enquiry about Kelly I think, or maybe Pete."

"Jeezus boy! You didn't ask?"

"Well no. They were asking Kirri questions when I joined them. It rattled me a bit."

"About that, why the hell did you tell them you were Tom Ariakas?" He demanded incredulously. "Why in the hell did you do that?"

I shrugged. "I couldn't think, I mean I just agreed to it."

"You do realize they probably already know who you are. I mean they found you here didn't they. Did they say how?"

"Well yes. They said someone from the Cross where Kelly stayed told them about me."

"What? How...? Did they know you?"

"Well no."

Big Jim shook his head, "This is not making any sense. I better come up to the station with you and sort it out. For them to come looking for you here they have to know who you are. You shoulda' realized that son. You gotta be straight up with the law. Straight up! But not stupid."

"I didn't think...!"

"Yeah that's bloody obvious. You shoulda' said nothing. Come on... get your gear together and we'll get up there and get this sorted out. You don't lie... but you don't say anything either. Let them earn their bloody money ... and you don't even know what it is all about!" He finished incredulous still, as he shook his head. "Bloody hell."

Hours later, sitting up at the police station we finally got in to see the officer who had the responsibility of the investigation that had for some reason led to me. It wasn't a comfortable conversation but at least Big Jim, who had remained with me, had some idea of what he was doing.

The interview was informal it seemed and still at the level of enquiry. They had said that they wanted to establish a few facts but as we got into it I could see that they knew much more than they had at first indicated.

My gut had begun to burn and I wasn't entirely sure if it was the Moogie Eye or adrenaline, but I rode with it as I begun to wade through the questions they asked of me.

"And you're Mr Ariakas?" The officer asked almost first up as we were introduced.

"Yes, and no... I often take my wife's surname, it's easier." I explained. "Here is my licence, you might do better to use that name."

The officer seemed surprised if not sceptical but accepted the licence I handed him and made notes. Big Jim had settled into the chair beside me easily. It had been his suggestion that I clear that problem up right away.

"And you're his father?" The officer enquired of Big Jim with consideration.

"No. I'm an Elder. Tom here is from up the Northern Rivers Way, a country lad. I'm just keeping an eye on him."

"I see." His look was none to pleased about Big Jim's presence but he accepted the information readily and settled back behind his desk.

The station was pretty open, not at all what I had imagined and it was none too private either. We of necessity kept our voices down to a minimum as the man took his time noting a few things.

Big Jim jumped right in however, impatient after a time. "Is there a problem, something we should know about then?"

"No. It is at this stage a general enquiry from the city precinct. They asked us to look into it. It seems it is about this acquaintance of ... of Toms. It is some kind of ongoing investigation and they are having trouble contacting the man."

"What you lost this bloke then?" Big Jim challenged, not without humour.

The officer looked up annoyed but instead of a rebuke, he offered a smile after a time. "Not this station or us fortunately."

Shuffling through the papers in front of him looking for something, the officer got back to us in time. It appeared that it was all in an endless parade of useless fax sheets and reports before him. These he was wading through with some impatience.

"It is concerning this … man. You know him then?" He asked handing me a faxed photo.

"No. As I told the officers I only met him once or twice. Pete is what I knew him as."

"Pete?"

"Yeah, he was a friend… of a friend. Bit of a bully really."

"A bully?" The officer asked as I got a small kick below the table from Big Jim, which accompanied a frown when I glanced his way. It was then that I remembered his advice not to volunteer information and nervously I looked back at the officer who was watching me.

"Yeah. He was in some argument when I met him, other than that I just saw him in passing really."

"This friend of yours, would that be this girl." Shuffling the sheets again he located the paper he was looking for. He handed me a blown up faxed photo of Kelly, one even more hazy than the photo the officers had if that was possible.

"I think so, it's hard to say." I handed it back to him nervously.

"This girl is of interest to us. She has gone missing as well."

"Kelly?" I said, impulsively, that earned me another kick.

"You do know her then?"

"Well yes. I have known her as a friend for some time. Nice kid."

"Our information is that she is a … close friend of yours."

"Kelly? … Well you could say that. As I said, I have known her for a while now. I believe she is in Melbourne, least that's what I have been told."

"Melbourne?" He reiterated surprised, as he made a note before looking back up at me searchingly.

I heard Big Jim's small annoyed sigh, one of frustration I thought and defensively I settled back into the chair while the officer sifted through the papers again.

"Is this going to take long?" Jim asked somewhat irritated. "The boy had to be leaving today, he needs to get on his way."

Looking up at Big Jim somewhat apologetically, if not resigned, the officer took another moment. "I wonder if I could ask you to wait for a moment. I just need a bit of information to be faxed through. We will try not to keep you longer than necessary."

He was an age. The hours ticked by as he shuffled about the office on some errand. The coffee wasn't even particularly good but at least it was refreshing in its own way. I had the sense that they didn't want to let us go without gleaning as much as they could. Perhaps they didn't think we would voluntarily come back in again and they were right in that at least.

I was well and truly over it by 1:30 in the afternoon when they bought us sandwiches and Big Jim looked even more irritated than he had previously.

"You know they only feed you when they want you to stay put longer." He whispered under his breath, as he never the less took up their offer. He was not happy, but he was also as hungry as I was no doubt.

Eventually after some time the officer in charge of the investigation got back to us and I wondered if he had even had lunch somewhere along the line.

"Mr Ariakas." He began as he settled in the chair across from me and handed me a fax sheet. "Do you recognize this car?"

"Yeah sure." Handing the sheet back I looked him squarely in the eyes. "It's my ute, looks like it's outside of Central Station I would say."

"It is. That was taken by surveillance camera on Saturday morning. The young woman in question was seen to get out of it. Can you explain that?"

For a moment I was puzzled and then it fell together for me. "Yes. But why would you want a picture of me or Kelly? I don't understand?"

"Could you just tell me why your ute was there."

"Dropping Kelly off obviously. I told you she is likely interstate by now."

The officer nodded. "And this?" he offered. Passing across another surveillance photo. It was somewhat clearer and you couldn't mistake my vehicle.

"That's me, parked up near the Art Gallery in the Domain near the gardens."

"At Woolloomooloo Bay?"

"Well … yes. The Gallery is near there. Look I know the car wasn't supposed to be parked there …"

Big Jim interjected at this point. "Just what is this all about officer? The boy has already said it's his ute. You gunna book him for parking or what?"

Irritated the officer glared across at him. "I'm not a parking officer but I could as well…"

"Well do it then." Jim challenged now obviously annoyed. "We came here to help you with some investigations and if you want to slap him with a parking ticket. Then you are welcome to it. If that is all then we will be going..."

"This is a serious matter we are dealing with here..."

"Yeah well how about you tell us just what this matter is all about?" He challenged again.

"As I said." The officer enunciated slowly. "We are assisting in an international investigation. Fida Majeed is a person of interest in regards to a number of serious matters..."

"Well I hope you find him then." Jim cut in with a reasonable tone frustrating the officer further.

"That is just the point. He is missing, as is his girlfriend and the only person who seems to have any link in this is Mr Ariakas. You can understand..."

"What?" Jim interjected as though shocked. "The boy drops off a friend to catch a bloody train and then goes and parks illegally and suddenly he is a 'person of interest' in some ... some rabbit chase? Is this what your saying? Where's the connection? I don't see it."

Raising his voice the officer cut Big Jim off curtly. "We have reason to believe that Mr Majeed was down at Woolloomooloo Bay on Friday night."

"Well then why didna' you catch him then? He's a dangerous bloke by your own accounting."

"His wallet was found in the vicinity, with blood stains. We are just waiting for the forensics to confirm..."

"You mean there are people down there that mug them's that go down that way? That's a bit dangerous isn't it?"

"Mr..."

"You aren't accusing my boy of this crime are ya?" Big Jim challenged, clipping his words in such a way that I struggled to contain my smile.

"That has not yet been established..."

"Well I should say not." Jim added cutting him off. "There was a lot of men down there that night, me included. We seen nuthing of the like... nuthin! I can call in those that were there if you like, they would be happy to help... happy. They could vouch for Tom here as well, he gave some of them a lift home, tired as he was after looking after that young girl. Keeping her from harm... what with men like that other bloke around...?"

"There is no need for that." The officer added somewhat annoyed now. "If we need your information we know where to find you."

"Young Tom here is gotta get going soon. He shoulda' gone today. He has business to attend to up at Hermannsburg.

"Well we have all we need I think. We can follow it through to Melbourne if needed and we know how to contact you. You will be available if we need you?"

Big Jim nodded graciously as he stood. "Well thank you officer. I hope we have been of assistance and please don't hesitate to call on me. Terrible thing this business with muggings... did they take anything from the wallet then?"

"The money of course, but everything else was there I believe. ID, license and other cards."

"Clearly they wanted the money. These druggies... ya can't trust 'em at all. Terrible thing it is." He added, turning to leave as the officer too stepped up to show him out. Though I wondered just who was showing who to the door.

"Well thank you again. I'm glad we could be of help. Any time... anytime at all, you just contact me is all you need to do." Big Jim added for good measure as we left him.

Leading the way to the car Jim was happy, if not at the lateness in the day, he was certainly pleased the interview had ended.

"Seem's the Djaranin was looking for spare change." He quipped as he buckled himself into the car with a chuckle. Waiting for me to do the same while he started the car.

"Do you think they'll be back?" I asked curious.

"Nahh... For what? Do you think they want half the Elders Council rocking up to their office? That would be a sight let me tell you," he chuckled. "They will likely wind it up I am thinking. An' if they don't ... well then what is there to tell? Friday night was a good night down at Woolloomooloo Bay, what with the men altogether for old times sake. We were malarkin' around we were, all in good sport. Saw nuthin' heard nuthin'. It's a simple matter it is."

The trip home was tedious, though once we left the traffic it improved rapidly. My belly was still giving me heat and easing it with my palm as I sat in the passenger seat I managed to attract Big Jim's attention.

"Still having trouble there?"

"Yeah. It has settled, but hasn't cooled any."

"Hmm... the sooner you get away the better I am thinking Tom. This business is what must have rattled the Djaranin into their hunt."

"We might leave tonight, it won't take much to pack what is left in the car. She is all ready to go."

For a moment Big Jim hesitated as he looked up towards the sun, which was setting steadily into a western spread of crimson sky. It was one of those truly beautiful sunsets that can spill across the sky.

"You should hold off until the morning maybe. If the Djaranin are still on the hunt they will find it easy to track you in the dark. I wouldn't want to be camping up anywhere tonight."

"So you think it could be a problem still?"

"There's no saying. With that heat still in your belly it's a bet they are still about. They don't give up these dark dogs, not easily or without cause. At least if you wait till tomorra' young Jeremy and I can help if there is trouble and I dare say Kirri would have something to say too if there was anything up. When you get far enough away from Sydney, they'll have no cause to hunt you. It's a bugger you couldn't get away sooner than this, all that fart arsin' around at the station."

Kirri looked to be in something of a tither when we finally reached the bottom of the track. She was sitting on the jetty step waiting impatiently. As we came into view on the stairs she immediately climbed to her feet to meet us, her eyes searching ours.

"Hey... what's up?" I asked amused. She simply took my hands in hers while her eyes held mine and was silent for a time. After what seemed like a measured moment she released me. The change in her was marked and I wondered if this was about this touching business of hers. However she smiled back at me confidently.

"What was that about?" I demanded refusing to move despite her coaxing.

"It is good. You are not concerned now about this thing."

"No? Well that is good to know." I laughed.

"It is good to know." She agreed turning towards the cottage. "Jeremy has been training his whip this afternoon. He worried for you both too."

"It's not his whip that needs the training, it's him." I corrected her chuckling again. At her curious look I elaborated. "You said it wrong... the whip thing."

Shrugging Kirri turned back to the cottage. "I think it is both."

That night over dinner we checked through our plans and I took time to have a quick look over the old book that Big Jim had given me. Gathering the last of the gear together that we would need, I decided on taking it over to the camper trailer tonight, in preparation for an early departure in the morning.

Having collected together the last of the gear I was checking through my wallet on how much cash I had. Planning on making sure Kirri had some cash on her for incidentals. Handing her a few notes I offered an explanation at her look of confusion."

"You'll need some money. I guess we should have arranged a account or something before we left?"

"No. I don't want to go to the banks. Thank you."

Taking the notes she slipped them into her shorts smiling complacently.

"Why not? A card would be good for you and it's easy to arrange."

Kirri looked up, her expression horrified. "No. This is not what I want."

I shook my head not understanding her protests or her reasoning. "Why ever not?"

"I don't wish to be enslaved."

"What!"

"I don't wish you to enslave me." She repeated with determination.

"What the hell do you mean?" I demanded, astounded.

"I have thought about it. What you said before and for me to use the money from the bank, they will want me to pay back more than I use, more than I have?"

"Well … yes, of course."

"No. This is enslavement. The money they want me to give them for using your money that they hold, doesn't exist. They create it and your government does not seem to mind. The banks do not get it from the government, but create it themselves so it does not exist really."

At my confused look she went on. "So I must pay back not only what I use, but extra, which isn't real. It does not really exist. So it is a debt I can never repay and I am enslaved to them. I help to enslave others when I give them this interest money because they will lend it to others. The debt is passed on to others from me. The bank makes you think this money is real… but it is not real. The government has not made this money, the bank pretends that it is there."

"That is crazy! Where did you get that idea? It is just interest Kirri" I asked still confused at her reasoning.

"Did they get this money from the government, this interest?"

"No of course not, it is interest they charge to use their money."

"It isn't their money, it is the governments money. Though they say it is theirs and they ask for more, for interest. You give them the money back you spend, and they create this … interest … and you must give them that also."

"They have created debt instead, it is not real government money." she persisted. "Something you must give them and they have done this thing from nothing. The extra money does not go away, it remains as debt for others to burden themselves with and it isn't real money. I do not want this as in paying back what isn't real, this debt... it enslaves people. This is wrong."

"That is crazy!"

"No; debt or this interest you accept or agree too is crazy. Your government ends up with debt that can never go away as they do not have this money. It is just debt that is passed on to someone else. I can't understand why your government allows this bank to do this, unless the bank is really the government perhaps?"

She took a moment, hoping that I understood her. Then realising I was confused still, she went on patiently. "The bank swaps this interest for real money that the government has and the debt becomes the peoples. It goes around and around and this is enslaving the people who must pay this interest that doesn't exist. They get nothing for their work in this thing and this is enslavement. I remembered that Aine told me that the government is the people in your world."

Totally confused by her argument I shook my head. I had trouble seeing it but it did make me wonder just what interest really was. Where did it come from, or even where it went too. "OK have it your way... no card. Not a problem Kirri."

The smile she lent me was strangely complacent and satisfied but still I grappled with her explanation while Jeremy too shook his head. Would I ever understand this strange woman of mine I wondered?

We took the last of our collection of gear along to the parking bay where the camper trailer was waiting for us later that evening. Choosing to take the dinghy around rather than hike up the path to the lower parking bay. It felt safer somehow to use the small boat.

It was a lovely night with the skies clear and full of stars, one of those truly bright night skies with a full moon to light the night and cloak it in long shadows cast across the ground.

The light danced across the water and while I had been happy to take the last of our gear around by myself, Kirri had decided to join me. Still full of nervous energy she was attentive to everything around her. As though it was to be the last she would ever see of the river and the small cottage.

"You don't talk much about the Inland. Do you miss it much?" I asked after a time looking for light conversation. I was rowing the boat steadily through the water wanting to settle Kirri down a bit as we travelled with the outgoing tide towards the landing. I had decided not to split the quiet of the night with the motor until we were on the return trip.

"Sometimes I do. I miss the simpleness of my people. The quiet of their natures," she said softly.

"Tell me about your home, your parents and family." I asked as I manoeuvred the old wooden paddles through the water.

Kirri looked surprised that I even asked this and it was a minute before she responded. "We don't live as you do. I have told you this. The Inland is more … more like the Community in some ways. It is quiet when you want peace. The balance of our world and peace is very important to us. There are fewer people there, than here in your city. Your world has become very crowded I think."

"Not all of it. We will see some very isolated places while we travel. Do you have any brothers or sisters then?"

"What a strange question. I have many."

"Strange?" I queried intrigued.

"Yes. There are many of us from the family, it is a strange question?"

"I mean like brothers or sisters which have the same parents."

Kirri set her head to the side, frowning. "I … I don't know. It is not something that interests us."

"Well from your mother then … has she had many children?"

Again, strangely enough she frowned. "I … don't know. There are many of us who have been together all our lives. It is now, as we mature that we go different ways. My mothers watch over me … our fathers take care of us when we can't care for ourselves."

I shook my head, seeing that there were obvious differences in our lives. Even the differences in trying to understand the meaning behind the words we used.

"OK… perhaps if I asked if there were special people in your family. Who are you closest too, back in your land?"

"My Old Mother. That is easy to answer." Kirri smiled in the memory and I could see that this person was special.

"Tell me about her then, perhaps I will meet her one day?"

Again she took a moment. "She is very old, but … but perhaps you will meet her. They say I am very like her in many ways and this is why she has taught me so much. I miss her the most I think, she speaks softly and I miss that. We often have no reason to speak as you and I do."

"Finger language?"

Kirri's grin was delightful but she shook her head. "No, it is a different language, it is of thoughts and of touch. You also speak in this way but you do not understand how to listen. You are like a baby in this who does not realize that they smile and at times you babble on like a gurgling baby."

"I don't? I mean … I do? I didn't know…?"

"One day you might hear me. You may learn perhaps to listen to what I say to you."

Chuckling at the thought and not understanding it much, I steered the small dinghy in towards the bank. As I thought about what she had said, wondering at it. I didn't know how to answer her. It was a strange conversation and I seemed to be having a lot of these lately though I still didn't know quite what to make of the things she came out with at times.

The few bags we had were light and easy to manage and as they were for every day use, we stowed them into the back seat of the forbie along with the small daypack for snacks and light meals.

"There... all done. That is the last of it I think. We should leave first thing in the morning, early light. Not before time."

"Not before what time?"

"That is a saying." I chuckled. "Sorta like saying not soon enough."

"Then you should say that," she scolded. "It is hard enough that you speak, but that you speak things that you don't mean makes it harder."

"Sorry." I answered slamming the door annoyed only slightly at her criticism. "You will have to teach me your finger language, that may make it easier."

Glancing about, her eyes reached out into the shadows around us impatiently. "We are making too much noise."

"Hardly. Barely any noise at all."

Imperiously she held up her small hand. "Listen... can you hear that?"

"Hear what?"

She shot me a look full of impatience and frustration.

"You're just jumpy..." I added teasing her trying to dismiss her concerns gently.

"I do not jump!" she whispered somewhat annoyed with me, which just bought a wider smile to my lips. We however both heard the low noise, a muffled growl and shuffling of leaves in the ground litter. It came from within the reach of the dark shadows cast by the bushes around us.

I froze, while Kirri on the other hand moved silently backing away from the sound. Seeking shelter in the solid structure of the camper trailer. It was the sound of a dog, a soft noise born deep down in a throat.

Subconsciously I reached looking for my whip that would have been wound about my shoulders before I realized that I didn't have it with me.

I should have had it and I felt a greater fool for the warning I had and had foolishly ignored. I had known, I had been told and yet I had chosen to discount the threat. I was a fool and I knew it in these moments.

I searched quickly through the dark shadows looking for any shape, any movement that could reveal the source of the sound we had both heard.

The burn of the Moogie Eye fired in my gut as I tried to dismiss the threats in my head that mocked me. However when my senses began to scream I reached from within myself, seeking the death stones strength. Drawing the stone towards the palm of my hand carefully I was reassured to feel its heat. It was the only weapon that I had with me.

It was a flick of movement, something dark and shifting with stealth in the deep shadows of the bush that suddenly alarmed me.

Turning to face the shift in the shadows my eyes searched for any movement or sound. The death stone was heating my hand, a comforting weapon whose growing strength I could feel in the sheltered depth of my palm.

I wasn't sure. I was not certain at all about what it might be, but I couldn't afford to be complacent. Not now that I was certain of the presence of something.

Kirri had slipped between the trailer and car where the two were hooked together. Stepping lightly I placed myself between her and the light pad of footsteps I heard, the shifting shadow in the darkness.

With my hand to my gut I carefully drew on the Moogie Eye and I felt the fullness of its heat reach my cupped palm.

It had been many months since I had drawn its strengths forward and the heat in my hand welcomed the weapon of the Kadaitcha, that which had been gifted to me. The first of my physical gifts, it was still the one I was most familiar with and its heat and weight in my hand felt good.

It was a low glow I held in my palm protectively, the red eye of the spirit men and the strengths of a world different to the one I was drawing it into. I saw and felt the slight movement of the vehicle at my side, the soft bounce and I knew Kirri must have climbed up to the top of the camper. But she would not be very safe there I thought.

The Djaranin would find it no barrier in the slight height advantage. Hearing again the pad of feet on bush litter I quickly swung to the sound.

The Moogie Eye glowed, spilling a deep red tinge of light across my gut. It was a light different to the one, when I had last used it as a weapon against the Numereji Serpent.

I didn't let that distract me now though, as I held the weightlessness of its form in my hand. Letting the red glow reach into the darkness in a threat all of its own I pulled the death stone from the shelter of my torso allowing it's light to spill around me.

I heard the stealthy pad of a muffled paw and then saw the sudden shift in shadow as the dark form crouched low, suddenly, stretched out against the ground as though to pounce at me. It was quick and sure in its movement, obvious in its intent.

Stepping forward in a swift dance I cast the Moggie Eye towards the shape and it flicked quickly around the form, illuminating the sleek blackness of the large dark dog flattened against the ground. Spilling its blood red light across the sleek shadow, exposing the form to the world.

It was one, only the one dog that I saw as the glowing orb returned to me in an arc, tracing the ground between us. I caught the orb in my hand easily and I knew I had the attention of the dark dog.

The red glow not only exposed him to the night, but it exposed me as well and I was glad of the exposure. It hid Kirri and I felt the satisfaction in that knowledge as I marked the movements of the Djaranin and prepared to cast the stone again. This time in a deathly blow as I felt its energies shift within my palm.

Its light swung between red, yellow and white feeling my intent and knowing the purpose for which I would cast it. Flicking my glance to Kirri I saw in a second the crouching shape of her on the top of the camper and was grateful she was but a dark shape, ill defined. Then my eyes flicked back to a sudden fast shift in a threatening shape. I quickly cast the death stone away from me with a fiery intent.

The Moogie Eye flew at the form in a flash as fast as the movement of the dog. But in that second I found myself crouched against the ground as the dark shape had leapt, sailing over my head. It swung back at me now, wild as a storm while it landed, hard against the ground, having missed my bulk. It was startled and angry in the same instant it landed.

White, as a spill of fire around its form, the death stone swept suddenly high between us, illuminating us both once more. We were like two adversaries facing each other off, under the spotlight of time.

The dog was dark and sleek, fine almost with the power behind its fore arms and in the broad girth of its shoulders. It was a beautiful thing but it was wild, angry and deadly dangerous as it bared its teeth to me hungrily.

It had crouched again to attack and I was barely within arms reach of its fangs as it braced itself to leap again at me. Facing it I knew in that second that I wasn't going to come out of this freely.

Having swept around us the white orb had quickly gained its height as it readied to dump its weight down upon the dark dog.

Then a high, wild scream hit the air between us and another shadow leapt through the darkness and into the fray.

It was a second before I realized what, or who it was when the slight form of Kirri landed in a scuff of sand and dirt having dived across the Djaranin's back. She unbalanced the dog as she caught and gripped it about the scruff, hauling it from its intent as slight as she was. She had used the momentum of her body against the hound and they both scattered along the ground now, rolling across the earth together.

The dog baulked and fought, twisting in fury while Kirri held on to the scruff of its pelt. Tossed about like a doll, the angle of her hold was the only thing that protected her.

I swept my hand high to try and halt the death stone in its drop from the heights. The Dog of Death had been almost in mid leap in its attack. Now the powerful dog scrambled against the ground unprepared, confused and wildly thrashing in an attempt to loose the lightweight disturbing its path.

The Moggie Eye ignoring me suddenly dropped from its height startling us all, in the same moment as I yelled a mad warning. In a flash of fire it flattened the creature of the night out along the ground barely missing my wife. In a shower of brilliance Kirri, as shocked as I, had released the hound on my yell and staggered back barely out of its way.

It was a brilliant flash of white light trimmed with red and blue as the orb shattered its form in a powerful crack. It split the stillness of the night apart in a terrible clap of what sounded of wild thunder, in a torrid strike from the heavens.

It was my bellow that tore into the night, mine that shouted a warning as Kirri once more scrambled and flew at the dark dog as it lay under the stun of the death stone.

She threw up her arms and bracing them together seemed to sink her clenched hands deep into the fur of the dogs gut. The glint of something she held in her hands sinking deep into the dog's dark pelt.

It was as though she was stabbing at and gutting the beast, swift and powerful thrusts with both hands driving a blade deep. Plunging her hands deep into the fur under the ribs of the animal as it lay stunned against the ground. The light of what remained of the Moggie Eye sparking about the two of them.

"Kirri! Wait...!" I yelled as I tossed my weight towards her, attempting to shelter her from the death sparks of the Moggie Eye, gathering the power of the death stone before it collected itself and descended again.

It was garnering its strength I could see, preparing to shift to a height again over the two of them. Flooding the ground with its building red light.

My movement didn't stop her as she plunged what looked to be a strange knife into the dog again and again with fury.

I stretched quickly over her to call the death stone to me. It's light had continued to gather alarmingly above the melee of movement.

Not wanting it near Kirri I willed the last of its life back into my hands with every ounce of power or strength I had. Then I struggled, crouching as I took it back into myself, protecting her even from the light it cast.

That it came was a relief and I gathered it once more into my body while I tried to regain my balance, struggling as I watched Kirri scramble away from the dying dog and up onto her knees in what was an exhausted surrender to the melee around her.

The relief I felt as my body swallowed the threat was intense. Kirri's breaths were laboured and her eyes wild in a display of fury and fear. This left me unsure of what I could do to help her.

It was a shock, a truly awful sight that twitched before us and yet still it was one you couldn't tear your eyes from as we both watched the Djaranin reel in its death throws.

"What have you done?" I whispered stunned at the sight before my eyes, still struggling for breath as I fought to quieten the stone within me.

Kirri was breathing deeply also, a heavy weight of realization in each movement of her chest. The weight and sight of what she had done lay between us.

"I don't know. It's dead … I killed it."

"You can't … can't kill a Djaranin." I protested still in a stunned whisper as I sat back on my heels. This despite the evidence of the dog, in its last death throws between us.

She looked up to me and proffered me the dark blood soaked knife in her shaking hands, holding it perilously.

"Yes, you can I think... with this."

It was a strangely twisted dark blade made of what looked like glass, gleaming dark against the night. It had an oddly knapped edge that was sharpened by the glint of the starlight. A flash that slipped eerily across that waving edge, where the coat of its victim had wiped the strange blade clean when she had pulled it from the dog's chest.

"What the hell is that?" I demanded as she too looked down at it as though it was an extension of her hand.

"My blade."

Edging forward towards the now deathly still Djaranin, Kirri stretched thoughtlessly to wipe the whole of the blade clean across the still glossy coat of the dog prostrate before us.

As she did so the death dog shifted, a twitch of life. One that had me lurching quickly too, dragging her back from its form in just the seconds it would have taken to reach her.

"I must keep it clean," she mumbled aimlessly now, almost confused.

The form of the dog shivered in the light of the night and amazed, we watched as it slowly began slipping into another place, another world in a shift of light and dark shadow across the ground.

I drew a ragged breath as I watched the light lose the form in the night and it vanished from our sight. Taking it even from our sense of its presence.

I was balanced against the ground awkwardly still gripping Kirri's arm, the same arm that had wielded the strange small, knapped knife.

"Jeezus I don't know if we should have killed it woman. It is the Serpents dog." I whispered as though to keep the truth from the night.

"It was going to attack you. I couldn't let it ..."

"Yeah well I could have handled it, I could ... would have dealt with it."

"No ... No Ariaka, it is the dog of death. It would have killed."

I knew then that it could have likely done just that, but it didn't help any now. Lifting her arm, pulling her hand to my view I stood silent as I stared at the strangeness of the small knife she still held gripped.

Then I released my hold on her realizing I was hurting her, letting her arm fall as I reached out again to help support her wavering figure. Pulling her into a circle of my arms safely as I dragged us both to our feet without any resistance on her part.

"I'm sorry, I didn't think... but I couldn't ..." she whispered softly moving against my chest.

"No you were right. I'm sorry ... I didn't mean to blame you it's just a shock is all." I said.

Wrapping her in my arms I tried to comfort her as I felt the small tremor in her movement. "Are you OK. That was crazy woman ... I could have hurt you... it could have hurt you. The death stone ... ?"

"I couldn't stand by and watch you die. You are mine." Kirri offered in a small voice.

"Jeezus woman." I groaned gathering her closer to me still.

For an age we stood there together, she was warmer and safe in the circle of my arms and I wanted her to stay that way until the shivers of her body had grown more settled.

Or that is what I told myself. It was hard to move, I didn't want to move and yet I knew we had to. After an age I mentally shook myself free of my inertia.

"Lets get back and find out what we can do... tell the others what's happened. I have a feeling they aren't gunna be happy about this somehow ... I don't know?"

It was with an odd sense that we made our way back down to where we had left the dinghy. Kirri was quiet, compliant strangely enough as I settled her into the seat of the dinghy and pushed us off from the shore.

For a moment we drifted with the outgoing tide but it was only a second. The motor fired easily and in no time we were racing back towards the cottage and our home jetty.

When I told Big Jim of what had happened he was oddly quiet, however I was more concerned with Kirri as I carefully handed her a small glass of brandy from the high kitchen collection of odd bottles and liquors we had stashed.

"Drink this, it will settle you down. You haven't stopped shaking yet Kirri."

"You killed it? Are you sure?" Big Jim demanded as he stood behind me.

"Yes I'm sure. It wouldn't have survived the knife Kirri had, and how she used it on the creature."

"Knife?"

"My blade." She said softly as though to explain. Kirri reaching into the loose folds of her top once more bought out the small blade she had tucked about her body. "I've been carrying it since yesterday. I could feel it... feel the threat that was around us, around Tom. Only since yesterday."

I crouched before her as she sat on the lounge, to better inspect the blade she held balanced in her hand. In the light of the room it looked much less threatening but I could see that it was the oddest of things.

It looked to be made of a knapped glass. The knaps of the blade were clearly distinct. It had a form that was made with a mastery of control. An art mostly lost to us in time.

It looked to be of a dark glossy stone, but at its edge it was almost a clear deep green in the colour of its glass. The centre of the blade was a deep opaque black and the handle had been wrapped in a tight, finely twined rope. The whole piece was simply beautiful.

"This is my weapon, it is ... I use this to protect me, as you use your fire. It is a gift from my Old Mother, it travels with me all the time."

Without any further explanation she tucked it back into the folds of her shirt, securing the blade into some type of holder she wore close to her skin by the movements of her hands.

"The killing of the dog ... the Djaranin was my doing. The blade is not an ordinary blade, it is a weapon against the creatures of the caverns. This was given to me many years ago now. Though I have rarely had to use it as I did tonight."

"You have such a thing? A thing such as a churinga?" I asked astounded. Still crouched at her feet as I watched her amazed.

"Yes. I am of the Illaparinja Tom. I am a woman of the Kadaitcha."

Astounded my jaw dropped. I was stunned by her words. "How...?"

Kirri smiled. "How?" she repeated softly. "How can you ask me this thing? I cannot answer you that."

I heard the movement of Big Jim behind me as he shuffled in his stance. When I looked over my shoulder he had his hand to his mouth, as he considered my wife with a strange look in his eyes.

"Apari knew this?" He asked slowly sorting her words in his mind.

Kirri just nodded once. "Not of the blade, but of my Lore. Yes."

"You didn't tell me." I scolded softly, still amazed at her words.

"You didn't ask me this thing. No one has asked this thing of me."

"Jeezus Kirri!" Still astounded I slowly stood to my feet.

Kirri watched me carefully as my thoughts raced through my mind. That Kirri was of the same Lore as I, had never even entered my head. Maybe she is confused but no... I knew the inherent signs of the Kadaitcha, and in turn the Illaparinja. The women of the Kadaitcha lore were a treasure, a Lore within the Lore and they were rarely identified as such. That was not their way.

The truth about this woman, my wife, was astounding. She sat quietly before me as the reality of her words flicked quickly through my mind. It all made sense suddenly, her way, her moods even. Astounded I felt the puzzle pieces fall into place.

Apari would not have told me of this, he would have expected me to recognize what I held within my reach. That I had failed to do so, that I had need to be told of these things was its own proof of my reckless arrogance and I couldn't deny it now.

"I am tired Tom, I need to rest," Kirri said softy as she stood slowly, my eyes following her.

"Yeah ... sure. I'll be in within a minute or two."

She moved quietly in that slight impish way she had. Two sets of eyes following her, our voices silent as she left the room.

A Reckoning

Tom

The night sheltered us all. There was a certain sense of safety in the house with all of us together under its roof. For some reason we felt safe from retribution for the moment but it was a fleeting thing.

Killing the Djaranin had been a defensive act, a proper business but that didn't help much when it came to settling down for the night. I was still stunned by the knowledge that Kirri was an Illapurinja woman of the Lore. I was difficult to truly believe such a thing of my woman and yet I had seen her wield that blade of hers with all confidence. It left my thoughts reeling. Her blade, the churinga of her Lore had done what no other blade could do. She had killed the spirit dog, the Djaranin.

What was the price to be paid when such a thing as this came about? Would the Wolgaru serpent seek vengeance? I desperately hoped not, for both our sakes. I wished with every fibre that I had, that this wouldn't see the end of us both.

I also wished that I could speak to Apari about this. My Grandfather was the only person I could think of who could advise me on the consequences of what we had done.

Neither Apari nor Jep seemed to have an ear to my worries and life at the moment. Then I remembered how my Jongorrie had mentioned that Apari didn't want him to disturb me now. Perhaps he had his mind busy with other things.

If only I had kept my whip with me, if only I had payed more attention to what I had been told, if only...

Kirri was sleeping curled up in the small room behind mine but I had found it harder to settle after the events of the day. A shower had helped some, but not enough and as I watched the restless flow of the river below the balcony I could feel the tickle of the breeze against my still damp skin. My towel was offering the only barrier between my damp skin and the cooler pleasantries of the night air.

It was quiet out here now and the Moogie Eye had settled its heat, that discomfiting burn beneath my ribs, so I felt no immediate threat about us. I should be able to sleep but I found that I couldn't. It was a necessity though, as I had a long days drive ahead of me tomorrow. Then on the other hand it would be good to get out of the city at last.

When I climbed into bed some time later I was still restless, as restless in my thoughts and as restless as the tidal pull of the river outside. I had left the long glass doors open knowing for the moment we were safe and the bite of the night air was refreshing, helping me settle in its own way.

For an age I lay mindlessly watching the night, enjoying the slight breeze but still unable to sleep.

"Tom?"

The soft voice whispered from the adjoining door to the bathroom and quietly. Pleased now for the company, I looked up catching sight of the slight figure. The curious look reflected in a set of sky blue eyes surrounded by a tussle of white blonde hair. Kirri stood there hesitant for the moment and I felt my odd tension relax. I realized then that I needed her to be near, at least for tonight.

Pulling myself up on the bed I lounged back against the head of the bed quietly and patted the space beside me in invitation. I didn't want to break the silent song of the night with loud greetings. She must have felt the same.

In her small, light step she joined me, climbing easily over my bulk to sit where I had seen her settle before, at my side. She too moved to lounge against the bedhead using the pillow for extra comfort.

"You were asleep. What happened? I didn't disturb you did I?"

"No. I am awake now."

Her words were like a lilting song, soft in the night. They were a part of the quiet and I smiled, keeping my own voice low and to a gentle tone.

"I can't settle. I can't seem to find a still place in my mind and I need to sleep. Any suggestions?" I asked quietly.

"You should lay down, tell me what is disturbing you," she answered. Suddenly sitting up she reached for my pillow behind me and I accommodated her intent as I shuffled about being mothered by my wife.

I let her arrange the bedding to her liking, me included, as I settled back down onto the bed and was pleasantly surprised when she too settled, nesting at my side.

It was a simple thing to welcome her into the crook of my arm and she snuggled easily there. Her head resting on my shoulder as she spread her hand softly over my chest near my heart. It was as though she was listening to the beat, hearing the tune of my life and I rather liked the feeling of it.

For a time we lay quietly, enjoying the night together. While we weren't quite skin-to-skin, the warmth of her hand had an intimate feel against my naked chest. She hadn't slipped herself under the covers though, instead she was comfortably settled on top and the night wasn't yet cool enough to drive her beneath the covers with me. I regretted that in the short moment between thought and rationale.

"You are worried about the Death Dogs?" she asked.

"Not really, not yet. The Moogie Eye is settled so there seems to be no threat but I don't know what they will do? It will tell me if there is a threat from the Spirit creatures nearby."

"The Death Stone? Your Grandfather told me of this, he said it was a weapon given you. I wasn't sure what it was though, but now I know."

"Can you feel this inside me?"

Kirri shook her head against my shoulder. "I have not been able to feel this at all and that surprised me. Perhaps because it is not a gift given to me, it is yours alone."

"I am still discovering its power, it is something I will become more accustomed to over time."

Kirri slipped her small hand over the muscles of my belly, from where I had drawn the Death Stone earlier. Flattening her palm there she splayed her fingers and rested the slight weight against me. It wasn't a sexual touch, but one of comfort. It was the oddest thing and my thoughts explored this light touch of hers.

"My touch does not disturb you, this is good." She said softly, pleased.

I chuckled. "Ohh ... I don't know about that?"

"No it is good. You are learning."

"What? What am I learning?"

It was quiet for a moment. I guess she was gathering her thoughts. "In the Inland, touch is a very special thing. It is something between two people. Our ritual."

"Hmm... in what way. I can think of a few rituals of my own that are pretty special." I challenged on a grin.

Immediately Kirri moved her hand, tucking it down in between us with a small sigh. I had to laugh; I couldn't help it. I knew my interest was beginning to stir and I could only guess that this was what had caused her withdrawal.

"You don't like that idea at all do you?" I challenged after a time.

I felt her small breath, a small indrawn sigh, silent almost and patient in some way. "It isn't that I don't like your touch. It is just that for me ... the way of my people is different. We have rituals that are a part of our union? It is somehow different, not real or ... or as it should be for me now. It becomes difficult."

"OK. Tell me about these things wife," I challenged with tolerance. I was still humoured but now I was also intrigued. "I am ready to hear all about these rituals of yours."

Kirri propped her self up on her elbow and considered me. "For Inlanders touch is special, ritualized and binding between two people. There is a great deal of ceremony we undertake when we choose to mate, to be together. I know for the Edgelanders it is different, more … more causal, less important. But for my people … it is very different."

"Like a ceremony or … or maybe an initiation into sex?" I asked. Thinking of a ceremony long ago deep in the Mimi Lands, which had banished the ignorant boy in me. It had been a rite of the Mimi People, those Spirits of the rocks in another land.

"Yes and no. We do not choose a mate easily. The constraints of touch over many, or much time have bought us rituals to help us and we do not stay together as you do commonly. For women these sensitivities, those in touch come easily but for our men it is more difficult. They guard and value this thing and touch, between us takes this away from them. It is for this reason that they do not take a woman into their lives often. The cost is too great."

Frowning I looked into her eyes, seeking answers to the many questions suddenly milling through my head. "Your men choose not to mate? Or… or not to take a woman, or even a wife? Well at least that is some sort of reasoning I guess."

Kirri nodded, watching me carefully.

I grinned. I couldn't help it. "Silly buggers!"

Then another thought occurred to me. "You… you have known lovers before though, haven't you?"

Again she nodded. "I am not a child. Our men do go through a time where they are vigorous, but then there comes a time when our sensitivities… where touch and knowledge become more favoured amongst us."

For some reason I relaxed again, though I couldn't have said why. Kirri was calm. With a delicate comfort and with ease she too began to settle back into my side.

"So tell me about this ritual of yours. I should know these things too." I asked quietly.

"You would do this thing for me?" She asked hesitantly.

Shrugging I considered her. "Not until I hear what it is."

"It is simple really. Not hard at all. It is a bonding, a rite of passage for two people who have decided to become one for a short time. A ritual of sharing and for the men in my world it is a ceremony that is solemn, one that binds them together in a special way for a time. I have been taught this thing. Every woman is taught this thing in the Inlands with her initiations.

When we become women and leave the child in us behind, we are taught this. It is an age and a rite where you may take a partner."

"How does it go?"

Her thoughts were considered and she developed a small frown before she answered me. "It is a gentle thing, it is slow and careful. It is when we are given to our teacher"

"No. I mean what do you do, what is done when you choose a man for yourself?"

"Oh. You should say this then if that is what you mean," she quipped with impatience. "When we enter the ritual of mating we wash the skin. The warmth and being at ease, these things are very important for the men, it helps them. Also oil, special liquid that will put both at ease. This I rub into your skin until it is time to complete the ritual."

"That sounds OK to me? But what of you, do I do this for you also?"

"No, not at first but it is a thing for both men and women. But for men it is their ritual initially. Then once bound, it can change between the two. It is a growing knowledge between us."

"So you prepare me?" I asked quietly, unsure of her meaning.

"Yes." Kirri smiled. "I think perhaps the men here are… different though. You are different."

"It sounds fine to me, I can't see that it would be a problem."

"You perhaps do not have the same problems the men of the inland have, I think?" She asked softly, obviously pleased.

"Oh?" I was intrigued. "Why wouldn't I?"

"It is not the way of the Edgelanders, I know this. They have little patience with these rituals but to us, to my people they are necessary. The ritual is very desirable for a man who is looking for a mate."

"So when would we do this thing … this ritual or ceremony of yours?" I asked thoroughly intrigued.

"We are not ready yet."

"There is more to it?"

"It … it is a want, a state of mind between us."

"OK. We can find that then; between us, can't we?"

"Yes. We can do this given the want or need."

Obviously pleased, Kirri settled once more back down into the crook of my arm. "Will you let me judge when we are ready? This is the way for my people. The women know these things, it is for them to say."

Then she suddenly added softly, uncertain. "For a man he needs to be prepared and ready. There is a great deal at stake for our men in this."

"I don't know if it is the same for us but… yeah, sure. If this is what you need Kirri, then it is fine by me. It doesn't sound a hardship at all and I am happy to help you in this."

"Thank you. This means a great deal to me Ariaka."

"Maybe it won't be too long." I added as I settled her against me carefully. "In my world, we would be more eager I think." The teasing in my voice was not lost on her I was sure.

"In my world, we are more careful. There is much more to consider, such choices are a very serious thing."

I thought about her strange request for a time, wondering what the ceremony she spoke of was all about in its meaning. There was the oddness of these things and her need to bring them into Edgelands. It would have taken a great deal of courage for her to leave her Country I decided in the end.

"You risked a great deal in coming here didn't you. I don't think I ever realized it as much, before tonight."

Quiet for a time, Kirri stirred with a small wiggle finding a sure place of comfort. "I was very unsure, which is why I was glad to spend time with Aine and Alex. Alex helped me a great deal."

Not sure that I liked the sound of that I wondered what had been said between the three women but then, that was a question all men have wondered at since the Dreamtime.

"I have changed since my time with Alex I hope." I added quietly.

"Yes." Kirri agreed in a whisper. "You are changing all the time Tom and this ritual will help you. It will allow you to grow perhaps towards a sensitivity your people do not feel. Please don't be impatient with me. Let me show you our way. This is the way I understand, it is the way I know between men and women."

I sighed with a patience I didn't always feel. "OK. I'm in your hands woman. I will try to behave."

Kirri giggled, a small soft sound that played in the heat against my skin. It was a delight to hear and feel. "You will not be sorry for the ritual when it is time. I promise you this Tom."

I slipped off into sleep at some point, though I couldn't have said when. My dreams were a strange journey but a pleasant one. One I couldn't recount either when I next stirred.

The sky was still dark when I woke and Kirri was curled like a kitten into my belly. During the night I had gathered her to me protectively and it felt good to wake up to the warmth of her, as I cocooned her with my arms and body.

I didn't want to disturb her when I moved, so with care I unfurled myself from about her. Taking particular care as I eased my weight from the bed so as not to disturb her, yet feeling the need to move.

It was on the edge of dawn and I felt that there was no point in returning to the bed, so instead I slipped quietly out onto the balcony overlooking the restless river. Kirri was still sleeping, still curled into a ball amongst the covers and as much as I would have liked to join her again, I chose instead to greet the dawn.

Outside the world was still in the deep shadows of the night, in the last of the spirit hours. I watched the first hesitant rays of sun spread over the river, brightening the day. It was then that I first recognized my Jongorrie nearby. He was settled in the corner of the balcony silent, watching me patiently in turn.

"Jep!" Straightening from where I had been lounging against the rails I turned to him surprised. "What the hell are you doing curled up there?"

"Tomtom. I didn't wanna disturb you... shouldn't do that. Apari said so. Said he did and he meant it."

"Yeah well I'm up now."

"I was just resting... just resting I was. But since you're here there is something I need to say. Something I need to tell you. That is why I am here... it is."

"What is it?"

"It's your woman. Bad I felt... really bad about that business."

"Jep will you just spit it out... say whatever it is." I cut in impatiently wondering just what he was going on about.

"The sickness, the sickness she has. Kintji should have protected her more. It is his fault really... his fault."

"Jep!"

"Yes well it can be mended it can. I can do this, help you. There is a place, the place of the Binoomea. An ancient place nearby that is of darkness, dark waters in the rock, dark places. This can heal... the healing waters. They told me about it, my people. They know these things. The Jongorrie know these things they do. You just need to ask... they'll tell me and they did."

"What the hell are you talking about?"

"Kirri. The woman... your woman. She needs to go there she does and the waters... the waters will help her. They said it is Gurungatch, a place of peace for the women."

"OK start at the beginning. You're making no sense to me Jongorrie!"

"The healing waters, they are nearby. Where the ancient waters have been lifted to the Edgelands. They are nearby Tomtom... I had forgotten. They will heal your woman... make her sound again. Strong and healthy like a woman should be. Your woman... that is important."

"Kirri is sick?" I questioned quietly.

"No... nono no... Not really. But she gets sick. This thing... this thing they gave her. The Oruncha, and it sits badly in her bingie." Rubbing his disgorged tummy the Jongorrie moved in an odd little dance. "The healing waters of the Binoomea will make her well. It's an ancient thing and I have arranged this thing for you Tomtom... arranged it for you soon. Soon. When can you go?"

"Go? Go where? And this thing Kirri has, it is nothing. Taipan said not to worry over it."

"Worry over it... of course I worry over it. Taipan doesn't know... doesn't know what it is like in the Inlands. Your woman worries over it. Taipan doesn't know everything... not all of it, he doesn't. He doesn't understand this. It's into the darkness of the mountains nearby, the place you need to go. They call it Jen-o-lan, Jen-o-lan it is ... big foot peak. Nearby, deep into the sacred caves there is a healing pool. She can drink of it and it will heal what is inside her. It's a special place the Binoomea, ancient and a special place for healing... special place for the women. You should go soon... soon. Before you travel far. That would be best Tomtom."

"Your saying I should take Kirri to this place. The Jenolan Caves, is that it?"

"Yes Tomtom... she needs to go. The healing pools will heal her. Make it better. You shouldn't be mad with Kintji either. He didn't know... he is only a young man yet. Not a Featherfoot yet, not been initiated yet. He missed the time, missed Wolgaru's dance he did. His time will come."

Slowly getting a grasp on what the Jongorrie was saying I shook my head wondering what Jeremy had to do with all this. I was still having trouble putting it together.

Perhaps my Jongorrie thought I was angry about Jeremy missing the recent hunt. Who knew how the mind of this little forest man really worked. It was a tangle of things, of ages, languages and time.

"This water, this healing water will cure Kirri of this... this thing she has. This ciguatera that worries her?"

"Yes. Yes it should. I can arrange it... arrange for you to meet the young Shaman. He will take you there... help you. He's only young, only young but he know the way to the pools of the Binoomea. It is his Country and he knows this thing, one of the few he is and they have told him this. The Spirits that talk to him have said they know these things."

Knowing how much this would mean to Kirri I considered his words seriously, picking what I understood from the gabble of time and talk.

"We are leaving today Jongorrie. But you say you can arrange this?"

"Yes... yes Tomtom. Arrange it I can, for soon."

"Two days. Is that soon enough?"

"Yes... yes. The night will be dark then too. It is a good time. We need the dark as the way is secret... very secret. The healing waters of the Binoomea is a secret place, the way is guarded... even the whitefellas guard this place but they do not know our ways. It will be a good time. This I can do... I can do this for your woman. She will like me then. Doesn't like me much and it's not good. Not good at all."

Frowning at his words I shook my head unsure of his meaning but prepared to dismiss it.

"OK. Two days, two nights. We will make our way to Jenolan Caves and meet the Shaman there tomorrow night."

"Yes. The main cave... the big one. Wait there in the spirit hours and we'll send someone to guide you, the youngest hours. I will arrange it Tomtom. I will do this for your woman."

Gleefully Jep moved. It was a swift movement, a shift of shadow and light and he was gone. For whatever reason, I could see that he was strangely pleased beyond his normal pleasure.

It still made little sense to me but I knew that Kirri still worried over her state of health and if this would reassure her, or even heal her of the ciguatera then it would be what we would do.

I knew of the Jenolan Caves, I had even been there once with my old school when I was growing up, some time ago now. Leaning back against the rail I tried to call the visit to mind from so many years ago.

The old caves house had intrigued me at the time. Even as a kid it had impressed me with its old world charm and the promise of meandering halls and rambling structure. It was tucked away into what had seemed to me at the time to be a secret valley hidden beyond a grand rock arch of what was a timeless place. That would have to be the main arch that my Jongorrie had spoken of.

I remembered the visit deep into some of the caves, the beautiful and ancient limestone formations and the eerie darkness. They were wet caves and I recall that there were subterranean pools but I had not heard of the healing pools.

Then it occurred to me that Kirri would likely enjoy a tour of the caves anyway. Such a beautiful thing was a rare place in the world and she perhaps would appreciate the caverns more so than anyone.

They were barely an hour or two from Sydney, deep in the Blue Mountains. Well hidden in the canyons and cliffs of limestone that was etched by time into the hinterland behind Sydney. It would be a good start to our journey, a good beginning for us both.

It could be a time when we could learn to be together as a team or a couple. Remembering her words from the night, I figured that it might help in someway. I still found it strange the things she had said. How being a couple, a man and a woman who lived together as a team was not something that was part of the Inlanders way of life. Perhaps this would be just the beginning we would need.

The idea grew in my mind in the short time it was before Kirri finally stirred. Looking for me, as the sun had begun to spill through the cottage, she found me deep in maps at the dining table in front of Jeremy's computer. I was planning for the following few days and even I was pleased with what I had managed to organize.

Settling down at the table with her small bowl of breakfast she was quiet, though obviously curious about what I was doing. Kirri hadn't mastered technology yet, it was still a mystery to her and she was wary of the computer. She was daily growing wary of many things she met with.

Having decided that she didn't like banks, didn't like to even touch the credit card or any banking card even, I was growing aware that she was building a small regime of behaviours which she felt protected her.

It was as though she thought these things would capture her or enslave her in some way and I was still wondering how I was going to help her get around these irrational fears of hers. I had come to see these as an expanding ill ease she was developing about some things in my world.

"Wanna know what the plans are?" I asked, trying to tempt her into an interest. I could see by her glance that this was something she was content to leave with me, as much as I wanted to inspire an interest in her.

"We are going to Etuta. To the Fire Mountain?"

"Yes. But first I thought we would visit the caves. I spoke with my Jongorrie last night and he tells me of the healing pools there, a special place in the mountains not far from here. I thought that it might be a place you would like to visit. It is also a special place for women, a place of peace and healing. We should take advantage of this while we are so close-by."

Suddenly interested Kirri sat up attentive. "This is in the caverns?"

"Yes. The Jenolan Caves are really a special place. They are not a place like the serpent caverns of Wollumbin, they are a place of peace, of healing and of water deep within the dark places. They are the Binoomea, a Spirit place also."

"You have been there?"

"As a boy, yes. It's guarded by the whitefellas law now. But still it is a place of peace. It is quite famous, though the healing waters are no longer used as they once were. A great deal has changed for the blackfellas."

"We can go there and the healing spirits will help me?"

"Yes. It is something the whitefellas don't understand. We can do this thing in secret. There will be someone to help us, someone who knows this Country."

"I have heard Jeremy, and now you talk of whitefellas and blackfellas. I do not understand this thing?"

"What? How do you mean?"

"It is all the same. And yet you say it is different. It is the same though, what is different between these... fellas?"

I laughed at her terminology and then shook my head. "There is a lot of difference."

Kirri frowned. "You are not black. Your skin is brown. Why are you not called a brownfella?"

"I guess it's a cultural thing... maybe the way we are bought up."

"It is not the same for everyone?"

"Well no. I guess it is where you are bought up, and other things too. There is a lot of difference. It is like the tea you drink, even if you add milk to whiten and flavour it; it's still tea Kirri. It is a life style, an understanding of custom. I'm considered a blackfella even though my skin is brown."

"We too have differences but we do not mark them as you do. Not in the colours of our skin, even when you are not that colour. That is a strange way to do this thing, these differences within your Dominions. Is it not enough that the Dominions are different?"

"Dominions?" I frowned, for a moment wondering at her meaning. "You mean country, lands?"

"Yes. Lands, places divided from each other. Why do you mark differences even inside your Lands. You are all of one land?"

"Well it is important. It is culture, heritage. What your own people do and how they live, how they think even."

"Those things are important too but to make so much of them is foolish. They are important only to you. You should not let these things divide the Edgelanders of your Country so much. Everyone has something to give, being different... that is a valuable thing. A great deal can be bought to your world by the differences people have. Your Land should be known for its differences, its tolerances. To divide yourself in your Dominion is wasteful of who you are. What can be gained by this thing?"

"You don't understand the history of it Kirri. Our history with the whitefellas has a lot of murder, the killing times for the Aboriginal people, my people."

The frown that grew on her brow told me that there were other questions coming. I began to go on to explain how we felt as a First Nations People, who were now disenfranchised in our own Country but she cut me off.

"The killing times? But the Edgelanders have always killed. It is what they do, what they have always done. This was my greatest fear, the violence of your world."

Surprised, I shook my head. "But it was different back then. You don't understand."

"Perhaps you cannot see this thing." She added softly. "Perhaps you are too partisan, too much apart. This too is something we know of your people. We see that the Edgelanders are still old in this way. You have not learnt to be one people together yet."

"What!"

"You are angry. Tom, please don't be angry with me."

Her voice was soft, hesitant and I drew a steadying breath. Flummoxed, I wondered how to get around this. "I'm not angry, just... just... I don't know? Frustrated with what you say."

"You are angry. I am sorry I spoke of this. I will not speak of it again. Please... show me this thing." Pointing to the map Kirri looked up hopeful of diverting me.

I drew a steadying breath and realized that it was true. I was becoming angry for some reason, or perhaps it was only my frustration.

When Big Jim walked through the door I must have been wearing an odd expression as he paused, tossing me a second glance when he entered, coming in from the boat-shed.

"Morning? Everything alright with you two?" He queried suddenly.

"Yeah... yeah sure." My response was more habit than answer.

"Tom is teaching me." Kirri said softly in a more honest explanation. "We are talking of how the Edgelanders kill each other. He is angry that whitefellas from other Dominions... Lands arrived and that they fight also. It is a difficult thing for me to understand. The colour of their skin is important for him but... I don't understand this thing either."

"A hard subject. It is a sorry business Kirri." Big Jim said as he moved into the room. "Tom should remember that your people don't do this. There are not so many of your people that the pressure for land is strong. Also, it was not only one lot... the whitefellas that invaded and killed. The whitefella were only the ones who thought themselves as boss. The yellowfella came also, and others. Tom too, like most of us has mixed blood running through his veins. You two can argue about this one till the cows come home. I am tired of this sorry business these days. So give it a break for now, save it for the driving times. All that adrenalin will keep Tom awake."

Kirri frowned confused, but Big Jim just headed into the kitchen area, then he looked up again to continue. "So what are the plans for you two. You should get away soon... very soon. Today!"

Binoomea – Dark Places

Tom

The ancient gorge in which Jenolan Caves nestles sits west, deep in the escarpment and deep gorges of the Blue Mountains behind Sydney. It's a beautiful drive from the time you begin to climb up the mountainous escarpment west of Sydney, right up until you pass beneath the Grand Archway of the Jenolan Caves, deep in one of the hidden gorges of the Great Dividing Range.

Kirri was entranced as we stopped often to take in the sights, the views from the mountains out over the coastal fringe of land between the Pacific Ocean and the long backbone of The Great Dividing Range. They are a long string of mountains that stretch for some four thousand kilometres following the eastern coastline of the continent.

At times I thought she felt overwhelmed, not only by the crowds in the well-known tourist spots, but by the view of the vast horizon. We had been watching the beautiful depth in colour of the sky and the swift scuttle in the drifting path of clouds.

"You look worried woman, what is it?" I asked quietly as we stood looking out over the view at the escarpment edge, near the small township of Katoomba. It was now a busy, crowded mecca for tourists.

"It is the sky. It is so vast. I was reading that the clouds... the rain clouds go around and around, travelling the Edgelands. It is strange for me. The mist of the Inlands don't travel across all the Dominions, they stay within our own place. Perhaps this is why when you foul your air, you do not feel the consequence. Others feel it and you do not care."

I chuckled at first, wondering how to explain this. "Maybe you're right." I surrendered with a shrug, giving up on explanations. "But we all share the air, all around the Edgelands so it is much the same I think."

"No. It is not the same, the air you foul travels away from you. It fouls the sea and... and other lands. You do not care, or maybe you do not see."

Shrugging I eased her away from the odd glance a couple were giving us, obviously having overheard what they would consider a strange conversation. "We can talk about it later." I said under my breath as I led us back to the car. "I don't know if you reading those books Big Jim gave you is helping. It seems to raise more questions than it gives you answers." I added on a rueful chuckle.

"They are helping." Kirri said quickly. "Maybe you should read them, you would understand what is plain to see too."

Laughing outright, I shook my head. "I have read lots of books Kirri. But you read them and see things... differently. I wonder if it's good for you."

"I will decide." She answered with determination. "You are my husband, not my keeper."

The look she flashed me was stubborn. Somehow it looked at odds with her size and the fineness of her build, but it made me smile none the less. Perhaps it was the sense of challenge I felt.

"About that." I added. "I could only get one room at the Caves House as I wanted to stay in the main building near the Grand Archway. You don't mind sharing with me?"

Kirri frowned for a moment. "We should stay together. Why do you think I would mind this thing?"

"Nuthin' No reason. Just making sure." I quipped as I climbed back in the car beside her.

"You confuse me sometimes Tom." She added softly after a time, obviously not seeing the problems of sharing a bed in our situation. That had me wondering some and my thoughts kept me busy for the next few hours as we wound our way around the mountains and down into the notoriously steep and precipice Jenolan Valley.

Kirri didn't see, or perhaps not understand the inherent problems in this arrangement and I wondered if she even understood it. I had come to the conclusion that the sex-drives between the people and of the Inlands, and those of the Edgelands were perhaps very different, as different as were their living arrangements.

Maybe it had something to do with the difference in life spans or perhaps it was custom. I had no idea of knowing and even less idea of how to approach the inherent problems for me, those in us living closely together.

For Kirri though there seemed to be little difficulty at all. In fact I seemed to be the only one having a problem here. The more I thought about it, the more it was a problem though, which was the ultimate irony.

I was going to have to do something about it in my head. I had also realized that since discovering that my wife was a Kadaitcha in her own right. One of the few, and one greatly treasured of the Illaparinja, I was more wary. I couldn't control her as I perhaps would have a woman of the Edgelands and that very thought alone had me smiling at the realities.

I was up against her Lore, her People as well as my own. Those who knew she was an Illaparinja would protect her fiercely and I understood that I should be numbered amongst those few. That was the very least of my understanding. It was also my main worry and I tried to settle the concept within my mind. This woman was beginning to truly get under my skin in a way no other woman had ever managed before.

Once we had checked into the old and somewhat grand Caves House near sunset, parking the car and camper trailer well up in the valley and out of the way, Kirri and I climbed the winding staircase to discover the secrets of the guesthouse from another era.

The dark woods, colonial colours and deeply cushioned chairs had an ole world charm from the colonial era. The house was an adventure in its own right with winding bannisters and unevenly stepped levels, where additions to the grand old building were added too and then added onto again over the century.

I was delighted to find we had been allocated one of the older front rooms of the building, one that looked down over the public area with the view flowing deep into the shadows of the cavernous Grand Archway.

The room was small by modern standards and wore a shabby grandeur that sat with ease in the cosy, comfort of the house. Even the utilitarian bathrooms were a share arrangement between levels and in the old time wooden wardrobe Kirri discovered the white bathrobes to be used in your passage between the bathrooms and your room.

Watching her try one on with amusement, I explained what they were for. Kirri was lost in folds of the white terry towelling and I laughed at the picture she made. While for me it was something of a tight stretch, particularly across my shoulders, and a challenge to hold the two fronts together. I doubted I would use it and told Kirri that she could use them both if she liked as I planned to simply get dressed as minimally as acceptable when I needed to.

The grand dining room was decked out in as quaint a décor as it had been a century ago in the old photo's that dotted the walls. The meal was friendly and relaxed and we felt the welcome of the old estate. For Kirri it was all a new experience and I enjoyed teasing her as she asked about the different offerings on the menu.

The young waitress thought me overbearing I think, until I explained that my wife was from the inland. Saying that she was from a remote township I waited for her reaction. The woman accepted this explanation readily and was more than happy to help explain the menu options without my help.

The evening was enjoyable and together we later took an adventurous walk well after dark. We ventured deep into the shadows of the Grand Archway that was lit with a soft street like lighting.

Taking the shadowy path down beside the iridescent blue lake we wound around the waters edge, watching carefully for platypus that lived and fed freely there.

Lounging about our room later I was stretched out on the bed with Kirri sitting cross-legged in her fashion beside me. We were pouring over the pamphlets and literature we had been given from the front desk, deciding on what caves and tours we would like to explore the next day.

"When will we get down into the Binoomea pool?" She asked after a time, having already chosen what cave tours that she wanted to join.

I looked up, watching her as she climbed under the covers beside me, settling down for sleep. "The woman said that the Pool of Cerberus was closed, it's been closed for a while. That is what they call the healing pool now. We'll meet the local Shaman tomorrow night, from one from the mob whose Country this is, the Wiradjui mob. He will help us."

"You know this man?"

"No. But he's expecting us. There are things that the whitefellas do not understand. We need the help of the mobs from around here who keep their secret business, the knowledge of the Binoomea."

"How will he know us?"

I smiled. "He will know us Kirri, that is not the problem. No one else will be waiting for him at that hour. I only hope we will be welcome. We will meet him tomorrow night in the archway, in the spirit hours when everyone else is asleep. It is the best way for this business."

Settling down she watched me and I was very conscious of it though I struggled to hide this from her. Not asking me if I was going to join her, she was soon asleep. It was a relief to settle my reading aside and instead absorb my mind in the mysteries of the woman at my side.

Curled up like a kitten she was a delight to watch and she moved little in her sleep. It was as though she had found a place where she felt no threat, understood all the questions and simply became lost in the mystery of her own secret world.

I wished for a moment that I could join her, be a companion in her dreams and discover more about the woman who was only now becoming so very real to me. Tucked securely into my life as she was now, and all without me barely having made an effort. What had once been an imposition on my habits was now slowly becoming a habit in itself. I was becoming accustomed to having this little wife of mine around me all the time and I even liked the idea a great deal it seemed.

I envied her the knowledge she held, the understanding she had gained and the questions born of fresh eyes in the mysteries that surrounded her in my world. Things I had grown too blasé to see any more. It left me wondering what she was really making of a world so different from her own.

I wished for just a moment that I could share the sense of mystery she was surrounded with. Instead, I fell asleep without really even being aware of it.

The following day was a pleasure. The beauty of the limestone caves really breathtaking and I was proud that I had found something that even a woman from the caverns was fascinated over.

The vastness of these caves was truly a mystery, one that kept us enthralled for much of the day. I asked about the healing pools, or the Cerberus cave and I got little satisfaction from anyone though they were very helpful and often curious, or wary about my reference and any knowledge I might have.

In the end I decided to keep my questions to myself and save them until we met up with the young Shaman. Instead we immersed ourselves into the adventure of exploring the truly magnificent caverns, which we were guided through.

Kirri was seemingly absorbed in the experience and kept asking about the references the guides made to the names they had given the beautiful limestone formations. When I explained to her that the names meant little too me and were drawn from another world, another experience, she found that curious. We had no time to discuss it though and so as not to miss all the information the guides were able to tell us, we said little.

Much later, deep into the following night we waited quietly in the dark shadows of the Grand Archway. I had no idea really what time we were to be met, aside from that it was in the spirit hours. This could have meant any time from midnight on until dawn and I was left wishing that my Jongorrie had been more conscious of my count of time.

The night was cool, though it could have been the recesses of the Grand Archway around us that kept the breeze damp as well. We had dressed for the temperate enclosure of the caverns, not quite sure what our experience was going to be although on the outside of the caves at this time of year it was quite mild.

Kirri was in high spirits and shifting quietly amongst the rocks on something of her own mission as she explored the slopes and hollows of the Grand Archway.

I didn't want to leave the light of the Archway, not with someone expected at any time so I had settled myself onto one of the cool seats provided there. Prepared to wait for however long that it was to take.

Kirri scarcely left off exploring the rocks even though she had managed to frighten a few of the small bushy rock wallaby's who had made their home here.

It was a curious thing to watch her explore and when she joined me she was full of what she had found, concerned mostly with odd scents, which seemed to be some kind of information source for her.

"Did you know there are caverns all about us, beneath our feet and nests, where the little animals live; there are dens and... and the air has that sweet taste of deep places... wet even."

"Yeah? What else did you find?" I asked interested. It was becoming a long wait and anything was worth the distraction.

"I don't know. I can't see properly. These little lights are not strong enough, they don't throw the light or even travel far at all."

Adjusting the small headlight wrapped around her head she fidgeted with it. We had held onto the helmets we had used earlier that day, along with the media self-guide but we had left the helmets and guides behind back in the room. We doubted we would have a use for them tonight, though the headlamps had been a good idea. They were something we now had strapped around our heads to help us once in the caves again.

"Maybe we should leave them off for a while. Let our eyes adjust to the deeper night shadows."

Kirri wasted no time in doing as I suggested and switched the small guide light off, then settled down impatiently on the seat beside me.

"Will he be much longer?"

I chuckled at her impatience, despite feeling much the same. "Give it time. He will get here."

It seemed to be a long wait though and when finally I heard the sound of movement coming down the path that wound through the vastness of the Devils Coach House, it wasn't at all what I had expected.

"Hi. Welcome. You waiting here for reason?" The middle aged Murri woman greeted us carefully.

I nodded, standing to greet her also but she moved once more with care. "Please come, up here this way," she said, indicating the way she had come. Seemingly unsure of whether or not we would follow her.

Both Kirri and I were silent as the three of us moved away from the public caverns, up through the Devils Coach House and then beyond that. We followed the Jenolan River with little difficulty in the open light under the moon and stars.

It wasn't far before we verged off from the public path and up into the bracken. We were following along a small animal track that led to a smoking fire we could smell well before we reached it. Here the woman began to gather green branches and I knew it was a welcome to Country ceremony.

The man there was tending to the fire and he helped her arrange the leaves into the ember bed encouraging the smooth billowing of smoke. Both of them said little and even then it was in a dialect I didn't understand. Kirri attempted a small effort in the silent finger language I was beginning to recognize so well but neither of them even recognized it, let alone understood what it was she had asked.

As the smoke swept around us I gave into the welcome offered us and followed the friendly ceremony, enjoying the melody of the words as they addressed the Spirit about us, their words singing through the air. It was reassuring to know we were welcomed onto their Country as family.

As the ceremony came to a close the young man stood and signalled for us to follow. He was a few years younger than I and there was something about him that reminded me of Jeremy. It was easy to see that he wasn't sure of what to make of Kirri as his glance hesitantly swept about her, then sank quietly to the ground.

"Thanks for meeting with us," I offered carefully to his retreating back as we retraced the path along which we had come.

His glance, seeking reassurance was quick. "I wasn't sure if you would come, but I understood you would have someone special with you. I am just surprised," he answered reluctantly almost. "She is not what I imagined, your girlfriend that is."

"This woman, my woman is a special person. Very different to what you believe." I added as hesitant as he, not wanting to offer any form of rebuke. If he was to be a shaman, he had to learn to accept things he didn't understand.

"She must be. It's unusual, taking a white girl down here like this on blackfella business."

"Can you take us down to the healing pools then?"

Surprised he looked back at me. "Yes. That is what I am here for. We will go down there now. The Elders have given permission for this and I'm to welcome you both to our Country." Then suddenly adding on a rueful glance he slowed. "I wasn't expecting … well a white girl."

"She's not a white woman, it isn't what you think."

His look was sceptical as he tossed his glance back. "No? You sure?"

"Very sure." I answered chuckling at his candidly expressed doubts.

"Funny business then. She looks like a white woman."

"I'm from the Inlands." Kirri suddenly said, jumping into our conversation without hesitation it seemed, having followed our conversation.

It surprised us both and I don't know why it should have, but it did.

"Hmph." Was all the man said, but he turned to lead us on regardless.

I knew he hadn't really understood Kirri but nor was he going to ask anymore questions. I had the feeling that we were going to get little out of him for some reason and I felt guiltily aware of his reluctance to talk of these things with a woman. Particularly one who he believed to be other than she was. For some reason this wrapped around my own frustrations of the past few days.

Steadily, however, we stepped on, back down through what was the Devils Coach House again, returning the way we had come with no more invitation to any conversation.

We were led on past this place in silence. Then we began to climb up around towards the entrance to the caves high on the other side. This I understood from the earlier tours into the caves.

The young Shaman had access keys to the caverns, something I wasn't sure to expect but as he swung the door too he took up the question in my eyes.

"You do understand that this way, down into the old healing pools is now a closed place. It's blackfella business down there for the time until we can decide what is to be done."

"Yeah we were told it was closed. Some development work I think." I added as he locked the way behind us.

"Hmm... That is what they told you." He answered with something of a gleam to his dark eyes.

"Why? What didn't they say?"

"You will see." Was all he said as he took up a lantern that had been left in a small box which he obviously had known to look for. As he switched it on the light flooded around us like a cocoon of safety. Despite this, Kirri stepped in behind me... moving into my shadow and even I was glad for the sweeping light the guide held high as we began to move deeper into the caverns.

It was a path we had stepped along earlier today, one we were familiar with. Though now instead of using the lighting of the caverns, which was designed to highlight the beautiful formations, the young Shaman just held the lantern high as he stepped ahead of us.

There were other locked passages, more steps and it seemed we moved deeper down into the caverns. Our steps silent almost and strangely muted without the accompanying sounds of others in a group.

As we reached a lower cavern the young Shaman seemed almost

reluctant, but never the less he indicated the way ahead, and that I should lead. We fixed our head lamps and carefully, we both moved ahead.

He kept hold of the brighter lantern and there was an uncertain consternation in his eyes, a concern or perhaps a reluctance it seemed.

I was glad of our earlier excursions as the caves were familiar by their features, but when we passed through yet another locked door this all changed. Silently I moved ahead with quiet directions from the Wiradjuri guide. Kirri stepped closely in my shadow as though she sensed something and I knew immediately what it was that had set her so ill at ease. I saw it when we stepped into a cavern with a high portal ceiling from which a long metal ladder descended.

It was a beautiful cavern, stretching high into the darker shadows but there was no pool of water evident anywhere that I could see. Our guide was silent, wary almost, perhaps conscious of something he couldn't see but could sense. It was the same sense that kept Kirri so silent and glued to my shadow.

I soon saw what it was that kept both of them quiet, high up in the cavern. He was squatting, silent and watching and I knew immediately it wasn't a man of our world. He was a hunter, a warrior and he wore what I thought was the clay markings of his time. He watched us as a hunter would watch its prey, silent and with stealth and Kirri moved in still closer behind me. So close, that I could feel the comfort of her body against my back.

I knew immediately that she could sense him, but not see him. It was as she placed her hands at the edge of my waist, and only then that I felt her calm. It was the strangest thing, as though she drew her calmness from me. Drawing on my knowledge of the shadow, the ghost of this underworld, as he perched high in the caverns here watching us.

Our guide however, had hung back with some respect and I wasn't sure if he expected anything of me or was just trying to avoid the cavern all together. Moving further along the pathway I encouraged Kirri silently and was pleased to feel her follow.

I could clearly see the shadow warrior of the spirit world squatting high on a cavern ledge, poised and waiting. His expression was a solemn as was his stillness and I felt acknowledgement in his stance. He understood that I could see him. He knew that I was part of his world and it was as though he welcomed me into the subterranean caverns.

He wore a crude form of dress, a simple hair braid about his hips from which hung the familiar tassels. His face too wore markings amongst the deep-set ochre colouring of his skin, though the white clay markings on his arms and chest were more predominant. Still he squatted silent as though waiting for something.

"Here, this is what I meant earlier." The guide said as he moved forward reluctantly holding the lamp high when we both swung towards him. With a quick tilt of his chin he indicated the floor beneath the newly constructed walkway that hovered above the base of the cave. There, welded into the rock as though part of the caverns lay traces of a human skeleton, carelessly placed by the hand of the spirits, or the hands of fate. "They have closed the cave out of respect for the old one. Until it can be decided what can be done. It is a difficult thing this. No one is sure of what should be done."

"He died here?" I asked uncertain as to his meaning.

The guide indicated a place high into the ceiling. "Yes. He fell they say, through some of those high shafts overhead, but they know he is from the tribes and the rocks have claimed him now. Bugga of a way to go." He added ruefully. "Not sure if he is Wiradjuri or Gundungurra? He could be any mob though. They used the healing pools for tens of thousands of years and the old people would bring their sick. They would come in from all across Country to this place. Could be anyone and he has been here for a long time. This is his place now, no one disturbs him."

Casting my glance back up towards where the shadow of the old warrior had squatted I realised he was gone. His shadow had moved on for the moment and strangely enough I felt Kirri's grip on my waist relax.

"He's still here." I said softly, the words echoing through the cavern. "Can you feel him?" Turning back to Kirri I waited.

Kirri nodded. "Like a cold breeze across my skin, he is not here now though… it has shifted, the breath of him. The sense of him has shifted to somewhere else."

I nodded in agreement. "He is still here though. He chooses not to leave the caverns for some reason. I can feel it."

Our guide shuffled about where he stood, uncomfortable with our talk. "It's further on, what you are looking for. This way."

Stepping ahead of us quickly, as though pleased to be leaving the cavern, he led the way ahead once more.

The walkway dipped slowly, passing a beautiful shallow pool with fine lace stalactites scattered overhead like a hundred delicate straws of light. It was like entering a grotto filled with the shadows of the spirit world. It was a place where all was quiet and sacred, where you trod carefully and with respect in your step.

We moved on however and soon found ourselves in a lovely bathing cavern, one with deep pools spreading their waters beneath the purpose built walkways. We stood, stunned by the beauty of the pools.

Our guide left us moving deeper along the path as we strained to see through the deep shadows. Kirri moved to my side in a silent awed wonder.

Suddenly the cavern was flooded with light and the scene was breathtaking. The pools were a beautiful turquoise through to a azure blue and the water crystal like I had never seen anywhere before.

"Watch it, it is surprisingly deep." Our guide said softly as I reached through the railings. His voice was low as though not to disturb the spirits we could feel about us. "Three to four metres they say. Were you planning on swimming? They would once soak in there, the old people, and they say the water is good, healing water. Good to drink."

"Well we could try it." I suggested to Kirri.

"They say they would drink from the shallower pool. You can swim in this one, sorta soak I guess. See over there... against the wall there is an old dive wire where some cave divers once swam between the caves. Under there somewhere there is a passage that leads out. It goes down to the river cave we're told. There could even be a current, so watch it. The old people knew another way out, there is a lot that is still secret in the caverns here."

I looked up at Kirri in question but she looked equally uncertain. So stretching to the water I cupped my hands and bought up a small draining cup of the water held in the curve of my hands, offering it to her.

Kirri knelt to the pathway and bent her lips to the fast draining cup, tasting the precious liquid. Then to my surprise she licked the last of the drops in my palms, cradling my hands in her own.

"It's cold, but not bad tasting. Quite nice, soft and fresh." She said somewhat pleased.

"Want more?" I offered, as the guide looked on uncertainly. Kirri nodded and then stretched her hands to the pool herself.

I sat back and watched attentively, pleased that she seemed to find what she needed while she scooped up small handfuls. Drinking deeply and satisfyingly of the cold water.

As we both watched her, it was with a strange sense that we became aware of, and then we heard clearer, the soft tones echoing about the caverns. It could have been the wind shifting, moving in a chorus but after a moment both the guide and I knew that this was not it.

It was a ghostly sound echoing like a soft intonation, a chant. One ancient in its tones bending to the hidden places about us as it shifted through the caverns. It was a song of ceremony and we waited as it slowly filled the chillness of the cave shifting about us. I glanced about, aware of something but not sure that I had seen a ghostly shade shift past the rock.

I knew my skin ran chill and the man beside me stiffened, aware of something about us that was not wholly of this world. He looked startled, while I was merely surprised.

Kirri too stopped after a moment and looked up, becoming aware of the soft chant on the air though she held no fear in her eyes at all. Merely wonderment.

"What is it?" She whispered, a question to us both.

I held up my hand to silence her, suddenly aware of movement about me. Seeking its source I carefully studied the shadows while our guide had shifted back as though trying to blend into the rock. The white of his eyes was wild as he looked across at the opposite wall and this made me turn suddenly towards what it was he could see.

"It's the dogs!" His voice strained, and harsh in its whisper as he quickly crouched low as thinking to hide from what he saw. "I didn't think... it is an old story... an old legend. Just bits... no one knows this thing..."

Turning against the light I could suddenly see what terrified him. I saw it the same time that Kirri did and she scuttled across the floor towards the guide in an attempt to escape what she too now knew.

Deep across the other side of the pool was the formation of rock in the shape and form of the head of a dog. Its eerie shade cast against the wall... a trick of the lighting I was sure.

But what held us transfixed was the shadow of the Djaranin emerging as though from a crypt of stone. The struggling dark shadow was like a ghostly dog stretching to free itself from the holds of the rock, its head tossing in its efforts as worked at its liberty. The shadows danced and shifted in a dark and foreboding fight in its quest as it fought for its freedom.

It was a dance, a stretch of dark light as the shape strained, emerging from its brace in the stone-shaped dogs head, that now came to life. The Dark Dog of Death had managed to free its forefeet and was bracing these against the rock as though to strain free from the fast hold. Its eyes as wild as the guides but it fought on, trying to break through the cold walls.

Kirri screamed and I wasn't sure if it was in terror or fear, her hands clamped over her ears, but I thought surely it was fear wild in her glance and this sent me diving towards her, sheltering her from the awful sight. It was then that I saw another shift of shade, a movement about us. The song of the caverns continued, that hallowed chant which had first drew our attention filled the cavern now. It was joined with the clap of sticks as though beating against rock in a sound pacing the time as I urged Kirri deeper into the shadows.

From nearby the entrance into the cavern emerged the tall dark figure, the spirit of the cave. He stood tall, a black shadow against the rocks as he began a slow dance. It was he who had sung the chant; he who held the clap sticks as he stepped high in a dance that drove the wild Djaranin to a new frenzy of movement. It was a gleefully savage dance that both dog and hunter paced. One they looked to have danced many times.

Kirri screamed again, and it was in terror of the deepening sound. I wondered then if she could see the shadow of the warrior, dancing deep in the entrance of the cavern. Or perhaps feel a threat, one I felt nearby, but which perhaps she couldn't see.

The guide dived for the shadows further along the walkway, away from the melee as he flattened himself now against the opposite wall, hiding in the shadow of the cavern with an unearthly sound throttled in his throat.

"We can't get out! ... It's blocking the way out, there is no other way!" He screeched as the deep shadow of the dog stretched itself further from the hold of the rock. The deep, sleek, chest of the animal was now beginning to break free. This allowed movement and threat in the grind of its jaws. The rock holding it silent for the moment as it was unable to stretch for breath just yet.

"The dive cave... the water! Where does it go?" I demanded tersely still aware of something else I couldn't see, but which I could feel in a cold breath about my skin.

"I don't know." He chattered, lost between fear and hope but I could see he thought it hopeless. "It must go somewhere though... the divers used it once." Confused and yet desperate he dug in his pocket for a small torch and flicking it to life reluctantly edged away from the wall as I took hold of a reluctant Kirri, trying to urge her forward to follow him.

We scrambled across the walkway decking and peered deep into the blue calm of the water while the deathly melee of movement and light shifted around us to the chant echoing along the cavern walls. It was growing stronger, more solid, filling the air and scattering the peace and stillness that had once been so much a part of the caverns.

The shade of the warrior continued to dance, tormenting the Djaranin as it tired to struggle free of the rock and I knew in that moment what held the warrior to these caves. In his dance and his chant he could control the dark dogs. It was likely this was what held him here down through time, guarding the men and women who moved through his world in wonder.

In the next moment I was watching the guide slip desperately into the cold once calm water, yet he was full of fear and uncertainty. The healing pools began to swallow him and his quick indrawn breath told us it was cold indeed.

Kirri scrambled to follow and I held her arms, helping to ease her down into the water. Plunging in after her, I caught the shadows of the warrior move closer towards the Djaranin, taunting it still. But the fear I felt dissipated, swallowed in the cold grip of the water as my body strangely warmed against the chill. It must be the Death Stone I reasoned but whatever it was, it was the sense of a sure thing that we were doing.

Able now to draw breath I heard the haunting howls of the dog as I too ducked beneath the surface to follow the others. Slipping beneath the cold waters at the urging of Kirri, who had released my shirt as she moved ahead of me in the wake of the guide. I was prepared to follow her into the chilling tunnel, even though I wasn't sure were we would end up, but I was also not willing to stay behind at the mercy of the Dog of Death.

We shifted quickly beneath the waters, Kirri's head lantern failed as I strained underwater to see her kicking ahead through the darkness. She was able to follow the shifting light of the torch ahead, which was the only guide we had. My headlight had faltered also, flicking long enough to announce the sudden upward sweep of her legs before it too had failed.

I was the last to break the surface of the small pool, where the dark tunnel of water had led us. It was a tiny space that seemed only to be a pocket of air but my chest was paining in the strain of the cold and the reach for a desperate breath.

I knew Kirri scrambled ahead of me pulling herself from the water onto a wide glassy bank where the guide had managed to gain a foothold. Wanting to be free of the icy water, seeing now only the small circle of light cast by his small torch, I too scrambled towards it and gripped the edge of the strange rock flow with some difficulty.

It was a shelf, small and slippery, that was a type of flow stone formation. It was one the three of us could barely fit onto as slippery as it was. The young Shaman was blubbering something, the sounds echoing in the small cavern and the meaning of which seemed incomprehensible.

Kirri however struggling with her hold on the slippery flow stone had moved ahead from us, disappearing in a scramble of feet and limbs into the gloom.

"Quick, this way... there is a scent of dry air." She chattered... her words sharp with the edge of cold as I heard the scuffle and scrape of her moving ahead.

We both moved at once, scrambling after her into the deep gloom. Only the guides torch between us able to light the darkness of the crawl space and I was still uncertain of what lay ahead. The floor of the space was muddy, slippery with slime but I didn't care. None of us did as we eased ourselves through tight spaces, scraping along barely able to squeeze at times.

It seemed an age, an impossible crawl and a desperate squeeze through spaces I couldn't see. Then suddenly we broke out of the earth. As I eased myself free of the ground emerging into the rough bush the chill of the night hit me but I was incredulous that we had even survived to break out into the night.

I couldn't believe that we had escaped the dark dog yet again... the Djaranin who seemed was intent on reaching us, as he too had tried to struggle free of the rock. Kirri lay crumpled against the ground, small animal sounds of distress and exhaustion filling the air and I scrambled over towards her.

"Kirri... Bub. What! What is it? Are you hurt?" I demanded for all that we hadn't just escaped from the grip of the hades.

With little thought she struggled up into the muddy circle of my arms, her hair wet and plastered against her skin as I tried to find her face beneath its tangle of muddied locks.

We sat there, curled against the last of the deep night. I pulled her carefully in between the protection of my folded legs as I sat heavily onto the ground, guarding her shaking body from within the circle of my limbs. Then looking up I realized that our guide was splitting the scene. I watched him scramble through the bushes, as he was quickly lost to our sight and I returned to the shivering curl of my woman, in my arms.

"It's OK. It's OK..." It was like a chant, a soft song that I whispered against her hair that was tangled about her. Pulling her firmly into my arms and chest, I cradled her, rocking her instinctively until her shivering eased.

"I think I will kill my Jongorrie for putting you through this." I threatened tersely, trying to find anything that would distract her. "He should have known! He should have realised what danger this would place you in."

I felt the anger building in me like a tide and I truly wanted to get my hands on that pest of a small forest man. Torture him some, as he had tortured us.

"It's not his fault Tom... surely he didn't know," she said shivering.

"We'll see about that." I whispered fiercely, the threat lacing my voice.

Kirri pulled from my arms hesitantly, exhaustion evident in her eyes as she struggled to free herself from my hold.

"No Tom. I am sure he really only wanted to help. He wouldn't do that... he couldn't do that." She said again in a shaky whisper. "He was trying to help... and he did. It just wasn't like he believed... what he thought. That is all... I am sure."

"Like bloody hell!" I spat irritated. "Kirri you realize you could have been killed back there!"

"I know. I know that but I wasn't. Neither were you. We are safe."

I felt her begin to shiver violently again, once free of my arms and I moved to shift her back into the warmth of my chest.

"No... no... we had better move. It will be your sunrise soon. It will get very cold and ... and others."

Seeing the sense in her words, I moved quickly to climb to my feet, helping her up along with me. "OK. Lets get outa here, back to the room then. Before anyone is about. Before that bloody dog finds its way outa the caves."

Scrambling, yet careful, we made our way around to the public walkway. We had broken free of the caves not far from the river and the light reflected from the seemingly still body of water was almost luminescent under the southern night skies.

We looked a sight I knew. Somewhere I had lost a shoe and I impatiently kicked the other off. Kirri began to shiver again as I checked the darkness of the pathway ahead of us and it was an eerie reminder of the caverns, as we made our way through the Grand Archway and back up towards the old guest house.

I still had the passkey, which had stayed with me buried in my pocket and we were able to get in easily through the back entrance. Making our way silently with wet and muddy feet through the old reception room with only a few muddy marks to give our path away, we reached the central stairs.

There seemed to be someone in the kitchen area off from the bar on the restaurant floor but we crept past silently, escaping on up the stairs towards our room. It was a relief to make the room and it was only then that I remembered we had no bathroom there.

Grabbing for the towels and robes I shepherded Kirri ahead of me and headed out again for the older of the washrooms further down the hall. It had a single shower, toilet and basin and it was rarely used I had decided yesterday. It was the bathroom I had chosen the day earlier as it gave me more time and more privacy than the newer more generous installation further along the other hall.

Once there, I locked the door as we both began to strip off. Running the water just bearably hot in the shower, all without saying a single word to each other.

Ushering her in ahead of me quickly, not waiting for her to fully strip off as there seemed little point to me. We just needed something to warm us; something to help break her free of the fine shivers which shook both our bodies and which had kept us both silent.

The shower of hot water was delicious and we took turns standing under its steaming flow, though I quickly gave up rubbing her down when she was under the flow of water. My body had a mind of its own in regards to Kirri and I struggled to control its wayward reactions.

"Do you think they will try and find us?" she asked in a voice soft and filled with fear.

"The Djaranin?"

"Yes."

I thought about it for a moment. "Did you hear the song of the warrior?"

Kirri took a moment before she answered. "Yes. Yes I knew what that was."

"I believe that it is he who controls the Death Dogs. Perhaps this is his place, to keep the Djaranin to the rocks. Think about it for a minute."

Taking the moment I swung from her, struggling for control of my body as I immersed my mind in the Lore and in legend. "It is a place of healing, but it is also a place of death, these caverns. It is a place where the Djaranin would come to judge if someone would die or not. Don't you think?"

"Yes. Yes... you're right. A place of healing would go in-hand with a doorway, a gateway into the spirit lands. You're right." Kirri's voice was soft, feminine and she was engrossed in my reasoning. It was not helping me at all.

"Perhaps then it is his song, and the dance of the old warrior that controls the dogs. It could be him that has given the Binoomea and the pools their reputation for healing. Perhaps this is what holds him to the caverns."

Kirri swung around considering my words, as she let the hot water run down through her hair, cascading as it did, down along her body. She had her eyes closed, enjoying the fine flow that tripped off the points of her breasts and slipped down over the fine line of her waist and the gentle curves of her tummy. It was all too much for my senses.

I had the overwhelming urge suddenly to gather her again into my arms and kiss her. Fighting my thought I quickly stepped out of the shower grabbing for a towel. "You stay in under the water a bit longer, I'm done I think."

"He was a kindly spirit I believe. There are those who are good in the caverns aren't there?" She asked of me as my mind struggled to revisit my reason.

"Do you mean the Uruncha men?" I stammered drying myself roughly.

"No. Men like Andrew and Apari. Men like you."

Kirri turned off the shower and stepped out after a scarce moment, reaching for a towel.

"You think I am kindly?" I asked surprised at her comparisons.

"You are kindly. Fair I think. Yes."

I grinned, liking the comparisons as I wrapped the towel firmly about my hips. Then reaching for her suddenly I slowly bought her up against my chest trying to read her thoughts in her eyes as I kept her warm.

My hands travelled gently down her still damp and naked back in a sweet caress, measuring the fine line of her. Her skin was soft and damp with heat and droplets of water. Her towel lay pressed between us, her hands gripping at it where she had been drying her skin.

Slowly I dropped my lips to hers and gathered them beneath my own. Kirri smelt good, tasted and felt even better against me and I could feel myself slipping towards the warmth of her with a delightful ease.

When I released her she was breathless, pink, warm and fully flushed. "It is hard to let you go." I whispered into her damp hair tempted beyond reason.

She drew a shaky breath. "How do you do that? Rob me of my breath..."

I chuckled. "You woman rob me of mine. How far away is the ceremony of yours?" I demanded softly, tormenting her slowly in a drawl that tickled along my throat with a low chuckle.

Looking up surprised, she caught my eyes. "I... I hadn't thought it close."

I dropped my arms away from about her, the disappointment running through me. "Then think about it woman. I don't know why we are waiting?"

Turning away quickly, frustrated, I forced myself to step away from her. Tightening the towel around my hips I grabbed for one of the robes then I slipped out the door in a determined stride. I couldn't have stayed and not argued with her over the whole business. Frustration ran through my body like a fire and I didn't even bother climbing into the robe. Instead I swung it over my shoulder and headed down towards our room with a frustrated and firm, if somewhat disappointed step.

Déjà vu

Tom

It was light when I stirred, daylight spilling through the window and there was the sound of movement, of people and noise milling below. It was a moment before I remembered that it was likely well into the arvo' by now, we hadn't made it into bed until near dawn and with that thought I swung about looking for Kirri.

Sitting there patiently was my wife, cross-legged on the bed watching me quietly and I smiled... déjà vu. Turning about onto my back I raised my brow in question while she just dropped her eyes for scarce a moment and then moved, climbing over me to step down from the bed and wander over to the window.

The night before, I had feigned sleep when she had come back from the bathroom. It was the easiest way for me, it was a cop out and I knew it, but any alternative was too hard. Nor had I been in the mood for chatter.

Kirri had just climbed into the bed beside me and fallen asleep it seemed, without any difficulty. Me... I had tossed about and turned for what had seemed forever before the dawn, falling asleep at last just before the rising of the sun had come over the mountain.

Now she stood looking out over the long drive and public area. "It is passed the lunchtime. Are you hungry?" She asked suddenly, turning back towards me.

"Hmm... yes. How about you?"

Climbing back onto the bed she nodded. "There is that woman down near the office area, she has been there for a long time. I think she is waiting for us."

"Woman? What woman?" I queried surprised as I climbed out of bed, making my way over to the window. I had left a pair of my jeans tossed over the chair in the corner, so I reached for them. Taking the time to climb into them before I moved over to look out of the window where Kirri joined me.

"There, over by the shelter. She is waiting I think."

Sure enough, the Murri woman from the night, who had led us up into the welcoming ceremony, was sitting quietly waiting. Around her milled any number of people, those who were on their way towards the Grand Arch and the caves, while others passed them on their way back.

Families shifted around her and occasionally a car would pass having emerged out from under the rock Arch... everything and everyone moved but her. She was as still as the rock, waiting.

"We had better get down there and find out what's happening. I hope to God there hasn't been trouble." I said running my hands through my hair trying to bring it to some order and grabbing for a shirt.

"I should have woken you. But you had such a difficult night."

I frowned, my eyes cutting across to her. "I didn't realize I woke you?"

"No. You didn't," she answered strangely.

Not waiting, she joined me as I swung the door open. Together we headed out, leaving me to stretch into my shirt as I followed Kirri down the stairs, still curious as to why the woman should be seeking us out.

The woman rose to greet us as we approached her. People continued to mill around us but as she stepped off towards the edge of the rock-face where it was quieter, we both followed her curious.

"I was hoping to find you. I had thought that perhaps you had left but I waited."

"Yes. We're still here. Is everything alright?" I asked of her, curious about her hesitation.

"Yes... the young man returned to us and told us what had happened. I wanted you to know that we had not expected that. It was something that we didn't know... the Death Dogs. These are things, which have been lost to us. We didn't know. The Elders, I was worried... for you."

I felt myself relax, relieved that there hadn't been repercussions or trouble. "We're fine, thanks." I smiled my reassurance and relief. "Please give our thanks to the Elders, for their help."

The woman nodded in acknowledgment. "The young man should not have left you." Her eyes shifted between us, looking for any sign of anger or perhaps disappointment even. Kirri however stepped forward, touching the old woman lightly on her arm.

"It is not his fault, it was... difficult. We understood."

"But he shouldn't have left you," she argued softly. "He is young, inexperienced but we thought he would be able to help. We didn't know ... about this business. You must understand that our mob, this Country. It is our Country but we have lost so much, so many of our old people when the whitefellas came. Death came with them, disease and loss. It killed so many of us. Our Lore, so much was lost."

"Yes. I know. I was told that the Wiradjuri, the Gundungurra suffered a great deal and lost many people, and much of their Lore and history. My father was a man of the Dharung... so many of my people also died with the diseases of the whitefella."

"You are a clever man of the tribes around Sydney? We did not know.

We were not sure if you would understand."

"Yes." I agreed, knowing the pain of not only losing someone but so many, along with the pain in losing the knowledge of your Country. Losing also an ancient and tried Lore to govern and guide you through your own Lands. I understood her loss and the loss to her mob, to her people.

"You are more than a clever man... one of high skills? I can see this."

I nodded silently. "I came to find a cure for my woman... that which keeps her sick."

The old Murri woman turned to Kirri. Her eyes searching her face, seeking something. "She is not as the others, this one. This woman is yours?" She asked, turning to me.

I knew she could sense something of Kirri, but Kirri stood silent. Carefully capturing the eyes of the old Murri woman and her hand reached again to touch her lightly.

Startled at Kirri's touch, the old woman looked down at her light fingers against her much darker arm. She was confused you could see, though silent as a frown marked her brow.

"You are sick?"

A small smile of affirmation touched Kirri's lips and the woman nodded. "Then the waters will heal you. The Death Dogs, we know little of them now as we only know some of the stories left to us. There are shadows only of the things we once knew. But they... they could not reach you?"

Kirri's voice was soft. "They did not reach me. My man, Tom, kept me safe and it was the guidance of the young Shaman who led us. This is good and maybe... perhaps I am getting better. I drank a great deal of the water." Chuckling she glanced up at me and then allowed the woman to take her hand carefully in her own, holding her attention once more.

For a moment it was as though they melded, became very aware of each others thoughts, conscious of their differences but as one, as women. Then the silence between them was quietly broken by the old Murri woman's next words.

"You must return when you have been through what you are here to achieve... and when you are done?" At her pause, her eyes searched Kirri's uncertain. "You have a task... one that is very important to you. I can see this. I would like to yarn with you though, you and your man must come again." Glancing up at me her look was one of enquiry, of hope also, before she returned her eyes to search Kirri's once more and then went on slowly, her words measured. They were almost a careful entreaty, one between women.

"We should know of these things. Perhaps you can tell us what you know of the Dark Dogs. We need to understand this thing. Will you return? Sit around the campfire with us perhaps, amongst the women? We would welcome you both and we can perhaps share the stories, the knowledge we have together."

Kirri too glanced up at me and then nodded in affirmation. "We have a great deal to do, much to see and understand. Tom and I, but we will return when we are done with these things."

Both the women then looked up at me and there was little I could do but agree. "Sure. If the women say so; who am I to argue? If it's what Kirri wants then sure; we can come back once we are done."

So it was that Kirri and I left the caverns, moving instead towards the deserts of the inland and on, to find out what we could of Etuta Mountain. The mountain of fire deep in the Macdonnell Ranges of the Central Deserts, the heart of Australia, our Country.

I had made a promise to return to the Country of the Wiradjuri and we would return. First though we had to find once more other secrets that had through time, been lost to us.

Would there ever return, a time when we would hold the knowledge that our ancient people had once held?

I hoped so... but it was a long arduous path back. It was also a path that could hold our very salvation and it is a path we were now on, together, Kirri and I.

www.ingramcontent.com/pod-product-compliance
Lightning Source LLC
Chambersburg PA
CBHW051507170626
46811CB00002B/692